THE
SHAAR
PRESS

THE JUDAICA IMPRINT
FOR THOUGHTFUL PEOPLE

A
Promising

A
SHAAR
PRESS
PUBLICATION

Past

A novel of
healing and hope

DOV HALLER

Published by **SHAAR PRESS**
Distributed by MESORAH PUBLICATIONS, LTD.
4401 Second Avenue / Brooklyn, N.Y 11232 / (718) 921-9000

Distributed in Israel by SIFRIATI / A. GITLER
6 Hayarkon Street / Bnei Brak 51127

Distributed in Europe by LEHMANNS
Unit E, Viking Business Park, Rolling Mill Road / Jarrow, Tyne and Wear, NE32 3DP/ England

Distributed in Australia and New Zealand by GOLDS WORLD OF JUDAICA
3-13 William Street / Balaclava, Melbourne 3183 / Victoria Australia

Distributed in South Africa by KOLLEL BOOKSHOP
Ivy Common / 105 William Road / Norwood 2192, Johannesburg, South Africa

ISBN 10: 1-4226-0906-5 / ISBN 13: 978-1-4226-0906-4 Hard Cover

Printed in Canada
Custom bound by Sefercraft, Inc. / 4401 Second Avenue / Brooklyn N.Y. 11232

Chapter 1

At eight forty-five on Motza'ei Shabbos, Max Frankel let himself into the empty shul. The large room, pulsating with energy and noise just a few hours earlier, was silent and dark. Here and there, a tallis lay, still unfolded and a pile of *sefarim* waiting to be replaced on the shelf. The tablecloths were in disarray and discarded tissues and candy wrappers littered the floors near the tables, waiting patiently for the janitor.

It was only a quarter to nine and the meeting wasn't scheduled until nine, but Max Frankel took pride in coming to board meetings early. Max Frankel was the shul's longtime treasurer, and the semiannual board meetings were a serious tradition in his life. He enjoyed putting on his hat and bidding his wife Eva a good night as he stepped out of their apartment.

He liked that she would tell the kids that their father was out at a board meeting, that even at seventy-nine years old he was still an active member of the community.

Max switched on the light in the side room and began to organize the chairs around the long table.

By five to nine, a large group of men sat in the small room, sipping tea and chatting pleasantly. Beneath the polite conversation there was a slight edge, a hint at the tense and heated discussions that would surely follow.

They were all dedicated and committed men, the members of the shul board of directors. Congregation Beis Aron Zvi was the proper name of the shul, but to everyone in Flatbush, it was simply called Rabbi Wiener's, after its illustrious Rav. It was a thriving shul with hundreds of members, and there was a whole stack of issues that had to be dealt with.

The secretary, Boruch Katzman, reviewed the agenda to himself. There was the question of allowing non-members to use the adjoining banquet hall for their simchos and deciding on the fee to charge. There was the discussion regarding expanding the women's section and resurfacing the tarred parking lot.

There was a day camp that was interested in renting space for the summer and the issue of whether to give the janitor a raise in salary.

The board members wouldn't actually begin deliberating these subjects until nine o'clock, because that's when the meeting was called for. And if that's when the meeting was called for, then that's when the president would arrive.

At precisely nine o'clock, the door swung open and the president entered. Though many shuls have presidents, and the title has lost some of its significance, in this shul it was different. At Beis Aron Zvi, the position of president was taken seriously; very seriously. The shul's president had his own parking spot and a designated seat up front. The old-timers would refer to him as such, saying "Good Shabbos, Mr. President," in respectful tones. True, it was a job that came with much responsibility and little by way of remuneration, but most of all, the title sounded prestigious. President.

And there was no one on the board, nor in the entire shul for that matter, who didn't regard Aryeh Markstein as perfect for the job.

For Max Frankel, the meetings were a little disappointing now that Markstein was president. When Grunwald was president, the meetings had been great fun; he would rehash every detail and viewpoint expressed. Grunwald had loved the ceremony of asking all of them for their opinions. Grunwald thrived on good debate and more often than not, he would tell the secretary to mark the issue unresolved, leaving it for the Rav to decide. Max had enjoyed the meetings then, had felt like a high-ranking government official as he shared his outlook in a weighty tone of voice. How much fun it was to return home after those meeting and share the conversations with his wife, his Eva, allowing her to feel a sense of his importance as well!

He had so much enjoyed sharing shul secrets with his married children; letting them in on things that others wouldn't know about for weeks. Why, he had been the one to tell his son that the Rav was considering issuing a rule that bar mitzvah boys would no longer be permitted to read the *parashah*! And he had told his son, Shimshon, the news a full ten months before the bar mitzvah of his son, so that he wouldn't waste time and money for nothing. Board membership had its privileges after all.

But now, with Markstein, everything went so quickly, so efficiently. He would listen as the secretary would relate the issue, and take notes as each of the board members would share his opinion. Markstein had rules. No one was allowed to interrupt, and each member had exactly two minutes to speak. Then, he would quickly flesh out the opposing points of view and invite one representative to state each one. Once it was clear what the issue was, he allowed ten minutes for questions, after which he would call for a vote. As president, he ultimately had veto power over any decision that wasn't to his liking.

There were so many rules, so much tension. Sure, the young people thought Markstein was something special. Things actually got done: decisions were made and problems solved. And of course, they got to rush out; they loved being in a rush, those young people. But for Max Frankel, who had sat on the Board of Directors since the late 1960's, the meetings were no longer fun.

A large crowd of teenage boys stood on the front steps of the yeshivah. It was late enough in the winter to be called spring, and with Purim on the horizon, their thoughts were on the impending Yom Tov and its promise of joy and merrymaking.

They stood there, elaborately casual, as they discussed the plans for the upcoming day.

Dovi Berman, one of the class leaders, was describing the costumes that his group would be wearing while they went collecting. "We are collecting for my uncle's yeshivah in Eretz Yisrael so we have these authentic Yerushalmi *bekeshes* that he sent especially for us."

A quiet boy named Gershy was unusually animated. "We are going collecting for poor families here in Brooklyn, and we are dressing up like soldiers. We got bona fide uniforms from an army surplus store."

A skinny boy, Tuvia, spoke up. "Our group feels that it is unfair to collect money for poor people and then use some of that money for costumes. Instead of renting costumes, we made up a hilarious song about Purim and the school we are collecting for, which is an afternoon program for public-school children." He smiled self-righteously.

Dovi easily took back the conversation. "I totally disagree with that. Interesting and original costumes make you a better group and you bring home more money that way. The institution that sponsored the costumes is the one that ends up gaining."

Tuvia spoke calmly, like an adult. "Dovi, you don't actually *know* that; you are just guessing. How can you have the right to spend *tzedakah* money on a guess?"

Dovi snorted good-naturedly as the boys around them voiced their opinions on both ends of the spectrum.

Ezzy Markstein stood with the boys, longing to join the conversation. To an outsider looking in, he seemed that he would be one of the leaders of the group. He was tall and handsome, with blond hair and soft, gentle features. Indeed, there was a time when he had been a leader, not just of this group, but of every other group in the school as well.

How the mighty have fallen!

These days, Ezzy pondered each word before he joined any conversation. He knew that if what he said even remotely offended someone, a whole arsenal of weapons was poised to put him in his place.

Since the incident, he had become an easy target, a sure way to feel better about yourself: squash Ezzy Markstein. He no longer had the luxury of expressing opinions in the assured, self-confident, way that he had previously. These days he only spoke if he was sure that his words were completely neutral and inconsequential to anyone. He couldn't risk being threatening to anyone; the resulting hurt was too great.

Aryeh Markstein sat at the head of the long conference table, his prized red pen in hand. There was a stack of financial statements before him and he was doing what he did best, seeking glitches and errors and circling them. Aryeh Markstein was a bright and effective accountant, and his specialty was rescuing mismanaged companies from the brink of bankruptcy. He would pinpoint the problems and fix them, bring the company back to solvency, then turn his attention to another beleaguered client.

He was immensely successful.

On this Tuesday morning, he was sitting with a young leather importer, who was watching his business self-destruct. The fellow was nodding eagerly, like a young child, grateful that the firm of Markstein and Company had accepted him as a client. Aryeh Markstein had a name as a superman of sorts, and his unique abilities had earned him quite a following.

As Markstein made another red line on the paper, he looked at his client and repeated his favorite phrase, his mantra: "The only important thing is the bottom line."

The meeting was interrupted by a buzz from his Blackberry. He frowned and looked at it, prepared to ignore it. Aryeh Markstein lived by his rules, and one of them was that he never answered his phone while meeting with a client. He considered it impolite and insulting. He noticed, however, that it was Malka, so he took the call.

"It's my wife," he excused himself.

Malka knew his policy, so she got straight to the point.

"Aryeh, that appointment with Ezzy is today, the one we've been waiting for all winter. Do you feel like joining us?"

Aryeh paused and considered the question. He could not know that Malka was hoping he would refuse, for she knew that Ezzy would be much calmer without his father present.

She could never really know what the thought of Ezzy, his only son, did to the organized, methodical planet of her husband. His perfect world began to turn at a dizzying pace when he would contemplate the boy. He was at a loss just when he needed answers.

"What time is the appointment?"

"Three forty-five, at 570 First Avenue."

He couldn't trust Malka to ask the hard questions that needed to be asked, so he said, "I will be there."

But of course, a boy isn't an account sheet and his problems can't be corrected with a red pen and a calculator.

Chapter 2

Ranjeet's mother had known how to read faces. Back in India, she had accurately predicted which of the neighbors would have happy marriages, which children would grow up healthy, who was prone to violence or anger.

Ranjeet hadn't fully inherited the talent, but he did consider himself to have some ability. So amid the traffic, noise, and pressure of his job, driving a New York City Yellow Cab, he entertained himself by briefly studying the features of his passengers and trying to figure out their occupations, interests, and futures. Then he would inquire what their favorite food was, or which color they liked. He would listen to the answers and congratulate himself on his perception.

At precisely three-thirty, a tall Jewish gentleman entered Ranjeet's car. Ranjeet studied the serious expression, the worry lines in the forehead, the hard eyes, and immediately decided that this customer wasn't one for conversation.

Mother would have been proud.

Aryeh Markstein was looking at his watch, making certain that he would be five minutes early. That was another Aryeh Markstein rule. Never come late and never come too early. Now Malka, she was apt to leave Flatbush at three-fifteen, and then stop to buy food for the trip.

I will probably be there before them, thought Aryeh grimly as he tensely thanked the driver.

Ranjeet smiled to himself as the door shut.

⎜▐▌█▐▐▐⎜▐▐▐▐▐⎜▐▐▐⎜

The waiting room of Dr. John Nikosi, Psy. D, was tastefully decorated in soft, soothing hues. There were comfortable cocoa brown leather chairs along one wall and a low couch in shades of peach facing them. Aryeh scanned the room for his family before selecting the chair farthest from the other patients, away from these people who were prepared to spend hundreds of dollars to speak to some … shrink. That's all he was, as fancy as his titles were, as highly recommended as he came, a shrink. People who ran their lives with order and responsibility had no need of such consultations.

At three forty-three, Malka Markstein entered, completely out of breath. She was accompanied by Ezzy, who shuffled in, looking every bit the unwilling teenager.

Malka noticed her husband and smiled brightly at him, "Thanks so much for finding a way to slip out of the office," she said.

Aryeh bristled inwardly at the suggestion that he could "slip out" of the office, but he smiled nonetheless. He knew that his wife meant no harm.

Ezzy nodded at his father and went to sit on the couch, where he picked up a *Sports Illustrated* magazine. Aryeh turned his attention to his Blackberry, and Malka, caught as usual between her two men, smiled gamely and mumbled something about the terrible traffic coming in from Brooklyn.

"Markstein," said the receptionist in a soft voice, and Aryeh almost shouted at her. How dare she use his last name, the one that he had invested with such distinction, to page the next patient? She should have found some other way to call him, such as "the millionaire father of the boy who felt compelled to steal two hundred dollars," or "the boy who was at the top of his class in everything and decided to throw it all away so that he could go to the bottom."

To add insult to injury, Malka had smiled at the receptionist brightly and said, "That's us."

Even Ezzy glared at Malka for that.

Aryeh opened the heavy, frosted glass door to the office and entered, expecting to be confronted by a couch. He was surprised to see that Dr. Nikosi's office looked very much like his own, neat and professional, no couches or knickknacks or inspiring slogans hanging on the walls. Malka, as Aryeh already knew, judged doctors based on one criterion; if they had pictures of their children and if those pictures were freshly dusted. That was it. It was good that he was there, if only to get a feel for this … shrink.

Dr. Nikosi rose to greet them, a short man, maybe fifty, with gray hair and a prominent, hawkish nose. He wore a blue vest and open shirt, very much the academic type, thought Aryeh. He smiled pleasantly and gestured toward the chairs clustered around his desk. "Make yourselves comfortable," he said.

After exchanging pleasantries about the weather, Dr. Nikosi turned serious. "Okay, Ezriel," he said, consulting the file before him, "let's hear a little of your story."

Almost immediately, Aryeh interjected. "Well, this whole problem started suddenly one day—"

The doctor held his hand up and looked at Aryeh. "Everyone will have a chance to speak. Let's start with Ezriel."

At that very second, Ezzy decided that the guy was worth a chance, just as Aryeh concluded that the fellow was a charlatan like all the rest of them.

Fifty minutes later. Dr. Nikosi had heard from both the son and the father. They had both referred to the same episode, but they seemed to have a very different take on it. The doctor was intrigued. He asked Ezzy to come by himself the following week so that he could hear his insight into what had happened.

To the doctor, it didn't seem like kleptomania or paranoia or any of the many other imbalances or disorders that compel people to steal.

Dr. Nikosi had often dealt with teenagers from wealthy homes who had been caught stealing, sometimes for kicks, sometimes for attention, but never like this; never just once. There was no prior history and no follow-up, just that one isolated incident. One that was enough to change the boy's life, maybe forever.

The following week, Wednesday afternoon, Ezzy prepared to leave school. "Where are you going?" asked Mendy, one of the nicer boys in the class, as he watched Ezzy rise. "It's only three o'clock."

Ezzy shrugged. He really was not in the mood of talking, but these days he couldn't afford to be picky. "I have a doctor's appointment," he said, heading for the door. Pinchas began to giggle and Ezzy knew that trouble was brewing. It didn't take long.

"Which doctor is it, your shrink?"

Ezzy ignored him, fighting off the urge to reply as he walked down the long corridor to the school's exit. He reminded himself that he couldn't really blame Pinchas, or any of the boys who were only to happy to hit him while he was down.

It wasn't that the boys in yeshivah were mean-spirited. It was just that, well, he hadn't exactly been so nice to them when he was on top. He had been the unchallenged king of the class for so many years that now they had all subconciously felt the tiniest thrill at his rapid slide downhill. Finally, each of them had a chance to become a star. The role was up for grabs.

All at once, the boy who knew all the answers , who could hit a baseball across two lots, who had the wealthiest father in the whole class, who was tall and smart and funny, was reduced to begging for friendship.

The boy who would turn competitive and fierce if someone dared oppose his opinion was suddenly looking at them with hopeful eyes, grateful for a kind word.

They were only human after all.

In the months following the incident, Ezzy hadn't even tried. He had rarely attended school, and when he did, he was withdrawn and silent. He had accepted the punishment that they meted out, seeming to agree with their unkind verdict.

During those difficult days, he had often thought of the time that his father had killed a mouse in their summer home.

He had swatted at it with a broom, and even when it was no longer moving, he had repeatedly hit it, again and again, until it completely stopped quivering.

He had wanted to make sure it was dead.

That was what Ezzy had felt like as he received blow after verbal blow, insult after insult, as if to make sure that he would never move again.

It was only in recent months, as he had struggled to regain his footing, as he attempted to be normal again, that he had felt the attitude, that he learned just how difficult it would be for them to forget.

Just yesterday, he had joined a basketball game and had easily stolen the ball from little Shloimy Perlman. It had been a perfectly legal move, but it was one that had left Shloimy looking silly, especially as Ezzy had moved down the court for a smooth lay-up and basket.

Shloimy stared at him angrily, as if in disbelief. "What else can I expect from a thief?" he had muttered, more to himself than to anyone else, but Ezzy had heard, loud and clear.

And that's the way it would be for him.

He would have to struggle much harder than anyone else and make sure not to offend anyone else and risk their wrath and cruel words.

There was a stain on him and it seemed like there was no way to erase it.

Ezzy entered the doctor's waiting room, feeling for the entire world like he was wasting his time. It wasn't that he didn't believe that Dr. Nikosi was a good doctor; it was more that he didn't believe his situation was reparable.

In the months following the incident, Ezzy's parents had accompanied him to a battery of therapists, psychiatrists, and social workers. Aryeh Markstein hadn't liked the idea of a frum professional knowing his family situation so intimately, but he had gone along with it.

Then, each of the people they consulted began to suggest that there was something deeper, some hidden rage that had to be exposed. That's when Aryeh pulled out.

Aryeh wanted a name, a title for the problem, call it bipolar, paranoia, kleptomania, it made no difference to him; he wanted a name. Then, he could find the solution, and just like one of his red lines going through a series of numbers, the problem would be gone.

These soft-spoken, wise-eyed therapists who spoke to him of childhood and history and the family dynamics made him nervous.

Thus far, it was close to a year since the incident and Ezzy was slowly changing, falling deeper and deeper into his abyss of despair, with no help in sight.

So, of course, Ezzy had little hope that the newest in a long series of professionals would bring him closer to a solution. Anyhow, Ezzy knew the truth. He had no problem, no chemical imbalance, no predisposition to damaging behavior. He had only been trying to make a point.

Chapter 3

That night, at supper, Aryeh cleared his throat and brought up the issue of summer camp. He felt that it would be beneficial for Ezzy to leave the city, to get away from the disapproving stares and bad friends. Last summer, he had made the same speech and Ezzy had gone. It had been a disaster.

He had arrived at camp suspicious and vulnerable. Every whispered conversation became something to fear. Were they talking about him? Telling his story?

After a week of camp, he started to believe that it might be possible to be normal again. His athletic abilities were distinguishing him, and he was slowly being reminded it of what it felt like to be smiled at, to be patted on the back.

Then one day it had happened, of course it had happened. Ezzy had left supper early and returned to the bunkhouse. As he approached he heard voices engaged in animated conversation, and he hurried up, eager to join.

There are different kinds of silence. There is a rich, easy silence that can spread between a couple of old friends like soft butter on a crisp roll. Then there is the hard, uncomfortable silence that hangs in the room like smoke from an exhaust pipe and just about smothers you when you enter. Ezzy entered the bunkhouse to the second type of silence, the type that told him all he needed to know.

They looked at the floor as he entered, wondering how much he had heard. Ezzy immediately realized that one of the boys, Sender, was looking particularly shamefaced. Sender, whose cousin was Ezzy's classmate.

"Did you guys hear about the water fight?" asked Ezzy, anxious to convince them that he hadn't heard them talking, that they could still leave it under the rug, that there was really no reason to expose the truth.

His voice was beseeching, pleading. "Did you? It was hilarious; the whole dining room was out of control."

"Sounds like we missed something special," a timid boy named Feivy finally said, and Ezzy knew that it was too late. They knew, and they knew that he knew that they knew.

Ezzy came back to the present.

"I appreciate it, Tatty, but if you think that if I go to a new camp they won't know about it, that's not the case. They always find out, and then it haunts me. There's no point in running away."

Aryeh answered in even tones.

"By this summer it will be more than a year later, a full year. Maybe by now people will accept that you have moved on."

"*You* haven't," thought Ezzy, though he dared not verbalize it.

Aryeh seemed to read his mind and continued, "And besides, I think it might be a good thing to get away from Moishy Winternitz and his gang."

Moishy Winternitz was the type of boy from whom parents instinctively shielded their young sons, a boy who was pronounced a bad influence even before he had a chance to speak. To be fair, the worried fathers weren't all wrong; Moishy was a tough boy with an innate contempt for all forms of authority. Early on, he had made it clear that he had neither the interest nor the intention to listen to anyone else, and he had quickly become the poster child for every alternative school that opened.

There was a long line of Rebbeim and teachers who had promised themselves that they would get through to Moishy Winternitz, but thus far, none had succeeded. He had been in numerous schools and programs, and at the age of sixteen, he was officially a dropout. Though kind-hearted storekeepers would hire him, those arrangements never lasted for more than a few weeks, and he would inevitably find his way back to the streets, where he mostly hung out and looked for attention.

Ezzy was actually his friend, for in better times, before the incident, Ezzy Markstein had been invincible; one of the few boys popular enough and confident enough to risk being nice to Moishy Winternitz. The old Ezzy would invite Moishy to come along with the boys when they went bowling and to the pizza shop, listening bemusedly to Moishy's tales of his antics. Ezzy had been his friend, but only as long as their roles were defined. Moishy knew that he was never really allowed to argue with Ezzy or to best him in bowling. He knew that the relaxed, easy air that Ezzy exuded was only evident as long as he was on top. Still, it had been worth it for him to accept Ezzy's friendship according to the terms that it was being offered. He was that desperate.

These days, the tables had turned. Moishy was the one being nice to Ezzy. And some days Ezzy was hungry enough, desperate enough for a kind word, to accept Moishy's friendship.

Ezzy rose to Moishy's defense.

"Tatty, Moishy Winternitz is my friend. He is nice to me."

"No Ezzy, he's not your friend. He tolerates you because he has no one else."

Ezzy suddenly pictured Moishy's face, his messy red hair, his long, skinny face, his sad basset-hound eyes, and he felt a surge of fierce loyalty to him.

"Tatty, he is my best and only friend. Please don't insult him."

They finished supper in silence and Ezzy went up to his room.

"The incident" was Aryeh Markstein's term, not Ezzy's. To Ezzy, it was no mere incident; it was the moment when fifteen and a half years of frustration had finally come to a head, when he finally broke free of his shackles. It was also the turning point, the precise instant when his perfect life ended. It was then that the bright, popular, athletic, personable Ezzy Markstein fell from his lofty heights, and he had fallen hard. He had tumbled down the side of a cliff, finally coming to rest, battered and bruised, among the broken souls at the very bottom. And there he languished, lacking both the strength and belief that he could actually lift himself up.

To his father, however, it was simply an incident. A thing that happened, and in his impersonal way, he had managed to isolate it as just a single episode and deny the voice that was calling out from just behind it.

Aryeh always managed to refer to it in conversation, say-ing, "since the incident," "before the incident." Even lying in the solitude of his room, Ezzy could hear the echo bouncing off the walls in his father's voice, "*the incident, the incident, the incident.*"

"No, Tatty," Ezzy would scream inwardly, "it was no 'inci-dent.' It wasn't about money or the latest music player. It was about you."

It had been a few days before Lag B'Omer of the previous year. Ezzy's tenth-grade classmates were eagerly preparing for a much-anticipated trip to Lake George. The trip was the prize at the end of a long and difficult contest and the boys were looking forward to enjoying the fruits of their labor.

In the days preceding the trip, the boys had talked of nothing else, planning with whom they would sit on the bus, what they were bringing along, what they would do there.

One day during recess, as the boys sat in a circle discuss-ing the trip, Nachman Oppenheimer had innocently remarked on how excited he was to bring along the brand-new portable music device that he had received for his afikoman present. Heshy Kagan immediately joined in with a description of his player, as did Nosson Kirshenbaum.

Ezzy felt like he had been punched in the stomach.

Ezzy Markstein may have been a nice boy with fine *mid-dos*, but that was as long as he was the king. He didn't own the new player and it was inconceivable that he would sit on a bus watching Nachman, Heshy, or Nosson, sitting proudly with the tiny earphones in their ears as he, Ezzy Markstein, would be using his old Discman. He pictured the humiliation of actually having to carry the discs along and bend over to change them repeatedly.

He knew that he needed the latest and the best. Fast. Before the trip.

On his way into the classroom, after recess, he tried a different tactic. He stopped Rabbi Kaplan and looked at him seriously.

"Rebbi?"

"Yes, Ezzy?"

"Are we allowed to bring music along on the trip?"

The Rebbi looked at him strangely. "Why not? I would actually encourage it. It makes the long ride much more pleasant."

Ezzy looked down. "I don't know, I just thought that, maybe for *achdus* and all that, the guys won't shmooze on the bus so much if they're distracted."

"That's very noble of you, Ezzy, but I think we'll leave it as is. There will plenty of opportunities for *achdus*."

It was a difficult day for Ezzy. He was slowly realizing how pathetic he was, but that didn't stop the frenzy of emotions, the need, insecurity, and worry that were gnawing at his insides. He imagined his classmates on the bus, all smug, and then suddenly one of them would notice that he, Ezzy Markstein, the king, was still using a Discman. They would remark about it to each other, and one of the more daring ones, probably Nosson, would offer his new player to Ezzy in a loud voice, relishing the brief moment of one-upmanship.

And then Ezzy would crumble.

What could he say? "I left mine at home"? They would laugh knowingly, mockingly, wondering if he really had one at all.

By late afternoon, during math class, he was unraveling, having repeated visions of the trip and his eventual disgrace. He felt himself growing ill at the thought, and, in desperation, grabbed hold of the one slim ray of hope that he had.

His father.

Aryeh Markstein could easily afford ten new devices, but there was little chance that he would purchase even one. Aryeh Markstein believed that prizes must be earned, not simply distributed to children who craved them, or to teenagers, for that matter.

Ezzy knew that he had his work cut out for him.

It was at this point that his memory grew vague, that his account of what had happened on that fateful day and his father's account differed, and Ezzy wasn't really sure anymore what was fact and what was fiction. It was painful to think about it, but the events of that day lived with them each moment and, it seemed, would not go away ....

Chapter 4

T hat Thursday afternoon, as Ezzy sat in class, tormented at the thought of not having what he wanted, Aryeh was sitting in the office of the debt-counseling organization that he had established. Several Rabbanim had asked him to use his expertise to provide practical financial direction to families that were struggling with crushing personal debts, and it was a responsibility that he took seriously.

That day, he was speaking with a middle-aged couple. Sholom was a computer programmer and his wife, Miriam, worked as a speech therapist, yet they simply couldn't make ends meet. They were itemizing the debts that had accrued from Pesach alone, and Aryeh was horrified. 'It wasn't like we did anything unnecessary,' she was saying. "We didn't go to any fancy hotels or anything like that. We just bought the boys new hats, suits, and ties, got new outfits for the girls, and brought home our daughter from seminary in Eretz Yisrael. That, along with the costs of matzah, wine, and food, put us over the top. We are already struggling with tuition, the mortgage, car payments, camp fees, and the work on the bungalow."

"And we haven't even started with *shidduchim* for any of our children yet," added Sholom dejectedly.

Aryeh was sickened. It was a story that he heard every day. Ordinary frum couples who had capitulated to every one of the demands on the list imposed on them by their children, neighbors, and an unforgiving society, collapsing under the burden.

Though being reassuring didn't come naturally to Aryeh, he took that route first. "You have to appreciate that the numbers here aren't so daunting. Others have it much worse then you do."

They visibly relaxed, and Aryeh took out his cherished red pen. "But this is where the cycle has to end. Now it's your kids pressuring you for clothes and hats; in a few years it will be cars and homes. You have to learn to use the most empowering word in the English language; NO. You can't afford to live this way. Why is your daughter in seminary if you are struggling? Let me guess. She cried and told you that all her friends are going and it would destroy her to be the only one that remained here."

The couple looked appropriately abashed under Aryeh's rebuke, but they couldn't deny the truth; he was right. "Had you said *no*, you would be ten thousand dollars richer today."

He continued. "You have to learn how to differentiate between necessities and luxuries. The boys probably got new hats and suits just six months ago for Succos, right?"

Again, the couple nodded miserably. Aryeh was gathering steam.

"And they go to camp for the two months of the summer?"

The expression on the husband's face answered that question.

Aryeh pounded on the table. "Today, May eighth, is the day that the party is over for your family. It's the day that you learn how to budget. Your children will complain at first, but in the long run they will thank you."

***

And directly from that meeting, Aryeh went home, still irate. Over supper, he shared the conversation with Malka. "We live in a society that is slowly destroying itself. Every day I see wonderful families coming apart. I don't know where it will end if people don't learn how to say 'no' to their kids."

It is unfortunate that Ezzy didn't hear the conversation, because had he known what kind of mood his father was in, he would have rearranged his plans.

But being unaware, he breezed into the house while his parents were eating supper. They greeted him and Malka set a place for him, serving him a generous portion of chicken and potatoes.

Aryeh shifted his attention to his only son. "How was school, Ezzy?"

"*Baruch Hashem*, really great. We have this big trip to Lake George on Sunday. The whole class is going, because we finished a mesechta this year, so I am really excited."

Malka beamed at her son. "That's so special. Do you need to bring food along?"

"Just a sandwich for lunch. We will be having a big supper there. The Rebbi said that we are going to gather wood and make a huge campfire."

Aryeh nodded approvingly. "That will be a useful thing for you to learn."

Ezzy mistakenly thought that his father was in a relaxed mood, so he launched right into his next question.

"Ta, a lot of the guys in the class have the latest gadgets to listen to music, no pictures or anything, and I would really love to have one. Do you think I could? It's not terribly expensive, maybe a hundred and fifty dollars."

Ezzy realized a second too late that it wasn't a good time. Aryeh pursed his lips deliberately in the way that he did when he was trying not to get angry but wanted his family to know that he really was angry, and it was just that he was exercising self-control.

"Ezzy, I have to tell you that I am appalled." He spoke in a low tone, but there was no mistaking the undertone of fury. "If you can ask, just like that, for a device that costs that much money, then there is something very wrong with your world-view. We don't just *get* things. People work very hard for money; it's not something that you just throw around every time you want something. You, Ezzy, belong to a generation that only knows the meaning of the word 'yes,' but when someone says 'no,' you wait a while and then ask again. It is inconceivable to you to think that you won't get exactly what you want."

Then, addressing the ceiling, but really seeing the miserable faces of the couple that he had counseled just an hour earlier, Aryeh continued. "Am I really just as guilty as everyone else? Did I raise a son who also thinks that way, that everything is his just because he wants it? Is my son so selfish and self-centered? Is his only thought, *Me, Me, Me? What I want, what I need, what I have to have.* Well, it certainly seems so and I'll put a stop to this right now. The answer is 'No.'"

Ezzy was aware of two things at that moment; he was disappointed that he wouldn't be getting the player, but much more than that, he was deeply hurt by the reprimand he had just received from his father.

Why couldn't his father just say *no* and leave it at that? Why the speeches and dressing-down? Ezzy looked down and spoke quietly. "I would like to be excused," he said, and without waiting for an answer, left the table.

He left a deafening silence behind him. Aryeh knew that he had gone too far, that he had laced into Ezzy in an unfair way. He should have gone after him and explained, but that really wasn't something that came easily to Aryeh Markstein. Instead, he muttered to himself about how some lessons must be taught, and Ezzy was big enough that he didn't have to take his medicine with candy.

Malka sat there, reeling from the blow her son had just received. She, too, should have followed him upstairs, and indeed, she wanted to, but Malka Markstein had long ago made a promise to herself.

Malka's mother had been a sweet woman, a good mother, and a caring wife. But there was one thing for which Malka could never forgive her. It was her practice of sharing her frustrations with her three daughters, her way of absolving herself of responsibility for their precarious financial plight. When the girl's would ask for money for something, she would smile sadly, and if her husband wasn't home, she would sigh expansively. "Your dear father," she would say, "a nicer man you'll never find. But a provider? Forget it. He simply lacks the ambition and cleverness of a true businessman."

Malka knew that her mother hadn't meant to be hurtful, that it was her way of apologizing for the lack and deprivation that were constants in their home, but Malka remembered all too well the feeling of rage that would overcome her when her mother would speak that way. She would feel her heart, a heart that was overflowing with love for her kind, unassuming father, contort. She would scream inwardly, protesting the assault to his honor.

And she had promised herself that she would never, ever subject her own children to any sort of negative talk about their own father, regardless of the circumstances. She knew that children would rather endure hurt alone than see their parents turn on each other.

So though she went up to Ezzy's room and brought him dessert, though she kissed his forehead and asked him if he had done his homework, though she smiled brightly at him and told him that he had grown again, she didn't once refer to what had happened. She didn't once say the words that Ezzy longed to hear: "Your father had a miserable day and was letting it out on you. He really didn't mean it …."

<hr>

After Malka left the room, Ezzy lay on his bed, staring straight up at the ceiling. He was hurt. His father had made him feel small and petty, like a silly child. He was also furious, feeling a strange, new kind of rage spreading through his body, as if he had sipped hot tea too quickly.

His father abruptly knocked at his door to ask if he was coming to daven Maariv. Ezzy was hurt. Nothing, not even a "how are you?" Just a businesslike question about Maariv!

Ezzy mumbled that he wasn't coming anywhere and then stood up from the bed, feeling dangerously empowered. His anger was fueling him, teasing him, challenging him to act on it, to assert himself for once and for all.

And so it was, that five minutes later, Ezzy had headed out his front door on the most dangerous journey of his innocent life.

He was going to get that newest music player, and he wasn't doing it for himself; he was doing it to teach his father, once and for all, that even with all his systems and plans and clear-cut lines, he couldn't stop his son from getting what he wanted.

Maariv was long over and the shul was quiet that Thursday night. Ezzy pressed the familiar numbers on the combination lock and entered the building, humming nervously, and perhaps, a tad eagerly.

He flicked on the lights in the center hallway and headed toward a small room off to the side. There, he approached a large metal door, Aryeh Markstein's pride and joy: the safe. Aryeh had conceived of the idea after realizing that the many *meshulachim* from Eretz Yisrael needed a place to leave the cash that they had raised, while they continued their rounds. The shul had constructed a large safe for their use. The entry numbers were known only to Aryeh, and as president, he would be the one to open it, twice each day. Each morning and evening, he would stand there, watching closely as each collector took the money from his private box or added more.

Only Aryeh knew the numbers … and Ezzy.

Chapter 5

H irsh Leib Koifman was a tall, jolly Yerushalmi Yid with
a short reddish beard and a gravelly voice. He had
never intended to be a *tzedakah* collector, and had
in fact tried his hand at various professions, including
bookbinding, kashrus supervision, and cooking for a yeshivah.
Somehow, the money that he earned never seemed to stretch
far enough to feed his ever-expanding family, and so, early each
spring, with the debts of Pesach weighing on his shoulders,
the practical Jerusalemite would travel abroad, first to Europe
and then to America.

In time, he developed a working itinerary and Rabbi Wiener's shul in Flatbush was one of his prime morning locations. The *mispallelim* were gracious and generous, there
was a hot urn and plenty of coffee, and best of all, they had

installed a safe especially for people like himself, collectors who weren't comfortable carrying around large amounts of cash. This Friday morning he entered the shul just after seven o'clock, anxious to remove the money he had placed there the day before.

He knew that Aryeh Markstein, himself a generous donor, would open the safe at precisely seven-fifteen in the morning. There were various boxes within the safe and each collector had a key for his private box, while only Aryeh could open the safe.

Hirsh Leib helped himself to a cup of coffee while he waited. His mind wandered back to his native Yerushalyim and the frenetic, pre-Lag B'Omer preparations that were surely taking place there. In his mind's eye, he saw his little Bere'le valiantly struggling with an oversized plank of wood, schlepping it to the neighborhood bonfire site. Hirsh Leib wished that he could be there, that he could see the light of the fire reflected in his children's joyous eyes, but alas, he had to be here, in America.

He comforted himself with the thought that he was going home that Sunday with enough money to buy a small American toy for little Bere'le.

Ezzy Markstein walked to school Friday morning feeling defiant. His mind was not on the fact that the money in his pocket was not his, nor was it on the fact that whoever's it was would surely suffer. In his mind, he could only envision one thing; the face of his father when he would open the safe and see that all was not right, that all his carefully laid plans weren't enough. Ezzy was immersed in the feeling of having broken free, of having empowered himself. And anyway, it wasn't stealing. It was just until he could get money from his bank account and then he would put it back in the safe. It was just a temporary measure, a way to make a point.

Aryeh Markstein walked to shul feeling horrible. He loved Ezzy. He knew that his outburst the previous night had been out of place and that Ezzy had been hurt. Malka had been uncharacteristically angry with him, and he had gone to sleep hoping that Ezzy would just forgive and forget so that they could move on.

When Ezzy had come downstairs this morning, however, Aryeh had seen that he had neither forgiven nor forgotten. Aryeh had planned on apologizing but something about the way Ezzy was looking at him — mocking him? — had made him pause. Then Ezzy had left to school. "Oh well," thought Aryeh, "If he is still upset this afternoon I'll explain it to him."

As soon as Aryeh opened the safe, it was clear that something was amiss. One of the boxes was wide open and empty. Whoever had forced the lock had torn open an envelope and taken out the money inside, leaving shreds of paper in the empty box.

Aryeh gasped as he realized at once that someone had tampered with his safe. But how could they? How could anyone open the door without the combination? He turned to the line of Yidden waiting for access to their boxes and asked them to step back a minute. He looked at the number on the box, 14, and checked his list. Koifman.

"Koifman?" he called out. The tall red-bearded Yerushalmi stepped forward. "I'd like to speak with you for a moment?" said Aryeh, motioning him to the side.

Aryeh put on a calm face and dealt with the waiting *meshulachim*. Then he locked the door to the safe and sat with Koifman in a corner of the shul.

He wasn't sure what to say. Seeing his carefully constructed plan fail, seeing his fireproof safe broken into, was something Aryeh couldn't handle. The only coping mechanism he knew was to start fixing, to find solutions.

He spoke firmly. "There seems to have been some minor problem with the safe, but we will immediately deal with it."

Hirsh Leib looked at him, uncomprehending.

"Um, someone must have fooled around with it, but in no time we will have the money back. We will make a quick investigation and find the culprit."

Hirsh Leib Koifman understood. Someone had stolen his money, the money for which he had traveled across the world and left his family, the money for which he was forced to endure the agony of humiliating himself again and again. The money for which he had to face the accusing stares of people, looking him up and down and wondering, *Why can't he get a job? He looks healthy and strong.*

Did they know how hard he had tried, how his salary had always been months late, how it was never quite enough, how desperately he wished he could find the job that would allow him to support his family in dignity? Did they know the feeling of a cold mattress in the basement of some well-meaning host, the sound of his wife's voice on the phone from across the ocean, the smell of delicious food emanating from a kitchen that wasn't his?

Someone had taken his money. It wasn't even that large a sum, for he had already sent the bulk of it back to his wife in Yerushalayim. It was just the little bit he had kept behind for his personal expenses, a collection of singles and fives and the occasional twenty.

A thought struck him. It was the money for his expenses. And to buy Bere'le his toy.

His Bere'le was schlepping wood with no father to help him and now he wouldn't even get his gift.

Hirsh Leib had a flare for the dramatic. In his youth, he had never been far from the megaphone at demonstrations. He rose to the situation that day as well.

"Yidden," he called out in the crowded shul, "can it be that someone would steal from a poor Jew from Yerushalayim? Can we allow such an outrage to be perpetrated in our midst?"

Aryeh sat there, horrified, as people began to gather round. "Stop it," he whispered to the Yerushalmi, "I will give you whatever it is, just don't make a scene."

But Hirsh Leib was enjoying the attention too much. He only wished he had a megaphone.

This was the story that the men talked about on their way out of shul, which they repeated to their wives at breakfast. Who would steal from a shul? And even more intriguing, if the thief could open the safe, why would he steal only one envelope from one box, and not more?

Friday afternoon, after school, Ezzy walked along the avenue. A few times over the course of the day he'd had second thoughts, but he had quickly pushed them out of his head. He knew that he wanted to avoid the larger stores that would be crowded with shoppers on this Friday afternoon. He walked several blocks until he came to the place he sought, Fogelman's Electronics. It was a small store, one that had never been able to compete with the glitzy new superstores.

Shea Fogelman looked up at the customer who entered. "Yes?"

"Do you sell the very latest in portable music players?"

Shea shuffled the length of the counter and showed the boy the only model he had. "I'll take it," said the boy, a little too eagerly.

"One hundred and seventy dollars," said Shea.

The boy reached into his pocket and pulled out a crumpled wad of bills. He started to peel off tens, fives, and singles, at last arriving at the proper amount. He looked around nervously, thanked Shea, and left the store.

On Shabbos morning in shul, Shea's seatmate was telling him about the theft in Rabbi Weiner's shul. "The strange thing is, why would someone steal only a few hundred dollars? It was just a pile of small bills; the biggest one was a twenty."

Shea thought about the boy for a moment and then looked back into his Chumash.

Pedro was sitting with Rabbi Weiner and Aryeh. For the fifth time, he vehemently asserted that he had no connection with the theft, and the men were inclined to believe the veteran custodian.

"Was anyone else in the shul on Thursday night?"

Pedro shrugged elaborately. "No." Then he remembered something. "Mr. Markstein, your son was leaving when I was coming in to clean, about ten-thirty at night. Maybe ask him if he saw anyone."

Early Sunday morning, Shea Fogelman hung up the phone after speaking with the president of Rabbi Weiner's shul, Markstein. He had felt compelled to call and tell him about the boy with the crumpled bills and the nervous demeanor. Markstein had asked him to describe the boy. He had.

"You never know, maybe some poor kid who really wanted the player and just couldn't afford it," Shea had said before ending the call.

Aryeh Markstein faced his closest colleagues at an emergency meeting in the Rav's home. He had heard from Shea about the tall blond boy who had purchased the device and paid with small bills. He had heard from Pedro about Ezzy's presence in the shul on Thursday night. He knew that Ezzy knew the combination to the safe. And most importantly, he had seen the mocking, challenging smile on Ezzy's face on Friday morning.

He said the words, speaking in his customary decisive tone, but as he informed the people around the table who the thief was, it was clear that he was shattered.

No one really knew how the word got out, but once it did, it spread. The fact is that by Monday morning, when Ezzy Markstein returned from his class trip, people knew. Maybe it was because Fogelman, proud of the role he had played, shared the story with his wife. Maybe it was because Pedro, resentful at having been suspected, told it to a few people. Max Frankel certainly hadn't told anyone, just his Eva. After all, she was his wife and entitled to know.

People were shocked.

Ezzy Markstein had been the thief in the much-publicized theft at the shul. He had stooped so low as to take the money out of the mouths of a poor Yerushalmi family. And his own father was the president of the shul at that. Who could believe it?

"The incident."

Chapter 6

I t was late enough in the winter that even the wind that blew carried with it a hint of the impending spring, a promise of warmer, brighter days. Moishy Winternitz was aware of the late afternoon breeze at the back of his neck as he walked, but he wasn't enjoying it. This daily walk to work was usually spent focusing on his own misery.

The route to his job, which took him past house after functional house, was a difficult one for Moishy. He would see mothers on their stoops, willing the sunshine to surround them in its embrace, smiling as they summoned children in for supper. He would see fathers pulling confidently into their driveways, their neckties loosened, as if to proclaim their freedom from another day's work. Everything about these images bespoke tranquility, calm, happiness; all the things that Moishy craved but would never have.

He checked his watch and realized that he was, once again, late. Tzion would be unhappy. *Well*, thought Moishy, *it serves him right for hiring someone like me. Who did he think he would get already?*

Tzion Batani was a good storekeeper. He had been raised at his father's feet in the small falafel store in Bucharim, a tiny storefront, but one that had provided for the family quite nicely. When Tzion grew older and felt the itch to go to America to seek his fortune, he already knew what he was going to do.

The small falafel store had opened to a receptive Brooklyn clientele. In time, however, the most traditional delis and even upper-class eateries began to offer his fare, falafel, shawarma, merguez, and kefta. He had to struggle for survival. He was never quite able to afford the gleaming storefront of his dreams, the spotless interior that he had so hoped for. Instead, he had to be content with the fact that his food was fresh and wholesome, his kitchen clean. He knew how to treat his employees so that they would feel proud of the place as well, that they would learn from him the importance of a smile to a customer. His staff was comprised mainly of teenagers in search of a few extra dollars, boys who didn't mind working his peak hours, from five-thirty until midnight.

Tzion looked at his watch with concern; it was already close to six and the new boy, Moishy, wasn't there yet. This was the fourth time he had been late in one week. Tzion briefly entertained the idea of speaking with him, but thought better of it. His father had always said that if you treat people with respect, then they would prove themselves worthy of respect.

Tzion noticed Moishy coming and smiled pleasantly. "Shalom," he called out warmly.

Moishy's eyes narrowed at the greeting. *Why was Tzion being so nice? What did he want? What did it mean?*

Moishy muttered a reply and struggled into his apron, ready to begin stuffing pitas, slicing shawarma, and frying onions. The noise of the first crowd of diners reached his ears as he worked without turning around, as if to drown out the sound of their happy conversation.

It was eight-fifteen and the supper rush was over. Tzion looked closely at Moishy and walked over to him. He laid a hand on the boy's shoulder and smiled. "Moishy, great job. Let me take you over for a little so you can go get a break. Take some food and relax."

Moishy felt it coming on, like a rushing wave in his heart. It was a mixture of self-pity, gratitude to his kindly boss, and, most of all, rage. And it was perhaps the most familiar sensation in Moishy Winternitz's life. He knew it already, knew it well. He would usually wait for it to wash over him, to pass him by so that he could get on with his life. Sometimes he would try to squash it, to dull it with cigarettes or beer, to feed it the way a lion tamer feeds a hungry beast.

Other times, like tonight, the rage seemed to have a voice all its own, and the voice spoke aloud. "What do you want from me already that you speak to me all nice, all gentle and considerate, when I know that you could"t care less about me? Leave me be, stop playing this game with me, let me do my job in peace. I am sick of this place and sick of how you treat me."

A lesser person than Tzion Badani might have been concerned with the hush that had suddenly come over the restaurant and its patrons, but the compassionate proprietor was more concerned with the pain of the boy who stood before him. Moishy ripped off his apron with a flourish and dropped it to the floor. "I don't need this," he said and stepped out into the cool night.

It was no use, thought Moishy as he walked aimlessly along the quiet stretch of the avenue. If he would have been capable of crying, he might have cried bitter tears of frustration at what he had just done, at another opportunity squandered, another victim felled by the rage within him.

The fury he felt so often would play a mocking song in his head, a song with words. It had a chorus that told him how unworthy he was, how he didn't really deserve anything he had, and that anyone who was nice to him really wanted something in return. Part of him knew that the contemptuous words were false, but the other part of him always responded, always gave into the anger and hurt like a frightened puppy cowering before its owner. Like tonight.

And, as always, when Moishy let the monster inside of him win, the pictures began to run through his mind in a haze of color and detail. If there had been captions on his mental album, the one next to this first set of images would have read "Moishy finds out the truth about how worthless and contemptible he really is."

Always, in his memories, he can smell that not unpleasant aroma of fresh-cut wood just after the rain has fallen on it, mixed with the odor of garbage bags left out in the sun. Sun, rain, garbage, they all come together in this mist.

Moishy is in camp, barely eleven years old, walking innocently behind the dining room just after a rain storm.

He has passed the large building and even walked by the garbage hut. He is going for a walk. Moishy likes the smell of the grass and trees while they are still dripping wet. It's not like at home, in the city. In the city, rain makes everything smell like oil and concrete; here, up in the mountains, the rain seems to be mixed with cinnamon and pine.

Moishy is alone, hoping to find a frog out here in this thicket. In the distance, he hears his bunkmates and the rest of the camp bentching, so he knows that he will soon have to hurry back to join them.

There are footsteps behind him and Moishy turns suddenly. Moishy is young, very young, and anyone in camp who is old enough to shave is seen as an authority figure. He knows that he is supposed to be bentching now, and he feels scared. Will he be in trouble? He begins to run. The footsteps quicken as well.

"Do you think that you are someone special, that you are somehow better than everyone else in this camp?" asks the figure suddenly looming large over Moishy.

Moishy recognizes him; he is the camp driver. Moishy recalls how, the week before, he had been riding in the van, headed to the roller skating rink, and he had angered the driver by throwing an empty soda can out the window. He recalls the frightening look that had crossed the driver's face as he had begun to shout at Moishy. Moishy recalls how he had laughed in the face of the driver's rage and how his giggles had caused his friends to laugh as well.

Moishy is suddenly brought back to the present as he feels fists on his back, pummeling fiercely. Strangely, Moishy is more fascinated than hurt, wondering why he is being beaten. Is he being mistaken for someone else?

Wait ... his assailant is explaining it. "You aren't any better than anyone else, so stop thinking that you are.

You're just a little —" Here Moishy feels a new round of punches beginning and he curls into fetal position, waiting for it to end.

When the blows stop, Moishy feels himself being lifted and dragged toward the garbage hut. He is shoved and he lands in the pile of garbage bags that surround it. "You are just a piece of garbage yourself."

And walking along the avenue on this March night, Moishy remembers the second picture. *He is sitting with his friends in the bunkhouse and the door opens. In walks a tallish fellow in a gray T-shirt. He looks right at Moishy.*

Moishy freezes. It's him, the driver. Had it really happened? Moishy had been convinced that it hadn't. Now that he sees the petulant face, the lips curled at him in a snarl, he knows that it had indeed happened. He also now knows that it had been his fault, that the figure standing over him and tapping him on his shoulder is right. He hadn't had any business being out back all by himself.

"Can I talk to you a minute?" asks the tall man, addressing Moishy in soft, almost pleading tones. Moishy rises respectfully, anxious for this person to tell him that it had never really happened, that it was a misunderstanding, that it wasn't his fault.

Instead he leads Moishy through the baseball field. He stops and tells Moishy an amusing story about hitting a ball in the wrong direction. Moishy laughs.

They continue until they pass the garbage hut and then go into the woods. Moishy follows. He isn't sure when to stop. Then he feels the blows raining down on him and he knows that it's time to remain still, very still.

"You still think that you're hot stuff, huh? I want to shake that feeling out of you. You are a rotten child, do you hear me?" Moishy hears and understands.

⏐▌⏐▐▌⏐▐⏐ ▐⏐▐⏐▐⏐▌⏐▐⏐ ⏐▐⏐▐⏐

And so it had gone for Moishy that summer. A slow, steady descent into a pit from which there was no escape. Sure, once or twice he had tried to cry out, to alert his counselor, but his message had never gotten through.

So when Moishy came home three weeks later, he brought with him several things. A haphazard model of the *Beis HaMikdash* that he had made in arts and crafts, some bruises on his back (*It's nothing Ma, just some scratches from falling next to the swimming pool*), and a consciousness that he was completely useless as a person.

He had heard it so many times. It had to be true. After all, no one else got beaten for it like he did.

⏐▌⏐▐▌⏐▐⏐ ▐⏐▐⏐▐⏐▌⏐▐⏐ ⏐▐⏐▐⏐

These days, Moishy didn't focus on any part of the story. These days, there were all kinds of people interested in helping him deal with it, concerned family and professionals whose expressions were horrified when he spoke. It was as if it was his fault that he hadn't been able to tell them all these years.

Either way, even if the story was ancient history, the feeling it spawned was his constant companion. And tonight those fists had claimed another casualty. His job.

Chapter 7

Mendel Wasser felt the familiar tightness in his neck as the bell rang, signaling the end of recess. He stepped out into the school yard and signaled to the boys that their break was over and that they were supposed to return to class. He squared his shoulders and walked into the middle of their baseball game, cupping his hands around his mouth and shouting, "Don't pitch the ball; recess is over *now!*"

Apparently, the boy with the ball didn't hear his Rebbi, because he pitched the ball even as Mendel stood there. The batter hit a sizzling grounder just two feet to Mendel's left, and Mendel had to make a quick decision. If he grabbed the ball, the game would be over and he could score a small victory. He would lead them back to class and hopefully have them seated before this escalated into a major mess. If, however, he missed the ball, then he would just feel foolish.

He decided. Mendel lunged for the ball just as it skipped by him and went into the outfield. He turned angrily and his voice came out shrill and unnatural. "The game is over this instant. Don't throw it, drop it now, I said something, leave it, I mean it, watch yourself ...."

Mendel's voice was lost in the excitement of the throw to home plate and an argument ensued whether the runner was safe or out. Mendel had the familiar uncertainty if he existed at all, if anyone saw his face or heard his voice. But of course, he knew the answer. The look on the face of the Menahel as he stood at the door to the building, staring right at Mendel, his face a mixture of disdain and pity, confirmed that Mendel was perfectly visible. The Menahel shook his head slowly and motioned for the ball. The game was over.

Ever since he had been a child, Mendel Wasser had wanted to be a rebbi. He loved Torah, he loved Jews, and he loved teaching. He so much enjoyed the thrill of taking a subtle, difficult concept and bringing it down to the level of his listener.

He had learned well in yeshivah and when he had married Gitty, it had been with the understanding that he would pursue a career in *chinuch*. Alas, a career in *chinuch* didn't pursue Mendel Wasser. He simply lacked that presence, that self-confidence that made *Menahelim* believe that he could succeed in the classroom. Sure, he had an abundance of warmth, empathy, concern, and patience, but these days, that wasn't enough. He was too short, his tie permanently askew, curled at its tip and pointing upward. The dandruff on his collar and the coffee stain on his shirt were part of his uniform, and his glasses were on a perpetual slide toward the end of his nose.

So even though his smile was full of hope and optimism and his eyes alight at the prospect of teaching Torah, his demeanor and carriage spoke otherwise. As endearing as he was to these interviewers, there was no room for a Mendel Wasser on their staff.

After years of searching for a position, he had accepted this one, teaching tenth grade at a school for scholastically weak teenagers. The odds were against him. The boys were unmotivated and cynical. The Menahel had only hired him in desperation, because it was two weeks before the beginning of the new school year and last year's rebbi had found a better job elsewhere. The Board of Directors hadn't been particularly impressed with him at their meeting. When they had asked him about his prior experience, he had smiled and said, "I may not have practical experience, but I have waited for this opportunity for fifteen years." The board members hadn't liked that answer. They'd found it trite.

The first day of school had been a nightmare for Mendel Wasser. He had come in brimming with exuberance and gusto, ready to meet his destiny. He had asked the boys to introduce themselves, thinking that it would break the ice. The first few boys shared their real names, but suddenly one said that his name was George W. Bush. There had been titters in the class and Mendel had made his first mistake. Instead of ignoring the challenge and moving on, he had stopped and looked at the boy curiously. "Come on, tell us your real name," he had urged.

"Okay, okay," the boy had said resignedly, "it's Rudy Giu-liani." Mendel hadn't been sure how to proceed, so he just made a note to tell the Menahel and continued with the list.

And that's the way the year had gone for him. Sure, the boys tolerated him, and some of them even liked him. Yet he had never really mastered the art of discipline, had never asserted real control over them. Mendel Wasser didn't realize a simple truth. With teenage boys, it's not merely enough to be liked; you have to be feared also. The boys genuinely liked the sweet, sincere, well-meaning rebbi, who truly had their best interest at heart. It just wasn't enough to get them to sit in their seats, or to stop talking, or to come in from recess.

The Menahel didn't care how much they liked Mendel; he cared that the class be orderly and well run and that the boys be kept out of trouble. Unfortunately, the class was not orderly and well run and he kept hearing about different acts of mischief that the boys had perpetrated. He had discussed it with Rabbi Wasser several times and each time, the rebbi would look at him pleadingly and tell him how close he felt to the boys.

From the Menahel's vantage point, the year had been a disaster. He had already begun to search in earnest for a replacement, and was planning on terminating Rabbi Wasser's contract as soon as he found someone qualified. Standing at the doorway on this late winter morning and watching the rebbi scramble for the ball as the boys continued their game over his protests made the Menahel think that the day couldn't come fast enough.

Mendel drove home slowly, still numb from his conversa-tion with the Menahel. "Rabbi Wasser," he had said, "you will probably be a great rebbi someday, but not here, and not yet. Go to a training seminar, get some experience, and maybe try getting a summer job. Then you can try your luck elsewhere. We will keep you until Pesach and then give you your salary for one more month."

The Menahel's tone left no room for disagreement, and he even looked surprised when Mendel asked, "But didn't you see that things were starting to go so well, that it was all coming together?"

He had nodded when Mendel said that, "Perhaps," he'd replied, "but not fast enough."

As Mendel made his way home, visions kept appearing in front of his eyes. David sitting at his desk after class last week, crying as he told Mendel of his father's illness. Shalom's eyes lighting up when he understood the first Tosafos of his life, the smile spreading across his face slowly and remaining there for the rest of class. Sammy waiting by his car as he left school, looking at the ground and muttering, "I am sorry Rebbi. You deserve better."

Didn't the Menahel realize that he loved the boys and they loved him? Did the Menahel honestly believe that some new rebbi with a cleaner shirt and more trendy glasses would have more room in his heart than Mendel had?

As Mendel's eyes filled with tears, blurring his vision, another thought struck him. Gitty. Energetic, successful, competent Gitty the overachiever. Gitty the super teacher, Gitty who had the whole world under control, who was constantly being asked to teach a higher grade, to take on new challenges.

His wife.

Gitty would look at him with sympathy and, instead of saying what he wished she would say, that "The Menahel is absolutely crazy, he had a future star in you and he is letting you go, we will fight this thing until the end," she would shrug and tell him, "Them's the breaks." She wouldn't be surprised.

||||||||||||||||||||||

Late that night, Mendel was still sitting in his dining room, wearing his tie and jacket, unable to summon the energy to head upstairs to bed. He had waited for the normal noises in the house to stop so that he could allow his tears to fall. His deep pain didn't come from the fact that he would soon have no *parnassah* for his family or from the humiliation of losing his job in mid-year. It didn't even come from the fact that the bond he had created with this crew of struggling teenagers was being severed so abruptly. He cried for his lost opportunity, for his dream of being a great rebbi that was being washed away with the tears that flowed freely down his cheeks.

Gitty had been predictably unsympathetic. Oh, she had clucked her tongue and told him that Hashem would send him something else, but she had never once said that it was a mistake, that he *was* meant to be a Rebbe.

She had merely continued washing dishes as she discussed various options with him, reminding him that she would be assuming the role of yearbook advisor at the high school where she taught, so there would be some extra income until the end of the year if things got really tight. Later on, Mendel had heard her on the phone with her sister, saying, "Well, Mendel finally lost the job," with an air of resignation, as if it had been inevitable that he would.

Mendel could almost imagine his sister-in-law's response. "*Oy*, that is hard," she would emphatically agree. "I know exactly what it's like. I still remember when they let Chaim Tzvi go from his old office. He was devastated, but we managed. I worked extra hours until he found something else, but it was still so hard. Good luck, Gitty."

Mendel couldn't be certain that she had answered exactly that, but he knew that her response would be along those lines. After all, she too was a Goldman girl, raised on the ethic of hard work and no play. They were all the same, this family of go-getters, the four sisters with their sweet, weak husbands.

Mendel sometimes felt pained at the knowledge that Gitty looked down on him because of his failures and unrealized dreams. He wasn't insightful enough to realize that Gitty had married him precisely because of them.

Chapter 8

itty Wasser checked off the next name on her list with a satisfied sigh. There were few things that Gitty enjoyed as much as tackling a list of jobs and watching the list shrink. This morning, she was systematically calling different *askanim* and businessmen to try and find a job for her Mendel, who would soon be jobless.

She dialed the next name on her list, a cousin of her sister's, who was apparently quite connected. He listened politely to her description of a pleasant, sincere, scholarly young yeshivah man in search of a job, and by the time she finished talking, his fingers were already working on the other line.

"Ari," he said into the phone, "I think I have the perfect guy for that job at Mishkan Shalom."

Moishy Winternitz looked at the clock: three o'clock. Ezzy would soon be out of school and Moishy hoped they would be able to chill together for a bit. Moishy was having a horrible day. He kept replaying the scene last night at Tzion's, how he had spoken so insolently to his kindly boss and effectively thrown away a good job.

It was easy to feel tough for a few minutes, but he knew that he wasn't tough at all; he was actually very weak, too weak to make anything work. He had spent the day berating himself *(You are a rotten child, do you hear me? You still think that you're something special?)* and allowing the fury to build up to the point where he had to silence it. He had taken a shower, letting the scalding water sear his skin, actually enjoying the sensation of pain, of inflicting punishment on the body that housed this mess.

He needed to talk to someone. There weren't that many "someones" who were eager to listen to Moishy these days. Only Ezzy. Moishy understood Ezzy, understood what it was like to be shunned and maligned by everyone else, and Ezzy understood Moishy and what is was like to be down on yourself to the point that it is difficult to look in a mirror.

They understood each other and needed each other like two American tourists lost in Australia need each other, two broken souls lost on an island of whole, happy people.

Mendel Wasser was having a bad day, one of his worst to date. The pre-Purim excitement had officially infiltrated his class. He was having a hard time competing with the current of excitement sweeping through the classroom as boys passed notes about costumes and fire crackers. He genuinely felt like closing his Gemara and confiding in the boys about what the

Menahel had said. He felt that these boys were his friends and they had a right to know. But Gitty had cautioned him to maintain his composure, to act professional and not like a crybaby and he knew that she was right, of course. Still, he felt like crying.

Ezzy walked out of his last class of the day, heading into the hallway. A large group was congregating near the school's front entrance and he stopped to listen to their conversation. Ezzy was already a pro at listening to conversations without trying to participate. He knew that if he would add something, then he would attract attention and inevitably some of them would think about him and his story. Then, they would grow uncomfortable and the conversation would disintegrate.

So Ezzy bent over, ostensibly to tie his shoe, as he listened to their carefree chatter.

"I plan to stay out till 4 a.m. this year, my father already said I could. He even said he would give me 25 cents for every dollar we raised over last year's total."

"Yeah, right, Dovi, that's what you said last year. Then you got dizzy and were fast asleep by midnight!"

Ezzy stood up and walked out of the building.

The sun was still shining, sending out its last few rays and proclaiming that winter was a thing of the past, but it wasn't enough to lift Ezzy's spirits.

There was another group gathered on the wide front steps of the building and once again, Ezzy bent over his shoes.

"We are going collecting at Motty Kleinberg's this year. Last year he gave out over fifty thousand dollars for *tzedakah* on Purim night."

"Oh, right, like you're his accountant, Shloimy."

"No, really, he davens in my shul and I heard him saying it last week. This year, he said, no group will walk out of his house with less than three hundred and sixty dollars."

Ezzy wished that he could join the conversation with some information of his own. Motty Kleinberg served on several boards with his father and they were quite friendly. He had told Ezzy's father that he was going to Florida for Purim.

Ezzy deliberated if he should share this information. He decided that it wasn't worth antagonizing Shloimy. You never knew how he might respond.

Ezzy was still hoping that he would be invited to go collecting with anyone of the numerous groups that his classmates were forming. In past years, he had been the one organizing the groups, deciding on who would come along, where they would go, and how they would dress up.

This year, he imagined the confused looks as people would open their doors. "Isn't that the Markstein boy?" they would whisper to their wives, "The one who ...."

Malka Markstein was humming a tune as she turned the key and let herself into her house. She loved this time of year, with the excitement of Purim and Pesach just beyond it.

Chavi, Avrohom Meir, and the baby were arriving just a few days after Purim and Malka could hardly wait. She hadn't seen her little granddaughter since the previous summer and the thought of the little girl with the wild golden curls filled her with glee.

Little Miri was cute, for sure, but that wasn't the only reason that Malka longed for her arrival. It was also because she was able to do what no one else could: turn Aryeh Markstein into the person Malka had always wished he would become.

| | | | | | | | | | | |

Twenty-three years earlier, Malka had sat in Prospect Park and made herself a promise. The boy she was dating wanted to marry her, and she wanted very badly to want to marry him. She just didn't want to.

Malka was the third in a family of five girls, by far the one with the sunniest, most upbeat disposition. Hers was a loving home, a happy home, and a very poor home. Aryeh Markstein, the boy that she was seeing, seemed to have many wonderful attributes. He was bright and respectful, serious and kind. Her father was ecstatic about this young yeshivah graduate with the accounting degree, seeing in him someone who would take good care of his Malka.

Malka found Aryeh pleasant enough; it was just that he seemed to be lacking the one thing she needed most: *simchas hachaim,* contentment and joy in life. She understood that his background hadn't really afforded him many opportunities for joy. His father had passed away when he was eleven. Afterward, his mother had moved her small family, consisting of herself and two boys, from Washington Heights to Brooklyn. In Brooklyn, they had changed apartments several times, always in search of cheaper rent. Aryeh began to contribute to the family income, working after school as a delivery boy for a local pharmacy and also found a Shabbos job setting up *seudah shlishis* at a shul.

The demands of school and work left him little time for friendship. Fun became something he disdained, something to be avoided at all costs. Aryeh couldn't allow himself to be anything but practical. By the time he was 20, he was juggling

yeshivah studies, a college workload, and two part-time jobs
— his mother relied on the income.

When Malka met this accomplished young man, she immediately decided that he was missing the "enjoy-life" gene, as she
later confided to her sisters, and she didn't see how she could
join her life with his when they were wired so very differently.

And she shared her misgivings with him one spring evening.

"I love to relax, to enjoy doing nothing at all, I love people
and places, and I feel that every second of life is something
beautiful to be savored. You think of seconds as grim reminders of how much you have to learn, to study, to work. How
can you say that we belong together?"

Aryeh had sat there quietly for a long while, considering
her words. Then he had spoken.

"It's true that I never really had an opportunity to take it
easy, and sitting and doing nothing is alien to my makeup. But
since when does being happy mean the same thing as relax-
ing? Why can't I derive happiness from my accomplishments
in learning and business?"

Malka had interrupted him, suddenly. "Look," she'd cried
out, "You can't miss this. Over there!" she pointed to a space
behind a thicket of bushes, "Stand up and see."

Aryeh was offended at the way that she had just cut him
off in mid-sentence. And it wasn't like they had been discussing the weather, either. They were having what was perhaps
the most important conversation in each of their lives, yet
still, she ....

He looked into the clearing and saw two little boys, perhaps six and seven. The younger boy had fallen of his bicycle
and had scraped his knee. He stood there howling, while
the older brother knelt next to him, and began to speak to
him tenderly. "Don't worry," he was saying, "it'll stop hurting
in a second." He was gently dabbing at the bloody area with

his T-shirt, all the while murmuring comforting words to his brother.

Malka's eyes were shining. "Look at the way that young child is caring for his little brother. Isn't that beautiful?"

Aryeh thought it was strange that she would interrupt a deep and crucial conversation to point out a routine sight. They were brothers, right? It wasn't all that exciting to him. Still, the fact that she could be so affected by the sight of love expressed made him realize ever so clearly that she was exactly what he needed.

Aryeh resumed the conversation where he had left off, but he found that he couldn't get it back on track.

Suddenly, the words came pouring out of his mouth, even before he considered them. "If you think that I don't know how to be happy, why don't you teach me how to be happy?"

Malka's features softened and tears filled her eyes. She smiled brightly at him. "Okay," she said softly, "I will, I will."

Chapter 9

The offices of Mishkan Shalom were alive with activity
and noise. Ari Engel was in the midst of intense negotia-
tions with a bureaucrat up in Albany when his secretary
signaled that his next appointment was waiting.

Ari smiled at the self-conscious yeshivah fellow standing
in the doorway of his office and gestured toward an empty
chair. Ari was surprised at the appearance of the gentleman
before him. Though he couldn't have been younger than thirty
years old, there was something about him that made Ari think
of a child whose mother had dressed him.

Ari wasn't far off base. Gitty had sent Mendel's suit to
the cleaners in anticipation of his meeting with Ari Engel and
had insisted that he wear his finest tie and his Shabbos hat.
She had primed Mendel on what to say and how to sit, done
everything short of actually coming along with him to the

interview. Gitty was perceptive and shrewd, and she realized — and struggled to make Mendel realize — that an interview with Ari Engel wasn't something to be taken lightly.

Ari Engel was the chief executive officer of Mishkan Shalom, a leading Brooklyn-based organization that served developmentally delayed adults and their families. The organization was totally funded by a New York State agency known by the acronym OMRDD, and Ari Engel was the one responsible for running the huge operation of group homes, case workers, and day centers. Ari Engel was an exceptional individual, a combination of empathetic listener and concerned friend on one hand, and a tough, hardened executive on the other. He had the ability to make snap decisions under pressure and his interviews tended to last mere minutes. Anyhow, the interview he was conducting on this afternoon was a simple one; he needed someone for the job and he was ready to give it to the first semi-qualified person he would encounter.

He introduced himself and shook Mendel's hand warmly, asking him perfunctory questions. He knew that after this interview, Mendel would join hundreds of other Mishkan Shalom employees and would cross paths with him only at the annual Mishkan Shalom Chanukah party.

Mendel finished talking about his background, using the word *chinuch* no less than six times, and Ari leaned forward in his interview pose, looking as if he was hanging on Mendel's every word. "Do you believe that *chinuch* has many forms and the world is full of classrooms, Reb Mendel?"

Mendel nodded eagerly "Sure," he responded.

"I am not certain how much you know about the job, so let me outline it for you."

"I understood that it was some kind of position that involved giving *shiurim*," said Mendel in that same eager tone. Gitty had told him that it was a job that he might enjoy.

"Um, do you know what we do here at Mishkan Shalom?" asked Ari gently.

Mendel looked as if he weren't quite sure, so Ari filled him in. "Well, we run all sorts of programs for special-needs adults. Most of our clients, or consumers, as we call them, are high functioning, and we find that they enjoy maximum productivity in group homes. We aim to create a warm, peaceful setting for them in these homes and allow them to contribute as much as possible. We also hope to make it as much like their own homes as possible. To that end, we have Shabbos meals and try to create a happy, homey atmosphere for them.

"Most of our consumers go out each day, either to work, to perform *chessed* activities, or for medical treatment. At night, when they come home, we like to have a learning session with them, which they particular enjoy."

Mendel looked shocked, and Ari continued smoothly.

"At our newest group home, in Kensington, we have a wonderful staff of dedicated professionals; we are only missing one thing. We need someone to daven with them in the morning and maybe learn something with them after davening, then learn privately with one or two of them, perhaps different consumers on different days. Then you would have to learn with them as a group each evening. You would also have to daven all the Shabbos *tefillos* with them and learn with them on Shabbos as well." Ari paused, and then finished, "There might also be some times when they just want someone to chat with them, or go for a walk with them.

"We receive our funding from the state and you will receive a respectable salary and benefits. You will also have a few hours off in the afternoon to prepare."

Mendel still hadn't spoken and Ari was getting a little edgy. He was used to working quickly. "Is something wrong, Reb Mendel?"

Mendel hadn't been ready for this at all, but he knew all too clearly that he hadn't any options aside from this. Besides, he was picturing a delightful scene in his mind, in which he was telling Gitty that she wouldn't have to work so hard, that she could turn down the extra job as yearbook advisor ... after all, he was earning a respectable salary.

"No, not at all," Mendel smiled at Ari. "It sounds very interesting."

"Great, great," said Ari briskly, pressing a buzzer on his desk. "Call Mrs. Schmidt to the office, please," he instructed his secretary.

Then he rose and patted Mendel on the shoulder. "Welcome to the Mishkan Shalom family, Reb Mendel. I am sure that you will find it to be a uniquely rewarding experience, a new way to reach Yiddishe hearts and minds. We are glad to have you."

Then he led Mendel to the door and introduced him to a tall woman with a clipboard in her hand. "Mrs. Schmidt, this is Rabbi Wasser, the new rabbi for the 18th Avenue residence. Please work out a schedule and list of his duties for him and answer any questions he may have."

Ari turned smartly and went back to his business, but found his mind wandering back to the sincere face of Mendel Wasser.

"This could work," he said to no one in particular.

Benjy Biller's eyes were shut tightly, and he was strumming on the strings of his guitar in ecstasy. "*Mama Rochel, cry for us again,*" he sang loudly, the sorry notes coming forth from the battered instrument bearing no resemblance to the song's actual tune. Benjy sang and sang, reaching a dramatic crescendo and trying valiantly to hit a high note. Then, he suddenly stopped and nodded at the crowd, his face shining with pride at the scattered applause.

"Thank you, thank you," he said grandly. He looked around the living room, as if hoping someone would ask for an encore. Someone did. Leizer. "Come on Benjy, play one more song for us," he urged. Someone groaned in protest, but whoever did was silenced by a sharp look from Leizer.

Each evening, after supper was over, the residents gathered in the large, spacious living room to unwind from the day. More often than not, Benjy, who fancied himself a musician, would regale his co-residents with his music.

Leizer was the staff member in charge of the after-dinner hours at this Mishkan Shalom group home, and he loved his job. Leizer Krause was responsible and hard-working, and had been successful at various jobs before this one. He had stumbled into the work at Mishkan Shalom during a slow season at the office where he had worked and, in the months since, had become an indispensable part of the newest home. Within hours of assuming his position at the group home, he had discovered that this job was like no other he had ever held.

Here, he was working with real people.

The struggles and battles waged by the developmentally delayed adults at the residence inspired him; the odds that they faced every single day touched him to the very core of his being. Quiet Leizer Krause became their most vocal advocate, and they in turn had begun to view him as such. They waited until after supper, when Leizer came, to voice their deepest concerns and hopes, looking to him for reassurance.

Now Leizer was getting married, and he was leaving Brooklyn for Monsey. In two more nights, he would have to bid farewell to this group of sweet, endearing adults who had become his best friends.

It wouldn't be easy. His only comfort lay in the fact that the people at the office had assured him that there was a great demand for compassionate, patient people like him in Monsey as well, and that they would find him a similar job there as well.

As Benjy started to play "Rachem," Leizer looked at his watch. They had told him that the replacement was going to arrive at seven o'clock so that he could begin training him.

Mendel Wasser was a man of faith, and firmly believed that everything that happens was exactly the way Hashem wants it to be. As he drove down Ocean Parkway, he wondered what the Divine Plan could be in sending him to this new post.

He was no doctor, had no training, and lacked the necessary skills to be able to teach anything to the residents at Mishkan Shalom. He had been overwhelmed by Leizer's suggestion that he would "soon be a professional," and had assured him that this was only temporary, until he found another rebbe position.

Then again, Mendel found his mind wandering back to Benjy, sitting with his beaten-up guitar, his face suffused with joy. Mendel felt a stab of affection in his heart as he recalled Benjy's huge brown eyes searching his face after he had finished playing, asking him if he had enjoyed it. There was definitely something about this new job that appealed to him.

He wondered what Gitty would say to a job that would take him out of the house during the early morning hours, the evening hours, and on Shabbos. She would probably just shrug and assure him that she would manage fine with the kids; in fact, she knew how to make *Kiddush* by herself if need be.

As soon as he had signed his contract with the people at the Mishkan Shalom office, Gitty had insisted that he inform the Menahel that he was done, that he wouldn't even stay until Pesach. Mendel knew that she was right, that in order to succeed at his new job he would have to immerse himself in it completely, but still, he wouldn't have minded finishing the *z'man* with his *talmidim*.

The worst thing had been that when he had informed the Menahel, he had quickly nodded, as if Mendel would change his mind, and said, "That's quite all right, I understand. I will handle them myself until Yom Tov."

Chapter 10

Ezzy walked down the hallway slowly, pausing to take a drink, delaying the conversation. There was one week left to Purim and the prospect of spending Purim night and day at home was increasingly unappealing. At this point it was clear enough that none of his classmates were planning to include him in their groups, even those venturing to neighborhoods beyond Flatbush.

There was one more hope, one that Ezzy was very hesitant to pursue. Daniel Becker. Even today, two years later, the mention of Daniel Becker's name would cause Ezzy to feel nauseous. It was perhaps that encounter with Daniel that best symbolized the "old Ezzy," and whenever Ezzy remembered it, he would feel overcome with self-loathing.

They had both been fourteen years old, a complicated and difficult time in a boy's life, and it hadn't been any less so for them. Ezzy had been trying to assert himself as the class leader, and was quick to quash any signs of rebellion. There were few, but Daniel Becker had made an attempt.

One of the teachers hadn't shown up for that period and someone suggested that they all sneak out of school together and go bike-riding. It was a daring scheme, and invariably, all eyes turned to Ezzy, waiting for him to render his decision. It was understood that they would all abide by whatever he would say, for such incidents of "civil disobedience" can only succeed if the whole class is united. If even one boy would choose to stay behind, then the plan wouldn't work. It was Ezzy's call.

Ezzy had briefly contemplated the consequences and then spoken. "Let's do it," he'd said breezily. "Nothing will happen to us anyhow."

Ezzy's quick decision had put Daniel Becker in a quandary. Daniel had desperately wanted a new bike; he had wanted one for his entire life. He had never owned a new bike, only second-hand ones that his mother had bought from neighbors or received from cousins. This year, his parents had promised, if his report card was exemplary, they would buy him a new bike. He had spent seven months studying hard, working diligently, and behaving impeccably, all for that new bike. He knew that there was a chance, however small, that the principal would come down hard on them and discipline them forcefully; that could cost him the bike.

So, in a small voice, he spoke up. "Um, I'm not sure that it's worth it. Think how upset Mr. Green will be and how he might react. I will stay back."

And just like that, voices were heard, silent murmurs of agreement. "Yeah, maybe it's true, maybe Becker has a point. Is it worth antagonizing Mr. Green so late in the year?"

Ezzy had been stunned by this unprecedented show of force from silent Daniel Becker, and, in desperation, he struggled to regain control. "Aw, Becker, what do you know anyhow?"

Daniel felt his face flush, but he knew he had no choice. "I know plenty, Markstein, maybe more than you."

Daniel was a good student, Ezzy thought, but this was unacceptable. "Maybe you know stuff about math and science, not about people. Stay out of it."

"Ezzy, you think you know so much? Don't you remember that you're the one that said it would be funny to pull the fire alarm by Gershy's bar mitzvah? Look at the mess that you got us into then!"

Ezzy had sneered, but inside he had been fuming and decided that it was time to put Daniel in place, for once and for all. He prepared for his cheapest shot, dragging it out the way an archer might aim carefully before letting his arrow loose.

'Well, Becker, I certainly know one thing that you don't. That new jacket that you're so proud of, the blue one with the hood … it's really mine. I wore it for a few days, but it didn't fit me right, so my mother just donated it to the Center. That's where your mother got it."

And as if to prove his point, Ezzy walked over to the corner of the classroom and lifted the windbreaker off the hook. He waved it aloft and pointed to a small, faded smudge on the inside pocket. It was easy to read what was written there: E.M.

Ezzy dropped the jacket on the floor and grinned wickedly. Daniel didn't even bother to get his jacket. He turned and ran out of the room.

Ezzy and his friends had gone bike riding. Ezzy had won, but it was a hollow victory.

On erev Yom Kippur, Ezzy had gone to Daniel's house and tearfully begged for mechilah. He had meant it, genuinely appalled at his own behavior. Daniel had said that he forgave Ezzy, but Ezzy knew that he could never really erase his sin. At least not yet. The wound was too raw.

Now, two years later, Ezzy approached Daniel in the hallway and walked alongside him for a minute. Finally, he spoke. "What's doing, Daniel?" he asked.

"*Baruch Hashem*, pretty good. How about you?"

"I'm fine, *Baruch Hashem*. So what are your plans for Purim?"

Daniel looked at Ezzy warily, as if trying to figure out what he wanted. Then it dawned on him. His group was composed of the less-popular kids, the ones who hadn't been asked to join with any of the more "happening" kids. Ezzy had obviously been rejected and was coming to him out of desperation.

"I think we will go collecting a bit," said Daniel slowly.

"That's nice, real nice," said Ezzy. Then, ever so timidly, he asked, "Would you happen to need an extra guy in your group?"

There was a moment of complete silence as Ezzy looked down at the floor and Daniel looked right at Ezzy and did something he would forever regret.

"Oh, Ezzy, what a nice idea. You can come collecting with us on Purim, and I even know what we can do for costumes. We can all wear your old clothing."

And with that, Daniel spun on his heel and walked away.

And Ezzy just stood there and closed his eyes, allowing the waves of pain to rush at him and overwhelm him. He slumped against a nearby locker feeling so, so tired. "Hashem," he thought, "I accept it, all of it." Ezzy felt small and insignificant, like a discarded tissue. But at the same time, he felt strangely liberated, a sense of closure.

He had come full circle.

Peretz Winternitz was better with computers than he was with people; it was as simple as that. Sometimes he wished that he could create a program that would allow him to communicate, to connect, to forge real and lasting bonds with them, but alas, it didn't seem like that time had arrived yet.

Peretz was blessed with nine children, and he loved each and every one of them fiercely. He just wasn't much of a communicator. He also lacked a crucial commodity: time. He toiled long hours to support his large family, working in New Jersey all day and then, at night, doing freelance work to help pay the bills. On Sundays, he spent hours at the various *mosdos* in which his children studied, solving computer issues as a way of lowering his tuition payments. With most of the children, his shortcomings as a parent hadn't made an obvious difference, and they had done nicely scholastically and socially. They had seen through his silent exterior, felt his love despite his lack of expression or eloquence.

Moishy was different.

Moishy had always been different, and even as an infant, he had been somewhat withdrawn and sullen. It had been difficult for Peretz to reach him, to make him laugh, and it became somewhat of a challenge, a game. Peretz would come home from work or from shul and look for little Moishy. Then he would start tickling him, working his way up his arms as Moishy would stand immobile, his lips set in a firm, straight line. Then, inevitably, he would burst out laughing, wild, hysterical laughter.

Laughter that would make Peretz very happy. It was only then that Moishy would really exhibit signs of joy and Peretz would cherish those moments, allowing the echoes of Moishy's peals to accompany him late into the night.

This joyous ritual continued even as Moishy had grown, when he turned eight, nine, and ten. Moishy was a tough kid, with a tough attitude; a walking challenge to rebbeim and teachers who all tried to break through to him. None of them could, and it was only Peretz, with his tickling, who could crack the impassive exterior.

In Moishy's laughter he heard a secret, only for him. It was a secret promise to love and live, to grow and flourish.

One day, the laughter had stopped.

Peretz would tickle and Moishy would squirm out of his grasp, running to his room. Peretz would follow and the door would be locked. No more tickling, no more laughter, no more secret.

Now Moishy was a teenager. The laughter was a distant memory, very distant.

Peretz spent most of his day working as a technician for a large telecommunications company. His devoted wife had prepared a disc with a collection of family pictures, culled from years' worth of albums. They swirled around his screen in a dizzying pattern, girls and boys, grandparents and grandchildren, graduations and chumash parties and bar mitzvahs and family vacations.

And Moishy.

Moishy sitting by his *upsheren,* unsmiling. Moishy at a Chumash *seudah,* a hat made of cardboard and golden paper at a jaunty angle, a marked contrast to his scowl. There was a picture of Peretz holding Moishy aloft and tickling him and here Moishy's eyes were dancing with unconcealed delight. There was one of Moishy, together with all of the other kid's one Chol HaMoed at the Bronx Zoo (it was a Wednesday, when admission was free) and here as well, Moishy stared straight at the camera, his face a mask of sullen defiance.

Then there were later pictures, Moishy on visiting day at camp, Moishy at his bar mitzvah, Moishy at Baila's *chasunah* last year … in these pictures, Moishy's eyes were no longer dark and brooding; they were vacant.

And at his desk on the fifth floor of a sprawling New Jersey industrial complex, Peretz Winternitz of tech support sat thinking, something he rarely had time to do. Phones buzzed all around him and memos were issued, but Peretz sat there with his head in his hands, motionless. His coworkers around him shared looks and shrugs with each other, but they were respectful enough to leave him in solitude.

They all knew that he had a whole bunch of kids. "Look," they mouthed to each other, "the pressure has finally caught up with him. Poor soul."

Peretz, meanwhile, was making a promise to himself ….

Chapter 11

I tzik the video man mounted his ladder, handling the camera with ease as he searched for the perfect angle to capture the joy of the wedding. Itzik loved his job, loved the action and energy, but most of all, he enjoyed the challenge of catching the perfect shots, the ones that truly captured the frenzied joy of the moment. Itzik knew that when the young couple would sit down to watch their wedding videos, they would relish the chance to relive the emotion of the *chuppah,* savor the joy in the dancing, but that wouldn't be the highlight. What they would enjoy most would be the surprise shots, the aspects of their *simchah* that they themselves had missed. They would be touched by the spontaneous dance of an uncle, moved by a clip that snared the happy smile of an old friend. And so, though Itzik made sure that he filmed all the important moments, he loved the opportunity to record those moments that would be pleasant surprises for the *chassan* and *kallah* later on.

And tonight, at the Krause-Wexler wedding, he had found the perfect shot. He steered the camera away from the *chassan,* Leizer, sitting on a chair amid a circle of stomping, sweating friends. He passed over the circle of Rabbanim and *mechutanim,* their circle slower and more restrained than that of the boys, but still, exuding a dignified joy. He even passed over the chance to record the exuberance of the three young children who had succeeded in obtaining pairs of white gloves from a kindly waiter. He went straight to the far corner of the large ballroom, focusing on a tight little circle.

What struck him about this little group was the look on the faces of the men dancing. All of them, Pinky, Naftuli, Danny, Heshy, and of course, Benjy, were dancing the dance of true *mechutanim,* free of inhibitions or insecurities. They were slightly off beat, and Benjy had his eyes shut tightly, but the aura of joy that pervaded their little huddle made Itzik realize that he had a winner. He drew near and saw that in the middle of the little cluster there was someone else, singing and dancing along with them; in fact, he was leading them in singing and dancing.

Itzik moved quickly. He focused on the look of intent concentration of the face of the leader, Mendel Wasser, and panned around at the group surrounding him, all of them sharing that same look of pure, unadulterated joy at the *simchah*.

And Itzik knew that he had his prize-winning clip for the night.

It wasn't that Malka Markstein didn't like Purim; sure she did. It was more like that she was disappointed by Purim, or at least by what her Purim had become.

She remembered that first Purim after they had moved to this block, her eager anticipation of how Purim night would be here, amid her affluent neighbors. She had spent the days before Purim baking, certain that there would be a steady stream of hungry yeshivah *bachurim* traipsing through her dining room. She would be ready for them!

But Purim night, just after Megillah *laining,* Aryeh had broken his fast and begun to rearrange furniture, moving his chair and a small table out into the entrance foyer and closing the glass doors to the dining room.

"They will almost undoubtedly be high, and who knows what kind of damage they can cause if we just allow them into the house like that," he had said primly in response to her curious look. She had heard the notes of distaste mingled with the self-defense in his words. She understood. Aryeh wasn't someone who was concerned with carpets and stains. It was something deeper, some need to keep any sort of true joy out of his house and life.

"Aryeh," she had protested, "the carpets will have to be cleaned anyhow for Pesach." He had agreed then, and grudgingly reopened his dining room, but she had already lost her enthusiasm and had spent that Purim night in a dark mood.

How could she explain to him that she actually wanted them to break something while they danced? How could she express her desire to look on mock horror as they would toss baby Ezzy up into the air, ignoring her noisy protests to be gentle?

Would he ever understand what it had been like, all those years before, when she would lie on her bed late on Purim night, listening to the singing and dancing through the thin wall? Though her father had been hard at work in his shop, the neighboring apartment, where Rabbi Levine lived, would be filled with action and energy; his talmidim, teenagers defiantly refusing to accept the fact that Purim was done. Late into the night, they would persist in celebrating, their strains of Shoshanas Yaakov filling her world, her dreams, touching her very core. One year, she had turned to her sisters with shining eyes and innocently expressed what was on her heart. "One day, my home will sound like this on Purim, and the whole neighborhood will come and listen."

They had snorted then, laughing at her and telling her to go back to sleep.

Now it was all those years later, and she was still waiting for her Purim, for the sounds and songs of her dream.

But how could Aryeh understand that? He had probably spent his Purim in righteous resentment of the boys who didn't have to spend the afternoon as he did, delivering medicine for the pharmacy while they delivered colorful mishloach manos.

And that's the way Purim had always been in the Markstein home. Sure, the groups came and Aryeh would generously distribute *tzedakah,* but Malka could never shake the feeling that they came not because they *wanted* to, but because they *had* to. So even as Aryeh smiled gamely and allowed them to hold his hand and dance around the table, looking at Malka proudly, as if to remind her that it was all for her sake that he was being such a sport, Malka was watching the eyes of these *bachurim,* eyes that were focused on their watches and each other, silently asking when it would be decent to leave without hurting their cause. She would notice their eyes peeking furtively through the window and across the street at the Newman's, where there was live music throughout the night.

This Purim would probably be even more disappointing than usual. For while in Purims past, at least she had been able to count on Ezzy to inject some *simchah* into the house, this year it didn't seem like he had any to spare. Though she dared not ask, it was clear that he had not been invited to join any of his classmates in collecting, and Purim was rapidly approaching. Her heart hurt at the thought of Ezzy going to sleep early on Purim night, or worse, looking out the window at his classmates coming and going to the Newman's house.

· · · · · · · · · · · · · · · · ·

Mendel Wasser drove down the nearly deserted Palisades Parkway, enjoying the serenity in the car and out. His five passengers were all fast asleep and he was grateful for the quiet. It had been quite an evening for all of them, and lots of work for him. Gitty had been apprehensive at the thought of him driving the residents of the group home to Leizer's *chasunah,* especially when she had learned that they were prepared to send a van and driver from the office. "Why do you have to drive them, Mendel?" she had complained. "There is a van ready to take them and the trip will be too much for you, to Monsey and back. Don't you remember how you got lost last summer on the way to visit my sister in the mountains?"

Mendel had explained to Gitty exactly why he felt a need to drive the men himself. "Gitty, Leizer Krause is getting married tonight, and to them, Leizer Krause is not just some guy who worked as a counselor in the home. Leizer is their friend and that means something to them, something real and meaningful. Sure, they can go to the wedding in a van that is shiny white, with bold blue letters that say 'Mishkan Shalom,' but that is not how friends go to a *chasunah;* tonight, they are the *chassan's* friends."

Gitty had given in; less because she agreed with his arguments and more because she was completely caught off guard by the fact that Mendel was arguing with her, and she was unsure of how to deal with this new phenomenon.

Mendel had gone to the home early, at five-thirty, and had helped each of the men select a suit and tie. He had told them how handsome they looked and even taken a picture of them once they were ready.

They had arrived at the wedding and Mendel had noticed Leizer's face when they came into the *kabbalas panim;* he had been waiting for them to arrive. They were his friends.

They had enjoyed the evening, and in the car on the way home, their voices had competed, each one describing the wedding in different ways, expressing awe at the way the food had tasted, the band had played, and the *bachurim* had danced. Benjy had been on a high because the *chassan,* Leizer, had requested that he go up on the platform with the band and sing a song. Benjy had complied, ("I wouldn't do it for anyone else but you, Leizer") and had insisted on singing the song again on the way out of Monsey. Now that he, too, had fallen asleep, Mendel finally had opportunity to think.

He loved these men, these new friends of his. Sure, he realized that Ari Engel hadn't exactly been straightforward with him when he had described a rebbi job. Mendel's work was more like that of a counselor, but still, there was much teaching to do. What had Mr. Engel said, that all the world was a classroom? It certainly was true, and Mendel very much enjoyed teaching the men *halachah* and Chumash, and even the occasional mishnah. He would take them to see how *tzitzis* were made and to a matzah bakery.

But what Mr. Engel hadn't told him was that he would not just be teaching; he would be learning too ....

Chapter 12

I n truth, Moishy Winternitz and Ezzy Markstein were an unlikely duo. Ezzy was insightful and perceptive, funny and personable, while Moishy was sullen and silent. It had started as a relationship of convenience — Ezzy didn't have anyone else to be nice to him so he settled for Moishy, who welcomed the chance for company- but it had evolved into a true friendship. These two teenagers had something in common.

Both were essentially good boys, unable to really allow themselves to fall, yet unable to climb back up either. For Ezzy it was the silent condemnation of his peers that was his greatest obstacle, while Moishy had to struggle with the dark demons of his past, reminding him of his inferiority and worthlessness. Both lacked the stamina to fight. Both wished they had it.

Some days were harder than others, and the Tuesday afternoon before Purim was one of the hard ones. Ezzy had been miserable in school, amid the air tangible with excitement of pre-Purim preparations, and every whispered conversation was a reminder of his sorry state, every passed note seemed to be mocking him. He had an appointment with Dr. Nikosi at four o'clock, but at twelve o'clock, he begged out of school for it, unable to handle any more. By twelve-thirty, he was sitting with Moishy and unburdening himself.

"I can't take much more of this. There is a whole army of people out there punishing me for years of misdeeds, and here I am, beaten and humbled, and still, they won't relent."

Moishy looked miserable, as he usually did.

Ezzy neither expected nor wanted validation from his friend, and he continued. "I basically gave up on being part of a group this Purim. I just don't know what I will do to pass the time ...."

Moishy's green eyes flashed momentarily, and he debated whether he should share what was on his mind. Ezzy caught the look and pressed Moishy.

"What is it?"

Moishy looked at the floor. "Nothing," he muttered.

Moishy had never had a real best friend, had never trusted anyone the way he trusted Ezzy, and didn't wanted to lose him. He knew that Ezzy was a good boy, a sincere boy, and in his desire to keep their relationship strong, he tried to be a good boy as well. Thus, when Reuven had come to share his plan with him that morning, Moishy had said clearly that he wasn't interested, though he was. He had said so because he knew that Ezzy would never approve of it and he wasn't willing to disappoint Ezzy and risk losing his friendship, the only taste of friendship that he'd ever had.

Reuven was one of his old buddies from the street, and Moishy had often hung out with him and his gang before Ezzy had come along. Reuven had long ago turned his back on yeshivah, and was outspoken in his anger and derision of that world. He had come to Moishy to share his plan with him, telling Moishy that it was his greatest plan yet.

He had begun with his usual speech about the system, the Rebbeim and *bachurim* who had wronged him, listing a litany of things for which he could never be *mochel*. Then he shared his plan.

"Moishy, listen closely. You know that this week is Purim, and all of them are, like, all pumped about it. I am sick and tired of watching all of them with their fancy rented cars and flashy costumes, all proud of themselves for raising a few bucks. I say that this Purim, we go to war, you know, just for fun. We will finally make our point."

Moishy had looked up from the floor, and Reuven had continued, growing increasingly enthusiastic.

"We will create real havoc for all the groups here, I am talking blocking the roads, releasing air from their tires, calling the police on them, just stirring things up a little, you know, just for fun."

Moishy had been taken aback. It was one thing to be jealous and resentful. It was another thing to be so filled with animosity that he was prepared to do damage. A single thought crossed Moishy's mind at that time. *Wow! Reuven must be hurting even more than me.*

Yet, at the same time, he wanted to be a part of it. Not because it was right, but because it was a chance to be connected, even in a most twisted way, with the activity of Purim night. He may not have been perceptive, but he understood. Reuven was stating, *Although we aren't allowed in the club, it doesn't mean that it isn't Purim night for us as well. We will find a way in.* Moishy had refused Reuven, because he knew that Ezzy would be horrified at the whole idea.

But that had been this morning. Now, Ezzy was sitting across the table from Moishy, sharing his own hurt and anger, and Moishy remembered Reuven's plan.

"Ezzy, you know Reuven Heller, don't you?"

Ezzy frowned briefly. "I know who he is, but I never spoke to him. Why?"

Moishy had a brainstorm. "Because he is planning to hang out with his guys on Purim night, not to collect, but to enjoy all the action and everything. I am a little worried that they can get a bit out of hand, and I wouldn't mind being there, just to keep things under control. You want to hook up with them?"

Ezzy was quiet, and, emboldened by his success, Moishy added, "It's not like you have anything else to do."

Ezzy looked at him sharply. Moishy had just violated one of the cardinal rules of their relationship. Ezzy was allowed to share his troubles, but Moishy had no right to express how vulnerable Ezzy was. He was expected to silently agree, not to comment on Ezzy's plight. Ezzy was still on top. *On top of the ant heap,* Moishy would often think — to himself.

Ezzy was considering how he, Ezzy Markstein, could possibly spend time in the company of Reuven Heller and his group, people with whom he had never even exchanged greetings. But on the other hand, he felt rejected and abandoned by the "good" boys. Everyone deserves to belong somewhere.

"Tell me the details," he said.

Ezzy and Moishy were deep in conversation when Ezzy noticed someone at the table next to theirs. The pizza shop was fairly empty, and it struck him as odd that someone would sit right next to them when there was no shortage of tables.

He gestured at the man and looked at Moishy quizzically. "What do you think that guy wants from us?"

Moishy looked up and studied the fellow. "I don't know, but he has the same coat as my great-grandfather."

Ezzy looked at the shabby blue raincoat, belted tightly at the waist. It was too late in the winter for a heavy coat, and too early for no coat at all, so there weren't many options; still, Ezzy had never seen anything like that.

It was clear to both boys that the man wanted to speak with them, but was too shy to initiate conversation. He kept clearing his throat and casting furtive glances at them, but when they looked at him, he would quickly avert his gaze.

Intrigued, Ezzy spoke. "Good afternoon."

The man nearly jumped to his feet, so excited was he to have an opening.

"Shalom Aleichem, boys, good afternoon to both of you."

Moishy was about to compliment him on the raincoat, but something about the sincere, gentle air of this stranger stopped him.

He offered his hand to Ezzy, a limp handshake, and then to Moishy.

He was short and slight, with a curly blondish beard and large glasses, which were slipping down his nose. He wore a hat and necktie and, of course, the shiny once-blue raincoat.

"My name is Mendel Wasser."

The boys were quiet, so he continued.

"Um, what are your names?"

Moishy waited for Ezzy to answer, and after he mumbled his name (he always said Markstein quietly and quickly), Moishy said his own.

Mendel was still standing, and he continued awkwardly.

"I have a proposition for you boys, an idea that I want to share with you."

Ezzy sighed, as if he were being interrupted in the middle of a crucial meeting, and shrugged. "Why don't you sit down?" he asked.

Peretz Winternitz was a straight shooter. He played by the rules, davening three times a day, learning when he had time, and raising a beautiful Jewish family. He wasn't the emotional sort, and didn't really go for outward displays of feeling.

As such, the regulars at the early minyan were surprised to see him wrapped in his tallis several minutes after davening was over, his eyes shut tight. It wasn't Peretz Winternitz's style.

But he had made himself a promise on that afternoon at his office. He had thought long and hard about his remote son, Moishy, and about the barriers that he had erected around himself. And he had decided on a plan.

He would ask Yankel Reich for help. Yankel Reich davened in the same shul as he did, and always seemed to have a *segulah* handy, the keys to salvation for any given calamity. He was constantly sharing stories of how this one had been cured, that one had found a *shidduch* for his thirty-year-old daughter, and the other had won his court case after following a *segulah*. Yankel knew what to say, where to give money, the details, and he, Peretz Winternitz would ask him for help. Maybe he would know of the *segulah* to open Moishy's heart.

After Maariv, he had called Yankel over and shyly asked for advice. Yankel had been totally caught off guard by the request from skeptical Peretz Winternitz, and suggested that he speak with the Rav.

So Peretz had approached the Rav, who had listened to this strong, silent man unburden himself. "Peretz," the Rav had said gently, placing a hand on his shoulder, "there is only one tried and tested *segulah,* one that can solve any problem. Have you ever tried *really* davening, opening your heart to Hashem and begging Him to shine His light on Moishy? Have you ever let your tears flow to Him?

"Peretz, I know that you never miss a *minyan* and that you are always on time. That isn't enough. I want you to start davening, really davening."

And so, each morning after Shacharis, busy, overworked Peretz would spend five minutes more, unburdening his heart, sharing his hopes and dreams with his Master ....

Chapter 13

Wednesday morning, at precisely nine o'clock, Ari Engel parked his car in his reserved space and entered Mishkan Shalom. Though Ari was the boss over many employees, he made it a point to remember each of their names, and as he walked between desks and cubicles towards his corner office, he had words of greeting for each of them.

He noted with satisfaction that his secretary had prepared his first of many cups of coffee, and even before he was seated, he was already scanning the papers piled up on his desk. There was a bureaucratic disaster that he had to attend to first thing, and as he removed his jacket, he asked his secretary to call his contact in Albany.

That was the way his morning went, one phone call after another, the blip of incoming emails persistent background noise, each one a near catastrophe, each one averted by his diplomacy and skill. At eleven o'clock, he rose and walked to the large plate-glass window that looked out onto the crowded floor of Mishkan Shalom. He had purposely had the window installed; Ari Engel, a man totally consumed by the cause, derived great joy from seeing his people working for that same cause. He gazed with satisfaction at the case workers at their desks, the secretaries and receptionists fielding phone calls and filing papers. He noticed that a gentleman was waiting on the small couch, just outside his office. The fellow looked familiar to him, and with a trace of annoyance, he realized that it was that new counselor he had hired to work in Kensington, Wasserman, he thought the name was.

Ari met all prospective employees, however insignificant, welcoming them to his fine office and sometimes taking them on a walk through the office, introducing them. It was a ploy designed to make them feel important, to allow them to believe that whatever job they would be doing was the very apex of power, to give them the opportunity go home and drop Ari Engel's name casually, (".Call me Ari," he would always say.) The fact is, that's all it was, nothing more. It was not an invitation to ever speak with him again, not a *drop by the office anytime, now you know where it is* type of thing. Ari was irritated that this Wasserman was just sitting there, as if Ari was waiting for him to enter.

He buzzed his secretary. "What's this, Chevy? Does he think that he picks up his paycheck in my office?"

"He came by and said that he absolutely needs a moment of your time. I told him that you don't have a free minute all day, but he looked so sincere and earnest that I just couldn't turn him down ..." then, suddenly feeling foolish, Chevy backtracked, "but still, I know how overburdened you are today. I'll tell him to come back another time."

Ari sighed. "No, no, it's fine. Let him come in right now."

Mendel Wasser walked into the office and shook Ari's hand warmly.

"Thank you so much for seeing me," he began.

Ari looked at him warily, wondering what he could possibly want.

"As you know, I have been working as a sort of rebbi to the boys at the Kensington group home for the past week, and have really been enjoying it."

Mazel tov, thought Ari.

"I have developed quite a nice relationship with the residents, and really like spending the time learning with them.

"I have, however, discovered something."

Ari involuntarily looked at his watch and then back at Mendel.

"These men can really learn a lot more than they are being taught. A few of them are quite bright, and they all deserve to be taught on their own level. The few minutes after Shacharis and at night that we talk about the *parashah* is not nearly enough. They are being cheated."

The last sentence was spoken much more forcefully than he would have liked, and he briefly wondered what Gitty would say if she knew that he had spoken that way to Ari Engel. He hadn't even told her that he was planning this visit. She would certainly have dissuaded him.

"I'm listening," said Ari.

"I want to purchase a bunch of new *sefarim,* and I want to start learning mishnayos with the men. There is no room in the apartment, but if you can rent the neighboring apartment — it's available and it's quite small — then we can set up a real *beis medrash.* I realize that it would be small, but it would be *theirs,* a separate place just for learning and davening. I think it would give them something to look forward to all day."

Ari smiled. And just as a mother, no matter how busy, will always have time to hear nice words spoken about her child, he, too, was touched by the fellow's obvious concern and love for the residents. "It's a nice idea, but it's really unfeasible. For starters, we don't have funding to do anything like that right now. It would take months to get government approval for your idea. Also, I am sure that there will issues with the neighbors if we seek to rent a second apartment in the building."

Mendel seemed prepared for this possibility. "I will personally get the consent of every single resident in the building, and I will raise the money necessary to launch the idea."

Ari knew a thing or two about fundraising, and he knew that this scrawny fellow in the ill-fitting suit who sat before him was no fundraiser. His tone was one of amusement as he leaned back and asked, "How do you propose to raise the money?"

Mendel smiled proudly. "Well, yesterday I made some inquiries, just to see if it was still possible to find some yeshivah *bachurim* that haven't yet made plans to go collecting this Purim. It took me a few tries, but *Baruch Hashem*, I found some very fine boys who might be willing to go collecting for us on Purim."

Ari leaned back in his chair and closed his eyes tightly, thinking. On one hand, as a government-funded organization, he didn't have to do much fundraising, and when he did, he invariably received cynical comments about how he was drowning in money and had no business soliciting funds, so he tried to avoid it. On the other hand, the extra money always came in handy for small expenses, and he had nothing to lose by allowing Mendel to implement his plan.

"Are they the type of boys who will do the name of Mishkan Shalom proud?" he asked sternly, happy to be back in a position of control.

Mendel nodded eagerly. "Absolutely. I met them yesterday and they made a wonderful impression on me."

"And did they agree to go collecting for us?"

"They said that they needed a little more time to think about it, and that I could call for an answer today."

Ari nodded. "Okay. Here's the deal. They can go, but you bring the money here before you decide how to spend it. Then we could talk about if and how to implement your plan.

"Have a nice day, Rabbi Wasserman."

Mendel was too excited to correct him.

Ezzy and Moishy were sitting at their table in the corner of the pizza shop, deep in conversation. They couldn't decide what to do about Purim, and they had been rehashing the same conversation for the better part of two hours.

Ezzy was thrilled at the opportunity to go collecting, to belong, to be like everyone else, and he wanted to agree. Moishy was more skeptical. Though he also saw the Divine Hand in the fact that the offer had come just as he was telling Ezzy about the plan to join Reuven Heller, he had a hard time committing to the strange guy and his strange organization. Besides, Moishy liked being angry. He liked the idea of spending his Purim with other angry people, celebrating their shared grievances, and nursing their wounds.

But still, he didn't want to lose Ezzy.

For the third time, he pointed out that Mendel was a little bit weird, and that the fact that he couldn't find anyone else aside from them just proved that his wasn't a typical organization.

Ezzy didn't care. Anything beat spending Purim night at home.

Mendel parked his old car in the only spot he could find, a good two blocks from the pizza shop. He almost ran to his meeting with the boys, and entered the eatery breathlessly.

"Hello!" he exclaimed, greeting them as if they were his long-lost friends, and Moishy shot Ezzy a warning glance.

"Well, boys, here I am. What have you decided?"

Ezzy smiled at him. "We'd like to do it," he said.

Mendel beamed at him. "That's great news, really great. Tell me exactly what you need, lists, drivers, anything."

Ezzy looked uncertain. "I guess if we stay here in Flatbush, then we can walk ..." his voice trailed off as Moishy kicked him under the table.

"We are *not* staying in Flatbush, Ezzy!" he said, with uncharacteristic firmness. Ezzy was momentarily surprised, and then he suddenly comprehended. If Moishy was going to go collecting like a big *tzaddik*, then he was certainly not going to be spotted by Reuven Heller and his gang. That would be too much for him.

"Okay, so we need a car and driver. We'll take care of costumes. I don't need a list; we'll just knock on doors in Boro Park. I guess that's all we need, I mean, it's just the two of us, right?"

Mendel hesitated, and Ezzy grew suddenly wary.

"Uh, yeah, it's basically just you two and a driver, except ... maybe .... I just thought ...."

"What is it?" asked Ezzy.

"The men in the home would love to go around collecting. They get such *simchah* from singing and dancing. It would be a huge mitzvah if you took a few of them along with you."

Moishy was about to stand up and walk out, even if it meant antagonizing Ezzy, but then Mendel said one more thing.

"I mean, these people never, ever get a break. Aren't they also entitled to enjoy Purim?"

Perhaps it was the way he said it, or maybe it was just the thought that they weren't the only people in the world that were hurting.

"Sure, we would love to have them with us ...."

Chapter 14

I t was late on Purim night, late enough that the last of the evening's merry-makers had already collapsed from exhaustion, and early enough that the footsteps of the first *vasikin*-goers, anxious to get an early start on this holy day, were not yet heard.

Moishy Winternitz lay in his bed, unable — unwilling — to fall asleep. He was experiencing something new; the rage that was his constant companion was blessedly silent, but for the first time, it wasn't because he had silenced it himself. Normally it would take a cigarette, or perhaps a shouted confrontation, to contain the fury, the ever-present beast that lived inside him, some sort of destructive act with which to squash it.

Tonight, much earlier — while they had been in the middle of collecting — Moishy had felt the familiar sensation of anger rising, had heard the voice reminding him of his own low self-worth, had felt the cold fingers of loneliness and melancholy reaching out and gripping his soul. He had looked around, wondering how he would fight it. He thought of simply stomping off and leaving Ezzy with the rest of them — after all, this whole thing was his doing — but at that very second, Benjy had placed a hand on his arm.

"Moishy, would you sing together with me in the next house? I need someone to do harmony and the others are growing hoarse."

Moishy had shaken his head in disbelief. Benjy hadn't stopped singing for one moment since they had started their evening, yet he was showing no signs of stopping. They would enter a house, and almost immediately, Benjy would be standing on a chair, leading the others in song. Always, the house would grow quiet, as the spectators would stop what they were doing and look on, enthralled, at this gray-haired, childlike adult, clearly hampered by emotional delays, yet so very happy, so real. With eyes closed and arms spread wide, Benjy would always steal the show. By the time Ezzy would approach the owner of the home, asking for a donation to help set up a *beis medrash* for the residents of the home, their hearts had already been softened by the sweet sounds of Benjy's off-key song.

So when Benjy urged Moishy to please come sing harmony with him, he hadn't had time to think, to focus on his unwelcome guest. He just allowed Benjy to lead him up the stairs to the next house.

The singing and dancing had quieted the fury the way nothing else ever had. The beast inside of him had remained in its black hole for the rest of the night, a night that had passed in *leChayims,* songs, and pleas for *tzedakah.*

It had actually been nice.

Ezzy was also in a good mood. The evening had gone well, really well. There had been a few moments when he had his doubts about the whole idea, such as when Mendel had suggested that he drive them in his car. Moishy looked at Ezzy and shook his head with vehemence, and Ezzy had searched for a diplomatic way to reject the gracious offer. In the end, Mendel had to withdraw anyhow; his wife was making a Purim party for her students and she needed Mendel to keep their children out of the way. Of course, she had assured Mendel, she would manage fine without him, but it would be nice for the children if he were there.

So Ezzy, Moishy, and the residents of the home — Benjy, Naftuli, Pinky, Heshy, and Danny — had been driven by Moishy's older brother to Boro Park, where he left them off on Sixteenth Avenue. Moishy had made it clear that Ezzy was in charge, so he ignored tense feeling in the pit in his stomach, walked up the steps to the first house, and rang the bell. As soon as he did, he was overcome by doubts and insecurities, wondering what he was doing there.

A middle-aged man with a curly gray beard and smiling eyes opened the door, welcoming them warmly. "A freilechen Purim," he had said enthusiastically.

Ezzy had motioned for the others to join him, and had suddenly felt very silly. Should he start a song? Should he begin to dance? Should he ask for a drink and say a short *vort*?

During that first moment of doubt Benjy moved in and established himself as the leader. "*LaYehudim, laYehudim ...*" he began, grabbing hold of Ezzy's hands and forming a circle.

It was only five minutes later, after a spirited dance and small *leChayim,* that Ezzy made his plea for funds, articulating Mendel's vision. The man with the smiling eyes filled in a check and pressed it into Ezzy's hands, leading him to the door.

"Thank you, thank you for coming," he had said.

The night had continued in that vein, with Benjy leading the way from house to house. After the sixth house, Ezzy had come up with an idea. His mother always said that the best thing to do when you are down is to do something nice for someone else. "Nothing can boost your spirits like giving someone else a lift," she would say, and Ezzy would usually roll his eyes.

Tonight, he was learning just how true that was, how exhilarating it was to bring joy to others. Every time he looked around at his crew, their steps heavy, their speech sometimes slurred, but their faces alight, he felt his heart soar.

He leaned over to Moishy and shared his idea. "You know, we keep following the crowds, going to the biggest houses, the ones with the open doors and loud music inside. What about the people with smaller homes and less money? Don't they also deserve the opportunity to be a part of this?"

Moishy shrugged. Ezzy was the leader and it was his call. It was all the same to him.

Naftuli's father was a prominent Chassidic Rebbe, one of Brooklyn's most revered. Naftuli was the Rebbe's oldest son, but when he was four years old, it was already clear that he was not to be the heir apparent. He understood little, and could barely communicate.

His father, the Rebbe, presided over a burgeoning community, with many families and several large institutions, and he rarely had a free moment. He counseled Yidden until late into the night and was responsible for a million-dollar budget; all this in addition to learning, davening, and teaching.

Each afternoon, however, the Rebbe went for a walk, and then he was accompanied only by his oldest son, Naftuli. True, Naftuli couldn't speak like his younger brothers and it wasn't clear how much he understood, but when they would walk, arm in arm, through the streets, when people would stop and nod in respect, *then* Naftuli was the Rebbe's son. He cherished those walks, the only taste he received of his birthright, the moments when he, too, got to bask in his father's glory.

He had grown older, and had begun to attend day-hab at Mishkan Shalom. He progressed wonderfully, and when the opportunity arose for him to join the new group residence, his parents encouraged him to take it. He understood that it was a way for him to learn more skills, to prepare himself for the rest of his life, and with a heavy heart, he allowed himself to be moved into the home.

He loved it.

He loved the cooking and cleaning chores in which he took part. He loved the responsibility and the fact that they depended on him for certain tasks. He loved his new day job at a fish store, placing labels on small containers of fish and making sure that they were straight.

But most of all, he loved that here, he wasn't "Naftuli, the Rebbe's son, *nebech*," but just plain old Naftuli, one of the boys.

There was one thing that he missed, however, and that was the daily walk with his father, the awe and adulation in which he basked during those precious moments in his father's company. He understood that none of the reverence was for him, but he didn't care; it was for *his* father. These days, he didn't see his father much, Sure, he went home for Shabbos once a month, just like everyone else, and his mother came to visit him at least twice a week. Assorted siblings and nephews were always dropping in, and there were frequent *simchos* or other events for which he went home, but still, his father had never visited the home. He wished that his friends, Danny and Heshy, Benjy and Pinky, and of course Leizer and Mendel, could have seen him in his glory days, could appreciate who he really was: the Rebbe's oldest son.

Tonight, Purim night, had been one of the greatest nights of his life. They had been walking through the streets of Boro Park, and had neared the street of his father's *beis medrash*. They had heard the singing and dancing from inside, and had stopped to listen. "That's my father's shul," Naftuli had said, a little shyly. No one had heard him, so he said it again, a little louder.

Ezzy had smiled at him. "Right, of course it is."

Naftuli had begun to feel self-conscious. Leizer Krause would have known that it was true, would have insisted they go in, but these new people didn't know who he was. It was Benjy who came to his aid. "It's really true," he insisted, "Naftuli's father is the Rebbe!"

Ezzy had looked uncertain, but they had entered just the same. Naftuli was welcomed by the familiar smells and sights, and, suddenly transformed, turned to his group. "Come," he said, "let's go up these stairs."

And now, as Naftuli lay in bed, reliving the memory of his father rising from his place at the head of three hundred Chassidim and welcoming the group, asking each of them their names and giving them *berachos,* he felt like a child, walking arm in arm with his father.

Purim afternoon, all the residents of Mishkan Shalom had gone home to their families for the day, so Mendel Wasser had a rare day off. Late in the afternoon, the two boys, Ezzy and

Moishy, passed his house and dropped off an envelope stuffed with checks and assorted bills. He counted the pile slowly, then counted it again: over three thousand dollars.

He enjoyed the way Gitty looked at him in astonished silence, and prepared the speech he would give to Mr. Engel the next morning when he presented him with the cash ....

Chapter 14

F amily conferences have their own dynamics, thought Frieda. Each of her siblings entered the room, sitting the way she knew they would, saying the things she knew they would, as if they were marionettes with strings being pulled by some unseen hand.

Of course, Shaul sat at the head of the table, clearing his throat repeatedly, scribbling on his pad, and altogether looking very much the executive. Motty did just the opposite, perching on the arm of the couch, kicking his shoes off, and cracking jokes and pistachio nut shells in quick succession. Chaim Dovid entered submissively, selecting an unobtrusive spot in the middle of the table, waiting patiently for the meeting to begin.

And her sisters. Toby was standing in the kitchen, preparing coffees at a hyperactive pace, stirring furiously, clinking saucers and spoons as she worked. It was her way of being heard. Elka was the only one of the siblings who had come with a spouse, and she kept looking to her husband, Dov Ber, for support.

Since their mother had passed away two years earlier, they met every few months to discuss their father and his situation, and Frieda knew just what to expect. She and Shaul were the only two players in the room. The rest were merely a supporting cast.

Though Chaim Dovid was the oldest, he was by far the meekest personality present, walking an obstacle course of sensitivities as he tried to avoid a confrontation with anyone. He said that he didn't like arguments, Frieda thought, but it was more that he just couldn't deal with the reality.

Shaul was next in age, and he clearly considered himself the head of the family. He was the only one to have succeeded in business, and he attended these family meetings as if they were administrative sessions, his tone always respectful and calm, yet with an intensity and force evident just beneath the surface.

Toby had done their father proud by marrying a *talmid chacham,* and indeed, she and her husband were a credit to them all. Between her large family and full-time job in a doctor's office, she had long ago lost the ability to sit and do nothing. Though she rarely had opinions to contribute to these family gatherings, she always attended out of a sense of duty, and immediately did the only thing that she knew how to do: get busy.

Motty was the youngest son, and as far as he was concerned, these get-togethers had not a scrap of seriousness. He always came first and left last, refusing to miss even one little exchange, one more springboard for his endless supply of distinctly unfunny jokes — or at least Frieda didn't find them funny.

Elka was next, a fragile, timid sort with a husband who considered himself an authority on just about everything. Frieda wished he would stay home, and learn from all the other sons- and daughters-in-law about proper protocol for these meetings: siblings only, no spouses.

Frieda herself was the youngest, and as such, the closest to her father and the most in tune with his needs. The meetings were always held in her home, to her, clear and incontestable proof that she was, indeed, the one who should be making the final decisions. She knew what the others said, that it simply "made sense" for them to meet in her home, and there was no special significance. With Toby living in Monsey, Shaul in Woodmere, and Chaim Dovid in Queens, and the others in Brooklyn, they reasoned, it was simply the most convenient to meet at her Kensington home.

Toby came in carrying a tray of steaming coffees — *The balabuste in my house*, thought Frieda — and Shaul cleared his throat yet again, calling the meeting to order.

And as they all focused on the subject of their meeting, the man they all loved so, her father, Frieda felt her uncharitable thoughts fading away ....

In a small, crowded apartment on Manhattan's Lower East Side, Reb Anshel Hammerman shuffled across his room, gripping the handles of a walker with both frail hands. He felt hot, very hot, and briefly thought about opening the window, but didn't have the strength to cross the room again. He sank into his chair with a sigh of relief and his hand reached for the worn Tehillim on the table.

A wayworn man with his wayworn book, as always, when his fingers turned the tattered pages, tears came to his eyes. He himself wasn't sure why they would appear so abruptly, like a faucet that suddenly springs to life. These days, his body did all kinds of things simply of its own volition, but he knew there was more to the tears than mere old age. They were tears for towns that had long ago been destroyed, their inhabitants swallowed up by a brutal beast. He cried for the *cheder yingelach*, his friends, back in the Pietrikov of his youth, for the *melamed* who would teach them songs, and for the itinerant wanderer who would sleep on the benches of the *cheder shtiebel*. He cried at the memory of the Rebbe's *tisch* at *seudah shlishis*, the sun's last rays bathing the room in a purple halo as their songs of yearning rose heavenward. He cried for his mother, always with a needle in her hand and a prayer on her lips, and his strong, sad father, the textile merchant who loved the *shtiebel*. He cried for his sweet, laughing sisters and his little brothers, *peyos* curled around their ears like tight little fists.

He cried for the lone teenager, really a mere wisp of boy, who had been carried on angel's wings, the one who was still standing when the fires died down and the piles of dead bodies were buried.

He cried at the memory of the guilt and loneliness that were his bread and butter when he first came to America, crying now the tears that he hadn't allowed himself then. He cried for those few cherished friends who had emerged from the same abyss of despair as he did, but who had left their faith behind and had built a new life so different from the one they had known.

He cried when he remembered the bittersweet moment that he had married his Mirish'l, sweet because of the promise of a new future, bitter because of all they had lost.

There were tears for each note of triumph over the *reshaim*, each child they were given a gift that eased some of the throbbing hurt.

He cried for the struggles he had faced and overcome, refusing to capitulate. He relived the wonderful years and remembered his dear, dear *mispallelim,* most of whom had already gone onto their eternal rest.

Oy, the shul!

For five decades, he had given himself to the shul and its people, teaching, strengthening, listening. For five decades, he had delivered *shiurim* and answered questions, helped them find jobs and homes, had shared their *nachas* and their sorrows.

But they had all gone, his people. His function as the Rabbi had changed one day, and instead of delivering *shiurim,* it meant visiting the hospitals and old-age homes. Then, with dreadful regularity, his job involved visiting and soothing recent *almanos,* each suddenly bereft of her life's partner. He learned to deal with the sensitivities of the children, often as not overridden with guilt and pain, their thinking muddled. His *hespedim* were profound and touching, as he would recall the suffering that they had endured, this older generation, invoking his own memories of the painful times and the merits that they had all accrued on that bitter journey.

And then even the flow of funerals had ceased, and once again, he found himself the last one standing, the Rav leading an empty shul, a shepherd with no flock. He would come down from his small apartment to the shul each Shabbos, and together with the few stragglers, await the required ten men, so that he could stand before the *amud* and begin *Ashrei.*

The preceding winter had not been kind to the shul, as the freezing weather had prevented even those few faithful from venturing out into the slippery streets, and the shul, Congregation Beth Shlomo Bikkur Cholim Ahavas Yisroel, an amalgamation of several local shuls that had disbanded and joined his own, had been without a *minyan* for the first time since its establishment.

They sat there, a few lonely souls in the large, cavernous sanctuary, a room suddenly grown cold and immense. The gray winter sky, filtering in through the stained-glass windows, darkened, and as it became night, the Rav, Rav Anshel Hammerman, too feeble to go daven elsewhere, rose and davened Minchah by himself.

That Shabbos had been the final one for the *minyan*. The next week the few regulars davened elsewhere, unwilling to take a chance at a shul that couldn't get a *minyan,* and the Rav simply lacked the stamina and the resolve to work the phones, imploring people to come and daven with him.

That Shabbos also the marked the point at which the Rabbi's health began to quickly decline. With no reason to prepare his beloved *shiurim,* without the impetus to write down his precious *derashos* each week, the Rav grew disheartened. He began to forget important things, and was often confused and disoriented. The Rav, who for so many years had refused to leave his *kehillah* for Shabbos, allowed himself to be led, like a little child, to his own children for Shabbos.

One week, Reb Anshel spent Shabbos at his son's home, and the perceptive young Rav asked him to deliver the *derashah* on Shabbos morning. Reb Anshel rose to the challenge, speaking clearly and eloquently, and made it clear that "he still had it." That week, he had remembered to take his pills without any reminders and had even gone to the bank and taken care of his paperwork.

But that had been weeks earlier and now, with Pesach approaching, Reb Anshel was once again lost in the throes of gloominess, remembering Yomim Tovim past when he had *darshened* to a full shul. He recalled the Sedarim, when his Mirish'l was still alive, and the table would be surrounded by guests, children, congregants, and many of the East Side's loneliest souls.

He focused on the pleasant picture for a moment, and, with a shrug, brought himself back to the present. He wasn't sure what time it was, but he knew that it was already late afternoon and he had not yet recited his Tehillim for the day.

He dabbed at his eyes with a tissue and wished that he had remembered to prepare a glass of tea before he'd sat down. He thought about each of his children, focusing on them and their needs, as he did each day before he said his Tehillim for them ....

Chaim Duvid'l, Shaul, Tobe'le, Mottel, Elke'le, and Frieda ....

The very same children who were gathered around a table, just across the bridge from where he sat, deliberating what to do with him ....

Chapter 15

All sorts of people milled around in the commotion. There were those who determinedly parked their luggage carts right near the ramp, as if actually watching for the suitcases would ensure that they would arrive faster. Others took the opposite approach, waiting casually at the far end of the carousel, looking deliberately unhurried. Some jostled to get their carts flush against the metal rim, so that they would be able to easily lift their luggage right on, while others had to content themselves with a position in the second row. A middle-aged woman exclaimed loudly in distress as her heavy suitcase slid beyond her grip, and immediately several helping hands rushed to her assistance, pulling back the runaway baggage.

Chavi Federman sat on the edge of the carousel, straining to locate her two simple suitcases. She had tied bright blue ribbons around their handles so that they would be easier to spot, and she congratulated herself on her foresight as she noticed the bewildered looks on the faces of her co-travelers as they studied each piece, wondering if it was, indeed, theirs.

Even though her husband, Avrohom Meir, was waiting with a luggage cart, little Miri perched on its handles, and she was finally able to relax, she felt a migraine coming on. She had been fine throughout the long flight from Eretz Yisrael, with its compressed cabin air and soggy food. She had kept a smile on her face when Miri had taken the shoes from the sleeping man across the aisle and dropped them into the garbage bag of a passing stewardess. She had watched the little white plane that charted their progress on the screen move forward at a maddeningly slow pace. Each time she opened her eyes, it seemed to be stuck in the very same place, with its nose hovering just above Greenland. Though she herself didn't watch the movie, she couldn't help but notice the Hebrew subtitles flitting across the large screen, and had spent the long trip wondering which English word or slang expression each of them represented.

Night had become day, the bizarre light filtering in through the small airplane windows, and Chavi had long since stopped counting the number of hours since she had last slept.

Still, it wasn't fatigue or exhaustion that was giving her a headache. It was the simple thought of the two couples — her own parents, the Markstein's, and her in-laws — standing outside together in the arrivals lounge that was sending crashing waves of tension through her head.

Aryeh Markstein loved airports. Traveling, with its myriad arrangements and logistics, appealed to his orderly nature, and he cherished the organized bustle of the terminal. When he himself was the traveler, he would be in a state of euphoria, constantly checking his lists and patting his pocket to ensure that his passport and tickets were there. He put great effort into selecting the perfect seat on the flight, not too close to the front in case of disaster, *chas veshalom,* and not too far back so as not to have to wait to disembark. From the moment the plane took off, he would be consulting his watch, relishing the tension of worrying about a connecting flight or a scheduled meeting.

This morning, he was not the traveler, but still, the anticipation of being in the airport had made him more animated and he was in high spirits as he drove down the Van Wyck. Malka, next to him, was excited at the thought of seeing her daughter, son-in-law, and of course, her *einekel,* and she was telling Aryeh about all the things they would do that day. Malka had two children, and the decision that Avrohom Meir and Chavi had made to live in Eretz Yisrael had been almost too difficult to bear. She had never really understood what was wrong with the *kollelim* in America that made her son-in-law feel that he had to live across the ocean. The thought of having them around for more than half of the next month had filled her with giddy anticipation. For the next two weeks, she, too, would be able to parade around the neighborhood stores with her daughter and granddaughter in tow, introducing them to anyone who would make eye contact with her.

She couldn't wait.

Judy Federman was tense as her husband made the short drive from Far Rockaway to Kennedy Airport. She, too, was excited to see the kids, and of course, her little *einekel,* even though they would be going home with her *mechutanim,* the Markstein's, and not her. She, too, was counting down the minutes until they would move into her house and she wouldn't have to share them with anyone else.

She carried a lot of resentment toward her *mechutanim.* Her Avrohom Meir was a diamond of a boy, and when he had come home after learning in Eretz Yisrael, she had been inundated with *shidduchim* proposals for him. She had been looking for the perfect girl to complement his many qualities, and indeed, Chavi was that girl. But Avrohom Meir had also made it clear that he wanted to remain in learning for as long as possible, and in order to do so, he would need in-laws committed to standing behind him. Judy's own husband sold insurance and she worked as a teacher, but there was rarely extra money. She knew that they weren't in a position to do sixty-forty, seventy-thirty — or anything-anything; Avrohom Meir needed a *shver* ready to carry the load, and have the *zechus,* on his own.

When the *shadchan* had mentioned the Markstein girl, he had listed an impressive array of *mosdos* that the father supported; obviously he was a man of means. He was the president of several institutions and ran a successful accounting firm; it sounded like the ideal family for her son. She had never bothered to find out what the Marksteins were prepared to do; after all, Chavi was an only daughter and they were wealthy people.

Oh, there had been warning signals, but she had been too dense to catch them. When she and her husband had gone to meet the Marksteins, she had been shocked at the simplicity of their home.

"Maybe they are renovating," her husband had shrugged.

After the engagement, Avrohom Meir had worried about how they would live, so she and her husband had gone to meet with the Marksteins. "It's our responsibility as parents," she had insisted to her unwilling husband.

It had been a tense conversation. Aryeh had explained his philosophy to them. He believed that the young couples of today live an unhealthy lifestyle, way above their means, and *his* daughter would never fall into that rut. If she wanted a husband in kollel, then she would work to support him and he could do some tutoring on the side as well.

"When I was young, kollel couples lived with real *mesiras nefesh,* and that's how they became great."

Judy had been horrified.

Avrohom Meir had shrugged it off, and he and Chavi had indeed created a beautiful life for themselves. Now, almost two years after their *chasunah,* they were living a fulfilling, productive life, and even Judy had to grudgingly admit that her son was thriving.

Still, she was resentful towards her *mechutanim,* wealthy people who didn't consider their children — her son — an important enough investment.

She kept the meetings between them to a minimum, and now headed toward the airport where they would be waiting; she braced herself for the inevitable.

But that was just one part of the picture that was causing Chavi such anxiety. She could visualize her father, his smile more like a tight-lipped grimace, greeting his *mechutan* with poorly concealed disdain and perhaps a touch of superiority. Her father wasn't the type to mask his true feelings. Her mother would be over-compensating for his ungraciousness by being over-friendly and gushing loudly, just exacerbating his irritation.

Her father-in-law would shuffle away and look around, trying to strike up conversation with potential clients by informing them of a special insurance plan tailor-made for "the kids in Eretz Yisrael."

Her mother-in-law, however, would be dropping hints left and right, as subtle as a bullet through the window, letting the Marksteins know how pressed for cash the kids were. "Poor Chavi, living in a fifth-floor walk-up with a million stairs and no elevator … I hope she enjoys this vacation, the sweet girl."

And Ezzy … *that* was bothering her most of all. Ezzy and Chavi. They had been a team growing up, and she knew that Ezzy was the most affected by her decision to live in Eretz Yisrael. She had been the only one who was truly able to understand him, who knew what it was like to have a father to whom there were no gray areas. They had both grown up seeing how Aryeh had stifled Malka's natural exuberance and cheer, and they had always tried to present their father with a facade, a more serious version of themselves in order to please him. Like Ezzy, she had chosen to keep so many of her true goals and hopes buried inside. And now … Ezzy had been unable to keep it in any longer, and the spontaneity that was his nature had shown itself in an awful way. She hadn't seen him since "the incident" and had never really had the opportunity to empathize or commiserate the way she would have liked to; the phone simply didn't allow for it, and she couldn't bring herself to express her feelings of solidarity in writing.

She knew that the way she looked at him, that initial eye contact, would tell him everything he needed to know: if she accepted him, or if she, too, was judging him.

Ezzy sat in the back seat of the car, lost in thought. He had been thrilled when his parents had offered to take him along to the airport, more because it was an opportunity to miss school than anything else. Malka cherished the fact that her two children had a close relationshipand used every opportunity to cement it.

Now, he sat in the back seat, wondering how Chavi would react to him. Had she, too, heard enough about "the incident" and formed her own opinions? Would she accept him? He davened silently that at least this relationship would remain the same as it always was.

And as he davened, Chavi's lips moved in prayer as well. "Hashem, please, please let Ezzy realize that he can count on me …."

Chapter 17

Fact is, Jerry Gelber was an angry man. He relished altercation, thrived on confrontation. When someone parked
too close to him, he would jump out of his car and start
shouting, and he would drive miles out of his way in
order to honk at a reckless driver. He was the one who would
call radio talk-show hosts late at night and rail against them,
unwittingly providing them with material for another half-
hour of air time.

Maybe he wasn't to blame. His life had been a rough
one. He had grown up in a tough neighborhood, a lone Jew
in a sea of Poles and Italians, and it had been survival of
the fittest. His predilection to conflict had cost him his first
marriage, and his second one wasn't faring much better. His
wife, Sara, was a timorous wisp of a woman, who lived for

those blessed periods when he was tranquil and calm. She, too, was on her second marriage, and was grateful that her children had a father who provided for them. She had borne him two children, both daughters, and had been grateful for the fact that they were not boys. He didn't take any of them seriously enough to attack them for their opinions, so most of the time, things were all right. Also, he was away much of the time.

Tonight, he was home, and actually in a good mood. Jerry drove a truck for a kosher food distributor, and this season, before Pesach, was one of his busiest. He had been gone for three of the previous four nights, delivering supplies across the tri-state area, and now, he had two days off to rest up. She had prepared his favorite supper, and he was enjoying the food while listening to his daughter tell him what she had learned about Pesach.

The doorbell buzzed and interrupted the peace. Jerry growled and lifted himself up. Sara immediately grew apprehensive, for any visitor was an unwelcome visitor to Jerry Gelber. It might be a *tzedakah* solicitor: *go work for a living like I do, lazy bum;* someone looking for one of the neighbors on the floor: *what does this look like, an information booth?*; or maybe some kind of delivery, which would be worst of all: *come on, I do this all week and I don't crawl in with one box at a time. Let's see you work.*

Jerry looked through the peephole and turned to Sara. "It looks like a *tzedakah* guy." He swung the door open, savoring the opportunity to unload his views on this unsuspecting visitor. Sara cowered in the rear, wringing her hands and quietly willing the innocent fellow to run.

Jerry was disappointed at the man standing before him. He had neither the look nor the demeanor of a fighter. Jerry had no use for this weak little man; he was no worthy adversary.

"Shalom aleichem, Mr. ... Gelber," said the man, consulting a paper in his hand.

Jerry's eyes narrowed and he didn't move. "Um ... can I come in please? I would like a minute of your time."

Jerry pounced. "Do you think this is some kind of drop-in center? I am not interested in the product that you're selling, the institution that you're representing, or the candidate you want me to vote for. Is that clear? You have no business here." The little fellow gripped his paper tightly, and stammered out a weak, "I understand, Mr. Gelber. I realize that you're busy and this *might* not be a good time."

"I am *not* busy and this is a *very* good time. Just not for you. Now scram."

The little fellow took a step back and then fished out a card. "Okay, Mr. Gelber. Can I just trouble you to call me at your convenience?"

Despite himself, Jerry stole a glance at the card and saw the bold blue print: MISHKAN SHALOM. This might be fun. Jerry hated Mishkan Shalom, the people who had decided that his apartment building should become a hospital. He vilified them every time he left the building, several times each day and didn't mind a chance to share his views with one of theirs. He looked at the retreating figure scampering down the hallway toward 3D and called out, "Listen, Rabbi, why don't you come in right now?"

In the early years of her marriage, Malka Markstein would share her dreams with her husband each morning. She would tell him the weird occurrences, bizarre situations, and eerily realistic episodes that she had encountered in the night, hoping he would shed insight on what they meant. A man patient enough to listen to his wife recount her vague memories of her dream from the previous night is a rarity. Aryeh Markstein certainly wasn't that man.

This night, however, Malka was dogged in her determination to get him to hear her out. "So we were out on the Avenue, okay it was kind of like the Avenue, but instead of stores there were caves, and everyone was wearing green, but whatever. Anyhow, there we were, just Chavi and me, and the baby, of course, and Judy Federman and we were all laughing uproariously."

"That's great, Malka," said Aryeh, "but I must get to shul immediately or I will be late for Maariv."

"No, Aryeh this was a message, not just a regular dream. I want to invite Judy to come out for lunch with us today. Chavi is her child, too, and she deserves to enjoy her while she's in town."

Aryeh's tone was icy. "No, Chavi is not her child. Miri is her grandchild, but Chavi is *my* child. Judy Federman is a simplistic, ungrateful woman who bad-mouths us to others and I don't see why you should be gracious to her."

"Because she is my *machutenesta,* that's why," said Malka, uncharacteristically defiant.

This had long been a dream of Malka's, to become friends with her *machutenesta* once again, but she knew Aryeh would resist. He could never forgive her for making him feel stingy, so he had made her into some kind of monster. Malka only had one *machutenesta,* and she wanted to be close with her.

"Malka, a *machutenesta* isn't someone you go out for lunch with. It's someone to call on erev Rosh Hashanah and wish a *gut yohr,* nothing more. Her son married your daughter. Big deal, it's like a business relationship."

Everything is like a business relationship to you, thought Malka bitterly, *your wife, your son, your friends, it's all plus and minus, checks and x'es. Emotions are nothing, feelings are insignificant, all business.*

"Aryeh please, don't be stubborn. I will be *ma'avir* on my *middos.* It will be a *zechus.*"

He couldn't argue with her logic, so he just shrugged. "I am going to be late for davening," he said.

Mendel Wasser cowered in a corner of the couch, listening as Jerry Gelber shouted out his litany of complaints against Mishkan Shalom. "And they have these people milling in the lobby all day, just walking around aimlessly, unproductive, slovenly …."

Mendel reacted. "Excuse me, our residents are extremely productive. They work hard, and lead fulfilling lives, despite serious obstacles."

"Don't tell me about obstacles," Jerry roared. "I know all about obstacles. It's an obstacle to my peace of mind to have these people walking around the lobby of my building, sitting on the stoop, thinking it's theirs!"

"Sir, they are model neighbors and you know it."

Jerry plowed on. "And what's more, those bums that they employ as counselors, or whatever they call them, are a terrible influence, boys who couldn't make it anywhere so they come work here, in this building, where I am trying to raise my daughters."

Mendel held up his hand. "They aren't bums at all —"

Jerry's eyes were bulging and he looked like he was going to lunge at Mendel. "They are simply horrible people, trash. I've seen them smoking and littering the floors with cigarette butts, and I have heard the awful language coming out of their mouths."

Sara was a little shocked by the last part of her husband's tirade. He smoked heavily and his language was appalling.

Mendel rose to leave. "Okay then, I guess we can't count on you for help. Thank you for your time."

Jerry scowled at him. "Help? You came in here to ask me for money for these thieves, who are busy wasting my tax money as fast as they can get their hands on it?"

"No, actually it wasn't money that I was looking for. It was something else."

Mendel headed for the door.

"What was it?" said Jerry, curious despite himself.

Mendel sensed a hollow victory. "It really isn't relevant; I don't think it's worth discussing."

Jerry blocked Mendel with his large, portly body. "What was it?"

Mendel reminded himself of the words of *Chazal* that no harm will befall one who is engaged in doing a mitzvah.

"We would like to take over the apartment adjoining our facilities on ground floor and create a *beis medrash* for our residents. I was just circulating through the building, asking if any of the tenants have any opposition to our proposed expansion."

Mendel smiled sweetly. "So far, no one has."

Jerry let Mendel pass, and watched him retreat down the hall. "Let me just go on record," he bellowed at the top of his lungs, "at being absolutely opposed to your corrupt organization and to having my life wrecked by your people in this building."

Doors opened up and down the hall at the commotion and elderly Mrs. Hirshkopf in 3E peered out from between several chains. She saw Mr. Gelber standing in his doorway, wearing what looked like pajamas, shouting at a short fellow, probably a *tzedakah* collector.

"*Oy*, poor thing," she thought and reached into her apron. She brought out a crumpled dollar bill and extended it through the crack in the door to Mendel.

Then she hurried to call Mrs. Moskowitz down the hall. "The poor wife," said Mrs. Hirshkopf, "why does she stay with him?"

It was a familiar conversation and as they both settled comfortably into it, Mendel hid in the stairwell, waiting for Jerry Gelber to return to his apartment so that he could continue with his rounds.

Only when he heard the door slam did Mendel venture back into the hallway.

Chapter 18

Avrohom Meir Federman wasn't the type to meddle in other people's business. Quiet, sincere, and unassuming, he enjoyed being in his in-laws' home because it meant that his wife was happy. He knew that it was difficult for her to live in Eretz Yisrael throughout the long year, and she did it solely because that's where he felt that he could achieve maximum growth in learning. He willed her to enjoy her time in America as much as possible so that she might return to Eretz Yisrael after Yom Tov feeling invigorated and refreshed.

Chavi rarely made demands on him, but this *bein hazmanin,* she hadn't just made a demand on him; she had given him a project. She had begged him to learn with her brother, with Ezzy, to draw him close and attempt to become his friend.

Avrohom Meir was a reticent type, and the task was daunting. Sure, his teenage brother-in-law was a sweet kid, and they usually managed to make conversation, but they had absolutely nothing in common. Nothing except Chavi.

So Avrohom Meir turned to the pages of the Gemara, there where he was most at home, and in that comfortable environment, he forged a bond with his young brother-in-law. He was surprised to learn that Ezzy was not only smart; he had a clear, analytical mind and was quite good in learning. This knowledge only served to confound Avrohom Meir: how could a bright, kind boy like Ezzy have acted like a thief?

More than that: why did his father-in-law insist on sending Ezzy to a psychiatrist when there was clearly nothing wrong with him?

It was a riddle that was bigger than he was.

It was official. Frieda had prevailed. Her dear father would be moving in with her, and before Pesach yet! There was so much to do, so many preparations for his arrival. Her house wasn't especially large, just one in a long row of attached homes on a Kensington block, and they needed a room for him. Her husband, Zalman, had graciously agreed to have his study converted into a bedroom for his father-in-law, and there were only two weeks left in which to complete the necessary renovations. Her brother, Shaul, had agreed to cover all related costs, which was very generous of him, considering that he had felt it best for their father to remain where he was. Shaul had battled long and hard, insisting that a change of scenery would be the worst thing for their father, that without the shul he would no longer have a will to go on. Frieda had countered that there was no shul of which to speak anyhow, and that he was slowly deteriorating in his own apartment. He needed the constant love and attention of a child, and she, Frieda, the youngest, was perfectly ready and willing to be that child.

Frieda knew well that the challenge facing her wasn't creating a comfortable room for him or a pleasant atmosphere; it would be to find her father a cause, a burning reason for him to get up and out, to give him a reason to live! He was a Rav, and somehow, he would still have to be a Rav here in her Kensington row house if he was to thrive.

Joel Brick wasn't young anymore and change was a difficult thing to consider. His life had basically been running on autopilot for the last few decades, with few changes. He had lived in the same apartment since he was born; but now he shared it only with his mother. His father had passed on and his siblings, unlike him, had married and moved away. Same job at the post office, same seat, same lunch break, same everything. The only bright spot in his life, the source of excitement and color, had been the shul. There, he was a major player. He was the first one in every morning, the one to prepare the massive urn of coffee and turn on the lights. He would lovingly straighten out the Rav's siddur and arrange his chair just so.

Erev Shabbos, he would spread out the thick white tablecloths and roll the Sifrei Torah when necessary, performing his duties with pride. In recent years, he had also been the one to slip outside just before services, when necessary, in order to pull in enough people for a minyan. He had watched as the Rav's condition steadily worsened, never believing that his beloved shul would simply cease to exist, that Rabbi Hammerman, the steadiest and most loyal of them all, would simply pack his bags and leave; leave him, Joel Brick, all alone, with very little to live for.

He was no fool. He had seen the developers, their eyes as eager as a child's in an ice cream parlor, walking through the old building. He knew that the day wasn't far off that the shul would go down and be replaced by a condominium, probably with a sleek Duane Reade or coffee shop on the ground floor.

Herb Sabrowsky donned his *kippah* out of respect for Shaul, the rabbi's son, as he entered the Manhattan restaurant. Gary Glassman came just behind him, a fashionable gray wool cap on his head. Shaul hadn't seen the other two men in years, and stared at them in wonder. Herb had turned gray and soft, his face resembling that of his long-deceased father. Gary, on the other hand, was tanned and fit, striding briskly in the room with sure footsteps and embracing Shaul with an iron grip.

Shaul returned their warm greetings and the three of them sat there in silent reminiscence. It was clear that they were all remembering, recalling the happy moments spent playing in the large annex behind the *aron kodesh* during services almost half a century earlier. They would play *chazzan,* donning the high black skullcaps and pinching their faces tightly as they would holler out the liturgy. They would play rabbi, wrapping themselves in the fringes of yellowed *talleisim* as they delivered mock sermons. Shaul could never forget how they played; laughing the laughter of innocent young children who believe the world will never change.

But today, they weren't there to play games.

Their respective fathers had been trustees of the congregation, and several years earlier, when both had passed on to their eternal reward, that distinction had been transferred to their sons. Thus, these two gentlemen, both lawyers, had full discretion as to what should happen to the ancient shul building and where the vast sum of money would go when it was sold.

The two of them understood exactly why Shaul had requested this meeting, and they waited for him to open the proceedings.

He chose to make small talk with them while they ordered drinks, and each of the men in turn gave an update on his life, his family, and his business while the other two nodded politely. Herb spoke of his children who had chosen to make *aliyah* and Gary discussed the new rabbi of his synagogue in Scarsdale. "Nothing like Rabbi Hammerman was … that was a real rabbi."

He was throwing Shaul a crumb and they all knew it.

Shaul took it as a cue to get down to business.

"My dear friends," he began, trying to find the appropriate pitch for the news he was about the share, "the time has come. Our beloved Rav will be moving out of the synagogue, and our dear congregation will close its doors for the last time."

Herb looked emotional, and even Gary stopped smiling for an instant.

"The building will then be vacant. My father, the rabbi, will be moving in with my sister in Brooklyn, and you, gentlemen, will have to decide how to proceed. I needn't tell you how serious a responsibility it is. Now I know that my father was an employee, and each month, he received a fair salary from the congregation, so we have no complaints or grievances. I realize that what happens to the money is not our concern. Nevertheless, he is the rabbi, and his wishes were always respected and carried out. Therefore, I will share them with you."

The two men were all business, sitting silently, listening, offering nothing, no clues, no encouragement, and certainly no commitments.

"My father mentioned that he would be horrified if the holy building would turn into a house of worship for any other religion, G-d forbid."

Herb nodded vigorously, "No, of course not."

Gary interjected, "You know, Shaul, we plan to give your father a settlement from the sale money, a few dollars to live out his remaining years, and maybe leave something over, if that's your worry." He winked as he said the last sentence.

Shaul protested immediately. "No, no,, not all what I had in mind. I just want to see the money go somewhere that is worthy enough to perpetuate the name and ideals of our holy congregation."

"You know what, Shaul?" said Herb, "Let's move forward. Let's sell the building and get our hands on some money. Then we'll talk again."

Gitty Wasser was traveling in uncharted waters. Mendel had always been so pliable, as flexible as the play-dough that the kids molded and shaped according to their whims and wishes. In recent weeks, however, he had developed a certain edge, and she wasn't sure that she liked it.

Mendel was sitting at the dining-room table, surrounded by lists and phone numbers, writing furiously. "Mendel," she said, "they didn't hire you to be their lawyer or representative, just to teach the boys. You have to stop what you're doing."

Mendel looked up for a moment, nodded distractedly, and went on writing his letter.

Gitty felt herself losing control. Mendel would be nothing without her. Was this her thanks for putting up with him, failure after failure, job after job, and remaining steadfast and encouraging? To think that he was now ignoring *her* advice!

Even as she pleaded with him, he was dashing off another of his "Dear Tenant, We at Mishkan Shalom ..." letters, as if he were the chairman or president.

"Mendel, please! You're just an ordinary employee. Just do your job and do it right. Teach them, learn with them, make them happy, but don't be so ambitious."

If Mendel had been a cynical person, he might have laughed aloud at Gitty, the most pushy and determined of them all, telling him to take it easy. Instead, he shrugged and turned his attention to the list of the building's fourth-floor residents.

Gitty was infuriated, and the next sentence was designed to hurt.

"Mendel," she said quietly, "do you want to get fired *again*?"

Chapter 19

The pile of mail on Zanvel Berger's desk was reaching mountainous proportions, and the overflow was beginning to slide off the side of his desk. It was time to confront the daunting task. Paperwork and bills are never fun, but for someone in real-estate management, as Zanvel was, it was an absolute nightmare. Each letter meant more work, each bill required more poring over fine print.

He started the job, as usual, by rifling through the mountain of envelopes in search of something light with which to begin, something interesting in advance of the monotony that was sure to follow. An envelope addressed by hand to "THREE STAR MANAGEMENT COMPANY—VERY URGENT" caught his attention and he decided to open it first.

To Whom It May Concern:

I am sick and tired of having my rights trampled upon. I work hard for my money and pay rent on time and expect to be treated accordingly. Since you people allowed that loony bin to open on the first floor of this building, my peace of mind has constantly been under attack. The staff members are also scum of the earth, and I don't like the fact that they are scrounging around my building at all hours.

Until now I was quiet, being a peaceful sort of person. Now, with signs about their planned expansion plastered all over the place, I refuse to sit by silently. I will personally lead the battle against this violation of my rights. No way will these misfits take over my building and ruin my quality of life.

Either refuse them permission or get ready for war.

Jerry Gelber

Tenants United Against Mishkan Shalom

Zanvel Berger was a cool customer. His only reaction to the threatening, crudely written rant was a quiet whistle. He placed the paper on his desk and tried to figure out what was going on. He knew which property it was, the one in Kensington that housed Mishkan Shalom. He knew that the boss was very happy with Mishkan Shalom as a tenant. It was a government-funded agency, so the checks were always good and on time.

He racked his brain to try to place the name, Gelber, so that he could get to the bottom of the situation before it spiraled out of control. Gelber … Jerry Gelber … suddenly, it came to him: the garbage story.

A few months earlier, the custodian of that building had informed him that there was one tenant on the third floor who left his garbage in the hallway, neglecting to carry it all the way to the incinerator. The custodian made it clear that he refused to deal with the problem any longer.

Zanvel Berger knew what he had to do. He drove over to the building and found a bag of garbage left haphazardly in the third-floor hallway. He opened it up and pulled out an envelope addressed to Jerry and Sara Gelber, Apartment 3F. He marched himself over to that apartment and knocked firmly.

Even before a word was exchanged, he felt the anger radiating from the disheveled man who answered the door. Zanvel was used to dealing with all sorts, from all backgrounds, so he wasn't impressed by the character in front of him.

"Mr. Gelber, I am Zanvel Berger, representative of the owners of this building. Placing garbage anywhere other than in the incinerator is a violation of your lease." He never raised his voice or stopped smiling, but his tone made it clear that he was in control.

Jerry stared at him with undisguised animosity and loathing. When Zanvel finished speaking, Jerry answered with a shout. "Get out of here, you little rascal! You come after me because I'm the only honest, hardworking tenant in this building of welfare recipients and pensioners. Don't threaten me, punk, or you'll regret you did."

Zanvel nodded politely. "I'm glad we understand each other, Mr. Gelber. Please see to it that the situation doesn't repeat itself, or else your lease will be terminated."

Zanvel grimaced at the unpleasant memory, and tossed the letter into the wastebasket. *There are all kinds of people out there*, he thought.

Henny Winternitz watched as her kids piled into the van and suppressed a sigh. "Have a great time," she shouted, smiling gamely. As soon as they pulled away, she went inside to call her husband.

"Oh, Peretz," she almost sobbed, "it was like he so badly wanted to join them. You should have seen his face. They were discussing plans all day and he was giving them ideas, participating as if he was one of them. But then, when it came time to actually go, he crawled back into his shell, muttering some excuse about how it wasn't a good time for him, and wandered off."

Moishy Winternitz walked down the street, his hands in his pockets, looking at the ground and kicking pebbles, the very picture of a depressed teenager. For the first time in years, he was engaged in soul-searching. Normally, when he felt like this, it was simplest just to get angry and tell himself that he just wasn't worthy or deserving of better. Today, he wasn't feeling angry; he was feeling disappointed, disappointed that he had deprived himself of a chance to smile, to enjoy life, to be normal for a day. It was a new emotion for him.

His siblings had been sitting around the kitchen this morning, the first day of Pesach vacation for all of them. Seventeen-year-old Devorah had just received her driver's license, and it was she who had come up with the idea. "Ma, if I took the kids out, would you give me the car for the day?"

Mrs. Winternitz hadn't hesitated for a moment; if it meant a chance to clean her home for Pesach with no kids around, then she would get her hands on an airplane if need be. "You got it," she said.

"Great, where shall we go?"

The ideas came pouring in, fast and furious. The aquarium, auto show, and museum were all rejected because of the steep price of admission. Fourteen-year-old Sruli suggested that they drive out to Bear Mountain and go hiking. The girls groaned at the thought.

Moishy shared a suggestion of his own, that they go to the military academy where they could watch a parade. Though they all responded coolly, each of his siblings was shocked at the very fact that he had offered an opinion at all. Henny watched out of the corner of her eye as he tried to convince them of how interesting it would be. She hoped they would seize the opportunity and go running to the car before he could change his mind, but alas, military precision marching was apparently not interesting enough to her brood, and they rejected this suggestion as well.

After much heated discussion, little Yochanan's suggestion carried the day, and it was decided that they would park at Newark airport and watch the planes take off and land.

They had packed supplies for lunch and, giggling excitedly, had selected CD's for their trip. Henny noted that they were already arguing and they hadn't even left the house. Just as they were bidding her farewell for the third time, Moishy walked out of the house, mumbling to himself.

"Moish, where are you going?" she had asked casually, her heart sinking.

"I have to be somewhere. I just remembered," he replied, and fled.

And now, as he walked the streets forlornly, Moishy tried to understand himself, why he had been unable to join them. He felt as if he was in a sort of prison, trapped, incapable of getting out so that he could live. He wished he could be as carefree as his little brothers, that he could experience their simple enthusiasm at the thought of seeing an airplane from up close. Alas, he was ruined forever. Many years ago, a savage beast had beat the *simchas hachayim* out of his little body, and had taught Moishy to distrust every single adult and authority figure in the process. But Moishy knew … Moishy knew … and he longed to scale the wall that prevented him from acting on that knowledge and rejoining his family.

Bogged down by his glum thoughts, he found himself walking in a new direction, down Ocean Parkway instead of up. He knew where he wanted to be: in the company of the only adults in the world that he could trust.

The Finestone boys had their own *bein hazmanim* activity. They were moving their grandfather and close to sixty years' worth of possessions out of his home and into their own. His apartment had been relatively easy: his clothing and numerous *sefarim,* large volumes with spindly, fragile binding and margins filled with his flowing script.

The shul had been much more difficult.

The aged Rav walked slowly up the stairs to the *aron kodesh* for the last time and fingered the faded green velvet curtain. The tears came and he buried his white head in its folds, the smell of polished wood and damp carpet mingling with memories of fifty Ne'ilah prayers, when he would reverently slide this very *paroches* aside.

The trustees had already given the Sifrei Torah to institutions in need of them, and as Rav Anshel looked at the empty ark, a home deprived of its inhabitants, a gaping void that still bore the imprint of holiness, he recalled the joyous Simchas Torahs of years past. Then, the empty *aron* seemed to be smiling the smile of a mother watching her children at play; now it seemed to cry.

At the top of these steps, the blood of generations of Jewish children had been shed as they were joyously welcomed into the covenant of Avraham Avinu. The Rav would sit on the oversized chair, cradling the newborn, whispering a *tefillah* of his own. He could still hear the echo of the infant's piercing cries, the dramatic moment of perfect silence before the father would whisper the name into his ear, and the exultation of "mazel tov" that would follow.

His eyes wandered over the brass *yahrzeit* plaques against the back wall, Zev Volf ben Chaim, Aryeh Leibish ben Reuven, Huddel Miriam bas Shmarya … names of dear souls long gone, these plaques the only record that they had ever lived.

Sure, the trustees had assured him that the *yahrzeit* plaques would be maintained and honored by whichever shul would be the beneficiary of their money, but that didn't satisfy him. Reb Anshel remembered Hirshel ben Nachman Ezra, and he knew that he wanted his *yahrzeit* plaque *here*, in the shul where he had so proudly served as *baal korei* for so many years.

Be strong, Reb Anshel told himself, trying to smile at his *eineklach.*

Chapter 20

I t had been years since Moishy Winternitz had engaged in thoughtful, interesting conversation. He wasn't the type. Yet, here he was, sitting at the edge of the sofa in the Mishkan Shalom parlor, deep in conversation.

Benjy was talking.

"Some days it's really tough to get out of bed. I know that I am not like other people, that I am starting each new day with the chips stacked against me. I watch everyone else running, so quick, so sure of themselves, and I feel overwhelmed. Everything takes me longer, everything comes a little harder, and I wonder if I should bother getting out of bed and trying to keep up."

Moishy was intrigued. "So why do you?"

Benjy shrugged. "I guess because that's my job. Hashem made me the way He did, so this is obviously what He wants from me."

Coming from anyone else the words would have sounded trite, even corny, and Moishy would have snorted aloud. Coming from Benjy Biller the words nearly brought Moishy to tears.

Pinky joined the conversation. "Everywhere I go, I feel that people are staring at me. Even when I am home for Shabbos, I feel that my brother and sisters are a little uncomfortable to be seen with me. That's hard. I didn't choose to be this way, to look this way, to walk this way.

"But if Hashem made me this way, then He probably loves me like this. That keeps me going."

Moishy was amazed. He had his own issues, and suffered deeply from being uncomfortable in his own skin. His body had become his enemy. But he could walk normally, talk clearly, run and jump and shoot baskets!

Moishy was inspired.

In the next room, the Mishkan Shalom staff member, a trained nurse in charge of administering the various daily medications, was shocked. Benjy and Pinky obviously had opinions and voices of which he, a professional, had been unaware.

The auditorium was hot and crowded. There were fewer chairs than parents and Chaim Weinstein was annoyed. Sunday was his day off and he had no interest in spending it shoving through hordes of parents and grandparents lugging video cameras, pushing to the front of the room so that they could get the perfect angle

He loved his kid as much as the next guy; he just didn't think that he had to spend a beautiful Sunday morning watching this Pesach skit. His little Shmuli could sing his songs for him at home. He would give him as many solos as he liked.

Didn't any of these women have to clean for Pesach? Didn't any of these fathers have chores to do, *chavrusos,* jobs? Was everyone here being held hostage by a bunch of six-year-old kids who craved attention?

Chaim scowled at a woman who walked up the aisle and whacked him with the immense bag swinging from her shoulder.

There were all kinds of children up on the stage. Some were openly hostile, pressured beyond endurance, simply too tired to perform. Others were crying, irritated by the uncomfortable costumes. There were, of course, the naturals, who stood on the makeshift stage with smiles plastered on their faces, singing on key with gusto. His Shmuli was none of those things, he was just a regular kid, excited to be on stage, waving to his mother on the women's side of the *mechitzah* every three or four seconds.

The piano player pounded on the keys and the children burst into song;

"*L'shanah haba'ah b'Yerushalayim … shoin, shoin, shoin Yerushalayim habnuyah.*"

And as they did, Chaim felt the pain that had been lurking deep inside of him burst forth, threatening to engulf him completely. He knew why he was so frustrated and irritable, and it was the song of the children that was serving as a mocking reminder; it was because he had cut himself off from that world.

Sure, Chaim Weinstein was *frum.* He put on *tefillin* each morning and kept Shabbos and sent his children to yeshivah, but he had become a stranger to Yiddishkeit. Simple joy in mitzvos and deep-seated acceptance were no longer part of his diet. He had forgotten the flavor of true, unadulterated joy, and *temimus* and *simchah* and all the other things that the children on stage represented.

So as the notes swirled around the room, *shoin, shoin, shoin Yerushalayim habnuyah,* tears began to form in the corners of Chaim's eyes. He had fallen, and fallen hard. He was cold and numb to meaning and truth; his heart was surrounded by barriers he himself had erected. The perpetual, incessant struggle to earn a living, which left him no time at all to devote to more spiritual pursuits; the images flitting across his computer screen, firmly planting themselves in his mind; the cynicism and despair about his chances of ever growing again ... all these were bricks in that wall.

And as he saw the sweet, innocent face of his son, so filled with purity and promise, he wished that he could do more for him, longed to give him a father who could lead him and inspire him.

The program was over. The rebbi took center stage and thanked everyone for coming, and the children made a mad dash for their parents. Chaim stood up quickly. There was a whole day ahead of him and he might still be able to get something done.

The workers had been fielding questions all morning from neighbors and passers by, inquiring what they were doing, when they would be finished, who had hired them, and how much they charged. Zalman Finestone was perhaps the first one who just hurried by, intent on getting home. He was simply not a nosy person. He wouldn't have cared if the new World Trade Center were going up right here, on a corner in Kensington. These things weren't important to him.

He would have been just as happy to hurry home for supper, but Mendel Wasser chanced to step out of the building just then.

He pounced on Zalman. "Shalom aleichem," he said enthusiastically.

Zalman looked up at him in surprise, "Hi" he responded.

"My name is Mendel Wasser."

"Zalman Finestone."

"Can I ask where you live, Reb Zalman?"

"Right here, across the street."

Zalman indicated a long row of houses and pointed to one of them.

"Oh, that's *gevaldig.* So let me tell you what we're doing here. I work for Mishkan Shalom, you know, the group home right here in this building."

Zalman was vaguely aware that there was some sort of facility in the apartment building, so he nodded. He was hungry.

Mendel continued. "So we are doing a little work here, adding a nice, spacious room that will serve as kind of a *beis medrash.*"

"I see," said Zalman, "that's very nice. It should be with mazel."

"No, no, I want you to come in and see it," said Mendel.

"I am sure it's very beautiful," Zalman protested, "but I really must get home."

Mendel persisted. "You don't understand, I need you to see it and I will tell you why." He lowered his voice conspiratorially. "The residents here, they really need this to work for their own development, but the only way that it can work, that we can really give them the atmosphere that they need to grow, is if the neighborhood people help us out."

Zalman looked at him, not sure he understood.

"I want to have a *minyan* each evening for Maariv and

perhaps, eventually, for one of the Shabbos *tefillos*. I want to give our people here a sense of having their own place, somewhere where they are not guests or outsiders. In their family homes they feel alienated, at work they are treated differently, in shul people stare at them; sure, everyone is very nice, but they never really feel like they belong.

"If you could just come join us for Maariv once in a while, or maybe even more than that, it would be a great service."

"Sure, sure. Let me know when you have the place up and running and I will make sure to be there."

And feeling humbled, Zalman Finestone continued on his way home.

***

The phone buzzed twice and Ari Engel punched the button. "Yes."

It was Chevy, his receptionist. "Um, Mr. Engel, someone is here to see you without an appointment. He says that he is coming in whether I like it or not."

Ari could tell that she was frightened, so he quickly assured her that he was not angry. "Tell him to come in," he said.

His door swung open and a large, disheveled looking man stormed in. Graying hair, a large potbelly, faded sweatpants and shirt, and bulging black eyes. Ari had no idea who he was or what he could want. If not for the yarmulke on his head, Ari could have mistaken him for a disgruntled maintenance man.

"How can I help you?"

"Listen to me, wise guy. I have lived in a building with your misfits and rejects for long enough. This here is the final straw."

Ari had no idea what the man was talking about, and looked at the paper that was thrust under his nose.

To All Residents in the Immediate Vicinity;

We thank you for bearing with us during this renovation. We assure you that all the work will be completed within the week, im yirtzeh Hashem. We are very pleased to announce that we will, be'ezras Hashem, be opening a small Beis Medrash here that will be open to all of you each evening. We hope you will join us for learning and Maariv.

For all questions and suggestions feel free to contact Rabbi Mendel Wasser at 347.998.0137.

Thank you for your cooperation

Mishkan Shalom Organization.

I really must talk with Wasser thought Ari as he faced his visitor.

"I see Mr. —"

"My name is Gelber, Jerry Gelber."

"I understand your frustration and we would be more than happy to work with you on this matter. I can imagine that you feel that your quality of life is compromised by the renovations, the noise, the mess —"

Gelber interrupted. "No it's not the mess and noise. It's the strange people and the creeps you hire to watch them that I can't handle."

Ari Engel rarely got angry, and when he did, he didn't show it. But Jerry Gelber had just spoken offensively about "his" people and he was irate.

"Okay, this meeting is over."

And Ari Engel, correctly assessing that Jerry Gelber would never allow himself to be thrown out of an office, stood up and strode out of the room, leaving a seething guest behind him.

"Mark my words. You haven't heard the end of it," Jerry shouted.

Chapter 21

The trip from New York to Tel Aviv is one hour shorter than the trip from Tel Aviv to New York, for some reason that Chavi Federman didn't quite understand — something about tailwinds. Her father had explained it to her several times. It made no difference. For her the trip back was miserable and endless. The thought of the landing and finding luggage, of the drive home from the airport, the unpacking and cleaning her dusty apartment didn't do anything to improve her mood.

Yom Tov was over and here she was, on the way back home to Eretz Yisrael for another lonely year. Avrohom Meir knew from experience that to try and comfort her now would be counter-productive, making his soothing words ineffective later on. He knew that she would sniffle all the way home, but within a day or two, she would be back to herself, happy and energetic. It was best to wait it out.

Chavi knew it too. She appreciated his willingness to back off and let her cry without trying to make things right. (It had taken him a while to learn, but better late than never!)

So as Miri slept and Avrohom Meir learned, she sat in her seat, hiccupping loudly and inelegantly into a stack of tissues. She reached into her carry-on bag, searching for one more taste of home. She located a foil-wrapped package of her mother's homemade cheese muffins and placed it on her lap.

A paper was folded awkwardly across its expanse, fastened with a piece of tape. That was odd. It wasn't her mother's style. The paper was marked with her name, and, intrigued, she unfolded it.

It was in Ezzy's unmistakable handwriting.

Dear Chavi,

It was real nice having you home for Yom Tov. I enjoyed learning with Avrohom Meir and playing with Miri — she's real cute.

A few times you mentioned that you wanted to talk and asked me if I felt like it. Of course I did. It's just hard to really talk — the way we used to — now that you're married. It seems like you're always running or busy with Miri. You can't force a conversation, like "now I have a few minutes, let's shmooze." It has to flow naturally.

Thanks for trying just the same. I guess it wasn't bashert.

Anyhow, Chavi, allow me to update you on some of what's been going on in my world over the last little while. You see, my life is kind of complicated right now. I am not much of a philosopher, but this

I can say: people are funny. They are very quick to judge and very slow to forget.

Almost a year ago — this Lag B'Omer will be the anniversary — I made a mistake. Reacting to a situation and acting out of anger, I tried to make a statement in a horrible way. Yes, I took money that wasn't mine. That was wrong and I myself don't understand how I did that.

I have deep remorse because my actions hurt not only me, but Tatty and Mommy, too. Tatty bailed me out and as soon as I earn some money of my own I inted to pay him back. But that isn't he worst of it.

What shocked me most of all was how people around me responded. Nice people started to look at me differently, judging quickly and harshly, despite themselves. Cruel people taunted me and fine people were silent, keeping their uncharitable thoughts inside. One thing is for sure: no one looked at me the same.

Once I realized that public opinion of me had plummeted so low, I no longer felt any motivation to let them think otherwise. I started to sink. There was no one to give me the kind words that I needed, no one to tell me how disappointed they were in me, no one to express shock at my behavior. I guess that Tatty had low expectations all along and Mommy was feeling too badly for me to add any pressure.

Whatever.

The point is that in the last few weeks, things have changed. On Purim, I met a group of people who do have expectations from me. They look at me as some kind of tzaddik, certain that I am just the most wonderful person around. They make me feel like I am their hero, and thanks to them, I have started to look at myself differently. They aren't your typical people, but still, they are refreshingly honest and sincere and they say what they think. I started to think that I owe it to them to be who they think I already am. They are always asking me questions in learning and having deep conversations with me, and I really enjoy that.

I have realized that what draws me to this group more than anything else is the way that they look at me. I want to be the Ezzy Markstein that they see. Of course I gravitate toward them.

That's more or less what's going on inside of me.

Also, Chavi, I wanted to say "thank you." From the moment you arrived, I realized that you looked at me the exact same way that you did last Pesach. Nothing had changed. That made me feel good, but best of all was when Avrohom Meir asked me to learn with him each day. To be honest, I haven't learned much over the past year. How could I, when the Rebbi wasn't looking at Ezzy Markstein, but at the boy who had stolen from the Yerushalmi meshulach, all the while trying to diagnose the problem?

With Avrohom Meir, I was able to learn again. It was nice to be taken seriously. He didn't try to be my psychologist (I certainly don't need another one!) or put his arm around me and go for long walks. He just treated me like a normal person. It was just what I needed and I enjoyed it.

Have a safe trip, Chavi. I hope that your flight goes easily and smoothly and that Miri doesn't act up. It's difficult to stay in touch when you're there and I am here, so I will ask you this. Whenever you make it to the Kosel, please have me in mind in your tefillos.

And Chavi, one more thing; my friends, Benjy, Pinky, Naftuli, Heshy, and Danny can also use your tefillos. They suffer from all kinds of illnesses and face many hardships. I don't know any of their full names or their mother's names, but Hashem will understand.

I miss you already,

Ezzy

Chavi looked over at Avrohom Meir. He had fallen asleep. That was a good thing. She needed space for this cry. She burst into a fresh flood of tears, crying for her only brother and his blatant cry of pain.

The blurry vision of a concerned stewardess loomed in front of her. "Oh sweetie," sighed the woman, "it's just a bad case of homesickness. Don't worry, you'll be okay."

It had been a strange week for Mendel Wasser. Mishkan Shalom was shut for the duration of the Yom Tov, as each and every one of the residents went home for Pesach. Mendel had enjoyed the break and got to spend some precious time with his children, but he also missed the group.

One night of Chol Hamoed, he had decided to invite them over for a small *mesibah*. Gitty was exceptionally gracious, welcoming them and asking each of them about their families. She was fascinated by Naftuli's *yichus,* and he had heard her on the phone that night telling her sister's about it. (*Can you imagine? The Rebbe's oldest son!*)

Mendel was gratified that she was coming on board. He needed her behind him in order to succeed.

Pesach hadn't been easy for Zalman and Frieda Finestone. They had watched their beloved father, Reb Anshel, decline even further, totally disoriented and befuddled in his new surroundings. The Seder itself had been a throwback to better times, and he had presided over the large gathering with stateliness and dignity.

The *tefillos* of Yom Tov had been much more challenging. Reb Anshel was not used to being anything but a rav. Though the rabbanim at the local shuls were respectful, even deferential, he was still not *the Rav*. Over Chol Hamoed he began to act strangely and disoriented. For the second days of Yom Tov, Zalman arranged *minyanim* in the house. He knew that it was a short-term solution, that he couldn't impose on his neighbors like this on a steady basis, but still, it achieved the desired results. His *shver* was the Rav, sitting at the front, speaking before *laining* and honored with the coveted *aliyos*. They waited for him before beginning *chazzaras hashatz* and lined up after davening to wish him "gut Yom Tov."

The problem was how to proceed. After *bein hazmanim* the *bachurim* who had so goodnaturedly participated in the *minyan* (it began at nine-fifteen!) would be returning to yeshivah.

Zalman Finestone wasn't an idea person. He was content to deal with this problem the way he dealt with everything else; by leaving it to the Master of the World and awaiting His salvation.

Zalman was a daydreamer, the kind of dreamer who would become totally engrossed in his thoughts and therefore oblivious to his surroundings. So when he was walking down the block one evening, just a few days after Pesach, the "Shalom aleichem, Reb Zalman" that came from just behind startled him as if someone had popped a balloon in his ear.

He looked up to see the fellow who worked at that facility in the apartment building, the one who had approached him before Yom Tov.

"How are you?" asked Zalman politely.

"*Baruch Hashem*, wonderful," replied the other, enthusiastically.

"I wanted to let you know that we are opening our *beis medrash* next Sunday night, on Rosh Chodesh Iyar. It would be great if you could be *mechazek* us, and if you could help spread the word throughout the neighborhood. We will be starting with an evening program, Minchah and Maariv and a *shiur*. If you could come learn there with your *chavrusa* that would really be marvelous."

Zalman nodded noncommittally and promised to consider it seriously.

It was only after the other had walked away that it came to him. It came to him so suddenly that it stunned him, like a ray of bright sunlight on a cloudy day.

He turned around suddenly and headed back home.

Chapter 22

When Chavi had been seventeen years old and Ezzy thirteen, the family had gone on a trip. It was just the four of them, Aryeh, Malka, Ezzy, and Chavi, and they had traveled up to the Poconos at the end of one summer.

Perhaps in an effort to be vacation-like, or maybe because she was feeling light and free, Chavi decided that she would have fun with her family. Instead of the usual nervous conversation about arriving on time, not getting speeding tickets, and keeping the back of the car clean, Chavi put herself out on a limb. She was just back from camp and she, Chavi Markstein, was going to create a "ruach" in her family, just as she had in her bunk. She decided that they would laugh, and laugh hard.

She started alone, but within minutes, Malka and Ezzy were having fun and laughing along with her as they imagined the lives of the drivers and passengers in the cars around them. They saw a small, red hatchback with an enormous man driving, and they regaled each other with imaginary details of his past and personal life. They saw a woman behind the wheel of a yellow pick-up and they created a marvelously ridiculous story of just how she had ended up behind the wheel.

Through it all, Aryeh sat silently, eyeing the road carefully and looking for signs of a speed trap. Then it happened. They were discussing an old man in a nearby convertible. The man was easily sixty years old, and the wind blowing through his hair made it painfully obvious that he had precious little left.

They were wondering what could possibly make a man that age drive a car clearly designed with someone much younger in mind. Malka suggested that it was a midlife crisis, his way of proclaiming that he was still young. Ezzy had his own story. It really belonged not to the driver, but to his son, he said, and when the son had gone off to serve in the navy the father had decided to drive it in his honor.

Aryeh had surprised them by suddenly joining the conversation. "Maybe," he said heatedly, "he grew up poor, so poor that he didn't even allow himself to dream. When he got older he was so busy trying to provide for his family that he still didn't have time to dream. And," he finished on a painful note, "now he finally has time and money to dream. So really, this car is not the dream of a sixty-year-old but of a sixteen-year-old."

They were all quiet for a moment and Malka looked as if she were about to cry. "This wasn't the way it was supposed to go," thought Chavi, but still, she felt good that he had joined their little game.

She knew that he was trying to be light with them, not heavy and serious. It was just that he didn't know how.

He had also felt bad about the note he'd injected in their game and he tried to salvage it. "But then again, maybe he should have looked in the mirror before hitting the open road. I don't think he has the hairline for it."

He was trying; he really was, so they all laughed dutifully.

Later on, when they had stopped for gas and snacks, Chavi was sitting on a bench. She had bitten off both ends of a licorice stick and was using it as a straw through which to sip her Sprite. Her father had noticed and looked at her in disdain. "Chavi, that's childish," he had said.

He had stopped trying.

This was the memory that crossed Malka's mind as she sat across from her husband in the quiet of his study. She was going through a rough time; she usually did in the days after Chavi and her family returned to Eretz Yisrael. Malka was a fanatical photographer, and to comfort herself, she had downloaded all the new photos and clips of her *einekel* onto a disc. She had brought it into the study to watch. Yes, she knew that after supper Aryeh preferred to sit there in solitude, either learning, reading, or finishing business, and the last thing he wanted was to be forced to smile along with her.

She didn't take it personally. It wasn't about her. It was about him and his perpetual struggle to connect on an emotional level, a task that came so easily to her and with such difficulty to him.

Now, as they sat there looking at the images of their granddaughter, Malka felt the familiar sadness rising within her. She was engaged in her life's endeavor, trying to bring her husband into her world, *their* world, the world of the family, trying to get him to share the joy and warmth and happiness, but it was as if he were in prison, unable to get out.

He was watching the little girl on the screen, enjoying her sweet antics as much as Malka was, but there was something almost disapproving in his eyes. It was if he didn't understand how all the other adults on the screen, his wife, son-in-law, and daughter could permit themselves such unabashed displays of delight. *Life is serious business*, the creases in his forehead seemed to shout, *stop laughing*.

Malka ached for him.

Frieda Finestone thrived on schedule. These minutes just after supper, when her husband was out learning, were busy ones. She listened with one ear as her oldest daughter spoke about her day, while the other heard her younger daughter's reading homework. Her hands never stopped moving, preparing tomorrow's lunches with precision and skill.

She was also in the middle of a load of laundry and had put two of the little ones to bed, which meant repeatedly checking on them.

Thus, when Zalman suddenly burst back into the house, completely breathless, she barely looked up. She knew he wasn't the type to run home for no reason, especially at the expense of his precious learning time, but she was really busy.

"What?" she eyed him wordlessly.

"Frieda, we need to talk," he exulted.

She sliced a cucumber deftly and placed it into a sandwich. Yanky hated cucumber in his sandwich while Kaila loved it. Usher Zelig tolerated it but only if it was sliced the long way. Mindy had specially requested a cheese sandwich for tomorrow and little Moshe Boruch was going on a trip to a park and needed an extra drink and snack. She really couldn't concentrate on whatever it was that Zalman just *had* to talk about right now.

But she saw that he couldn't wait anymore. Her Zalman wasn't the idea type, the sort who got inspirations that he needed to share. So she made one last check on the children and the laundry and went to sit down with him at the kitchen table.

"Frieda, I have it," he burst out, unable to contain himself, "the perfect solution for Zaidy."

The look that she gave him was ambiguous.

"Zaidy is a rav, so if we can give him a chance to be a rav again, we will be able to keep him young, to give him a reason to go on."

A hundred cynical remarks about Zalman becoming a therapist were on the tip of Frieda's tongue. She was, however, so touched by his obvious feeling for her father that she swallowed them all.

He briefly filled her in on the plans for the new shul that the people at the facility across the street were building.

"And then, once it's up and running, we'll ask them to let Zaidy be the rav."

Frieda consciously looked at up the clock, as if to signify that she didn't have time for this conversation. "Zalman." She said his name as a sentence by itself. "Surely you didn't come running home to suggest to me that my father should become a puppet at the Mizrach wall of a shul designed to make unfortunate people feel good about themselves. That's pathetic."

Little Moshe Boruch popped his head into the kitchen. "Ma," he wailed, "I can't fall asleep. I need a drink now."

He caught sight of his father and ran into his arms delightedly. "Tatty!"

Other kids came into the room. Frieda rose, making it clear that the meeting was adjourned.

Zalman wouldn't give up. He came back home at eleven o'clock and tried again. Frieda wasn't exactly relaxed, but she wasn't as busy either. She was annoyed at his suggestion from earlier that evening, but still, when he came home, she prepared his tea and sat down to talk as they did every night.

"Did you see Yanky's Rebbi during Maariv?" she asked, as if to make it clear that there was no returning to the old conversation.

Zalman didn't reply. He made a *berachah* and sipped his tea, studying her carefully.

She repeated the question, wondering why he was acting so strangely.

Zalman Finestone, quiet, indifferent Zalman Finestone suddenly began to speak, and it was a voice Frieda had never heard.

"Frieda, listen to me," he said, slamming his tea glass on the table. "This is serious and I insist that you hear me out.

"I love and respect your father, maybe as much as you do. He lives in my house and it is my responsibility — a sacred responsibility — to do my best to honor him and treat him with love. I intend to do that.

"For over half a century, your father has gotten out of bed each morning with a plan, a cause, a task. He knew that they wouldn't start *berachos* until he came. He knew that there were people waiting for his 'good morning' and others that couldn't go off to work after davening until he wished them a good day.

"Being a rav is not what he did; it's who he was!"

Frieda listened, tears forming in her eyes.

He felt encouraged to continue.

"Frieda, let's face it. Your father's mind isn't what it was. He can't speak the way he used to or answer *she'eilos* with the same sharpness and clarity as he used to. There's not exactly a market for elderly rabbanim in their eighties with failing memories.

"He doesn't need the workload of a rav; he needs the station of a rav. He needs to walk to the front of the room, to greet the people when davening is over and to deliver an occasional *shiur.* Sure, that's not a real shul, but a real shul wouldn't take him either."

Frieda wasn't sure she liked it, but she nodded nonetheless, hearing the truth of his words.

Then, ever practical, she asked the question that had to be asked.

"And who says that they will take him as rav?"

Chapter 23

Reb Anshel Hammerman's room was small, but it more than met his needs. There was a bed and a dresser, a small bookcase with *sefarim,* a comfortable chair and numerous family pictures on the wall.

Up on top of the closet, where he kept the box with his Shabbos hat, he had his secret envelope. Each month, when his pension check would arrive, he would take it to the bank. He would separate *ma'aser,* and then ask for one hundred dollars in cash. The rest of the money would remain in his account.

He would go home with the cash and place it in his special envelope.

His *levayah* money.

Over the years, Reb Anshel had seen much heartache and misfortune and had been called in to resolve many conflicts.

Living as he did on the Lower East Side, a neighborhood with a large population of elderly people, many of his duties involved situations surrounding death and funerals. The most heartbreaking among his responsibilities was arranging for a funeral and burial when there was no money to pay for it. All too often, he had been confronted with *meis mitzvah* situations, where there was neither money nor family members interested in helping accord a Jew the ultimate *chessed*. Then, it would be up to the rav to call in the favors of the funeral-home directors and cemetery officials. He would be the one to ensure that there would be a *minyan* at the funeral and the *kevurah,* that Kaddish and mishnayos would be recited for the soul of the departed.

It was one of his hardest jobs, but each time that situation arose, he was reminded again of just how fortunate he was to be serving the Jewish people as a rabbi, where the opportunities to help people abounded.

So now Reb Anshel lived with his daughter Frieda in Kensington. He understood his own situation well. He felt it on the days when he was sinking fast, when there were cobwebs in his brain and he just couldn't get rid of them. He had seen enough of his friends and congregants travel this painful route to know that there would be rough days ahead.

So although he knew there was money in his bank account, he hoped to leave it to his dear children after he departed the world. He had but one worry, and it consumed him. He needed to know that he would not be a burden, that come time to pay *him* final respects, there would be money to cover all the necessary expenses. He didn't want his dear children to sit *shivah*, grieving, and also worrying about money.

His place in the cemetery, right near his dear Mirish'l, was already paid for; the money in the envelope was for the funeral. In fact, the envelope was marked in his handwriting, "For my *levayah.*" When they would need the money, they would find it.

***

Gitty Wasser looked out the window and saw her husband walking up the steps. "Look at him," she said into the phone, "so calm and relaxed, while I am such a nervous wreck."

She couldn't understand how Mendel could take so much on his head. Here he was, basically opening a new shul, and he wasn't even making the necessary arrangements. He should have been on the phone, making calls to ensure that everything would work out.

She felt that it was her responsibility as his wife to help things along, to see to the smallest details of what he was planning. After all, she wanted him to succeed.

He came into the house, setting his *tallis* and *tefillin* on the small table in the foyer and entering the kitchen. "Good morning," he said, sniffing appreciatively. "You baking something?"

"Yes," she said, her pride evident. Mendel wasn't sure what her new attitude was all about, but he couldn't say he minded. She put on her oven mitts, removed a fresh chocolate cake from the oven, and placed it gingerly on the counter.

Mendel looked on with pleasure as she cut him a large slice and even served it to him. She prepared a cup of coffee the way he liked it and placed that in front of him as well.

Then she pounced. With enthusiasm she could not hide, she slammed her notebook down on the table and removed a pen from the pocket of her skirt.

"Okay, let's go through everything that needs to be done before the grand opening next week."

Wow, when Gitty is on board, she is completely there! thought Mendel.

Jerry Gelber was on a mission, and like a man possessed, he stomped up and down the halls of the building looking for flashes of yellow. The papers were everywhere, a cheery shade of yellow with the Mishkan Shalom logo in large blue letters on top, mocking him;

TO ALL RESIDENTS
Please Join Us
on Sunday night, Rosh Chodesh Iyar,
as we dedicate the brand-new Beis Medrash of
the Mishkan Shalom Group Home.

We appreciate your graciousness
during the renovations
and hope that you will avail yourself of
this wonderful new addition to the building.
Program at 7:30 sharp.

Jerry wasn't content to simply rip the papers from the walls. He wanted it clear that there was serious opposition to the plan, and he tore each paper into shreds and dropped the pieces on the floor. *Let them see,* he told himself, *let all these meek, voiceless losers see that there are some real men left in this building.*

For the elderly widows of the building, it was all very exciting. They watched with horrified fascination through the chains on the doors at the figure storming through the halls, muttering and cursing, and when he was gone, they ran to call their neighbors and rehash what they had seen. Mrs. Hirsh-kopf didn't mince any words. "You know, I think it is so nasty to let this happen. We've been living here for so long, it's time we made our voices heard as well. I say that we go to the event and show our support, a united voice for the cause."

Mrs. Nevinsky on the second floor, another veteran of the building, (*her Sol, olav hashalom, could have bought the whole building for next to nothing, back in the Fifties, if only he'd listened to her. But no, bless his soul, he had insisted that it would be better to invest their money elsewhere*) also got into the act. She assured Mrs. Hirshkopf that she would show her support and almost immediately, sat down with a pen and her special stationary.

We are so pleased to be invited to the wonderful affair and thank you for including us. We most certainly will be there. We think that it is wonderful that the building will have a little shul and we are completely behind you.

She read what she had written with pride. She still had it. Her handwriting was elaborate and flowing, just as it had always been and she was proud to be the one to represent all the girls in the building. She called back Mrs. Hirshkopf and read her the letter. Then, they spent the better part of an hour discussing and arguing over which of their friends should be invited to sign their little petition in favor.

Sadie's name should be first, after all she was a big-wig in the shul sisterhood for over forty years, and her name will mean something. Why, they even honored her at a luncheon last year.

No, no, we have to put Pauline on top. Her son is a state senator out on Long Island and it will impress them much more.

It took a few more minutes for all the maneuvering to be completed satisfactorily, and then they had to work the phones, gathering signatures for the cause they were coming to love.

If this was war, then they could still fight.

Don't count us out, thought Mrs. Nevinsky as she made the trek down to the first floor to deliver the letter, walking with more energy than usual.

⬛▮▮▮ ▮ ▮ ▮▮▮▮ ▮ ▮ ▮ ▮▮▮

Chaim Weinstein's head appeared, then his chest, and then the rest of him emerged from the subway station stairs. It was already evening, and he quickened his pace as he headed up the block. These few minutes, just after he arrived home, were the only peaceful moments in his day.

His sweet children would greet him at the door, ever so eager to tell him what they had learned in school. He would sit and hold them close as they would fill him in, showing him how to make a *lamed*, or solemnly recounting the story of Yosef and his brothers.

Then, just after their bedtime, he would sit down to supper and be thrust back into the real world. At work, it was his boss hounding him, harassing him, judging him, and pressuring him. At home, it was Chana Rivka doing the same thing. But where Michael from the office did it with snide remarks and critical comments, Chana Rivka did it with silence and mournful grimaces.

He wasn't sure which was worse, but he was slowly breaking from the combination.

Some women needed money and expensive clothing in order to make them happy. Chana Rivka needed a husband who learned and had *yiras Shamayim;* that was it. He was zero for two. He had neither the strength nor the desire to learn anymore and whatever *yiras Shamayim* he had once possessed had been buried deep within him, hidden under the residue created by the perpetual struggle to make a living.

He was weary, bone-weary.

As he headed toward his house, focused on these unpleasant thoughts, he noticed some unusual activity at the apartment building on the corner. The residents of the facility that was housed there, some kind of place for developmentally delayed adults, were gathered around in a little cluster, whispering excitedly.

As he approached their group, he was suddenly offered yellow flyers by five different hands, each one beckoning him to take his. He smiled graciously and took all five papers, reading the top one just to be nice.

Come Join Us for the Opening of Our New Beis Medrash, it cheerfully invited him.

He looked up, bewildered. "Huh?"

One of them, a shortish fellow with curly graying hair, was the spokesman.

"Yeah, we're opening our own shul, a Mishkan Shalom *beis medrash*, and we hope that the people in the neighborhood will come learn and daven with us."

Just great, Chaim thought, *another shul that I won't go to. Chana Rivka will love this.* He hid his feelings from the five men.

"That's great. Good luck," he said, smiling warmly and walking on.

Chapter 24

Mendel Wasser was a *Litvak* through and through, descended from a long line of people to whom that heritage was a sacred mandate. Mendel had always been a little wary of chassidim, and his contact with them was minimal. Sure, they were all friendly and kind, but when it came to religious matters, well, it simply wasn't his *mesorah*.

Yet here he was, sitting in the waiting room just outside the Rebbe's chamber. He was looking around, trying to take it all in so that he could describe it later for Gitty; after all, this whole escapade was her idea. She had even called the Rebbe's office to make the appointment.

Mendel was thinking that it didn't look so different from the waiting room at his doctor's office. There were chairs lining the walls, almost all them occupied. Unlike the doctor's waiting room, however, where people busied themselves with magazines and the contents of their handbags, here even the waiting seemed to have a purpose.

Mendel couldn't get enough of his surroundings. It wasn't that he was nosy; in fact, Mendel Wasser was anything but nosy. It was just that he was in a new environment, doing something he had never before done, and he wanted to understand why people came to Rebbes and what they did there.

In the corner an old man sat, his eyes closed tightly in nervous concentration. Mendel wondered how much older he was than the Rebbe and how often he came here. His was clutching a *kvittel* so tightly that it was saturated with his perspiration. Next to him sat a father and his young, barmitzvah age son, clearly here for a *berachah*. The fellow next to them didn't look chassidish, but he was no less anxious than the others. Mendel had overheard him discussing the details of a complicated surgery with the *gabbai,* who had assured him that the Rebbe would be intimately familiar with the procedure.

Over on Mendel's side of the room, two men were engaged in a serious, whispered conversation. It seemed that they were business partners, there to ask the Rebbe to resolve a dispute in which they were involved. Immediately next to Mendel sat a teenage *bachur* who looked like he didn't fit the traditional chassidishe mold, yet he too was sitting with a solemn, respectful expression as he waited his turn.

The *gabbai,* a tall, leathery man whose eyes never seemed to be more than half-open approached Mendel. "Are you well?" he asked in flawless English. Mendel gulped and nodded. He wasn't usually this inquisitive, but he had to know.

"Is it like this every night?" he asked the *gabbai,* motioning at the full room.

The gabbai smiled at him. "It's usually much fuller than this. These days after Yom Tov are quieter, because many people were here over Yom Tov."

"How can the Rebbe concentrate on each person?"

The gabbai looked at Mendel indulgently. "That's what Rebbes do; they listen to Yidden and try to help them. Would you like me to help you write a *kvittel*?"

Mendel couldn't imagine bothering the Rebbe for any more time than was absolutely necessary, so he shook his head. "No thank you. I will just ask the Rebbe to come and then I will go."

The gabbai looked at him strangely. "Come? Come where?" Mendel was unaware that, suddenly, all ears in the room were straining to hear his answer.

"Oh, we're making a *chanukas habayis* over at Mishkan Shalom, where I work, next week. We're building a new *beis medrash* and I wanted to invite the Rebbe."

The *gabbai* lifted his hands, as if exasperated. "No, no the Rebbe doesn't go places. He is not the type of Rebbe who goes around banging in *mezzuzos* for whoever asks. If you would have told me what you wanted, I could have saved you all this time that you've been waiting. The Rebbe will definitely not come."

Mendel thought of Gitty and how excited she had been at the idea. He was so happy to have her working with him. He shrugged. "I would prefer to ask the Rebbe just the same."

The *gabbai's* eyes narrowed. "He won't come."

Mendel's glasses were slipping down his nose, as they tended to do when he was nervous, so he peered up at the *gabbai*. "Perhaps he won't. But if he doesn't, it will be because he decided not to."

The *gabbai* hurried to greet a new arrival without looking back at Mendel.

The old man in the corner smiled with secret delight. He had never before seen "Leibel *gabbai*" maneuvered.

It was late, very late when Mendel finally had his opportunity to enter. The room was larger than he had expected, and the Rebbe was seated at the head of a long table. There were *sefarim* all around him and a pair of half-glasses rested on an open Gemara. The Rebbe looked up at him with wise eyes. His beard was streaked with gray and his forehead was wrinkled, but he projected a certain youthful energy. Even at the late hour, he didn't seem tired.

He extended his hand. "Shalom aleichem."

Mendel suddenly felt a strange, inexplicable sense of awe as he accepted the outstretched hand. The Rebbe motioned for him to sit. Mendel did, and the Rebbe turned to him with an expectant face, as if inviting him to speak.

Mendel felt that he could tell this man anything and had to refrain from veering from his prepared script. He felt a strong urge to start crying, to tell the Rebbe about all that he wished he could be, about his unfulfilled hopes for himself, about Gitty and the children, but instead, he reminded himself why he had come and kept to business.

His Yiddish was yeshivish, picked up in *shiurim* and *shmuessen,* and he wasn't really confident speaking it. The Rebbe interrupted almost as soon as he began speaking to tell him that he could speak English.

Mendel smiled appreciatively and introduced himself. He couldn't resist saying that he was really a rebbi, but had taken this temporary job at a group home, Mishkan Shalom.

As soon as he said the words, the Rebbe closed his eyes tightly and sighed. "Naftuli," he said, "how is my son?"

Mendel beamed. "He is a wonderful young man. Just last night we learned Pirkei Avos together and he really enjoyed it."

The Rebbe grasped Mendel's hands tightly. "What a wonderful *zechus* you have," he said. "I would love to learn with him, with my dear son. You see what kind of life I have, how busy it gets, and how hard it is to find time, but I try. My mind is never really far away from Naftuli and he comes to visit every few days. We talk, he and I, but ..." the Rebbe's voice trailed off into a whisper, "but I have never learned with him."

Mendel noticed that the Rebbe's eyes were wet. "Your *neshamah* has touched him in a way that mine never has. You must be a special young man. May *HaKadosh Baruch Hu bentsch* you for it."

Mendel nodded humbly. "I really enjoy learning with him, with all of them. They are so eager for any idea; every drop of knowledge is so valuable to them."

The Rebbe nodded. "How can I help you, Reb Mendel?"

"Well, next Sunday, we are making a small *chanukas habayis* for a new *beis medrash* that we are building for the residents. We really want to create awareness in the neighborhood so that others will come in, so we hope the event will be attended by many of the locals. We would be honored if the Rebbe would come and participate."

The Rebbe closed his eyes for a moment, thinking.

"What time is it called for?"

"Eight o'clock with Minchah first and Maariv after."

"For how long do you want me to be there?"

"Perhaps fifteen or twenty minutes. We would be honored if the Rebbe would just say a few words and give us a *berachah*." Mendel wasn't the calculating sort, so he continued. "Also, if we announce on the signs that the Rebbe will be there, most likely we will draw a bigger crowd."

The Rebbe smiled. He liked the young man and his inno-cent forthrightness. More than that, he liked that this fellow learned with his Naftuli, a job he felt he should have been doing himself.

"I will, *im yirtzeh Hashem,* be there, but I have one request. Don't put my name on any signs until I tell Naftuli about it myself. I want to see his face when he hears that I will be visiting him at his place. I should have done it long ago."

The Rebbe rose and walked Mendel to the door, giving him a parting *berachah* before opening it.

A lesser man then Mendel Wasser would have given the *gabbai* a triumphant look on the way out. Mendel didn't. He simply hurried out, hoping that Gitty was still up so that he could tell her that she had been right.

Aryeh Markstein was well-connected, but he wasn't the type of person to use his connections. He did the mitzvos he did without asking for favors in return, so it was with no small degree of hesitation that he lifted the phone to call Rabbi Hirschman.

Rabbi Hirschman was the *menahel* at a yeshivah where Aryeh served on the board of directors. It had been Aryeh who had come up with the money for him to give his rebbeim a much-deserved bonus before Pesach and Aryeh who helped him meet his payroll each month.

They spoke yeshivah business for a few minutes until Aryeh finally came out with it. "I know that you run some sort of summer program for teenagers," he began.

"Yes," Rabbi Hirschman replied proudly, "we have one of the best *masmidim* programs in the mountains. We have been full since before Pesach, *Baruch Hashem.*"

"What about waiters? Would you need waiters?"

Rabbi Hirschman paused. "I think I have some space. Why?"

Aryeh felt a headache coming on. "Well I have a sixteen-year-old son, Ezzy, and I would like him to go to camp this summer. He wants a change of scenery, a new camp, and I think your program might be nice for him."

"Reb Aryeh, we would love to have your son. I will have someone from the office call you for the particulars. The fact that he is your son is enough for us not to need references for the boy."

Aryeh laughed weakly.

"Thank you."

But he knew that the real battle was still ahead of him: convincing Ezzy to get off the streets and go to camp.

Chapter 25

The black Highlander was the perfect car for its owner; sleek and impressive without being showy or opulent. "That's all I need," he would tell his wife, "a fancy car so that people will say that the government is stuffing us with money and we don't know what to do with it."

This morning, the man behind its wheel, Ari Engel, slammed on the brakes as he drove up Eighteenth Avenue. He made it a point to drive by each of his group homes and day-hab centers as often as possible, and to him, no news was good news. He didn't want to see his consumers or staff hanging around, looking any less able or productive than any-one else. Ari Engel had spent years convincing landlords and neighbors that a Mishkan Shalom group home or center was a "good neighbor" and that there was no reason to discriminate against them. His goal was that they remain unnoticed, that there would be no evidence of the fact that they were there.

The yellow banner just outside the apartment building was a violation of every one of the rules dear to him. *Join us this Sunday night,* it called out cheerfully, *for the dedication of our new beis medrash. Be mechazek this new makom of Torah and Tefillah for our neighborhood.*

Ari briefly considered parking and ripping the banner down, but that really wasn't the way he did things. He called Mrs. Handler, the staff member on duty that morning, and in a deceptively calm voice asked her about the sign.

"Oh, I think Mendel brought it in last night. He and the boys were up until late hanging it up. They told me all about it this morning, and though they were tired — a little too tired, if you ask me — they were all in such good moods."

"Is Mendel there now?"

"No, he isn't," she said. "I will leave him a message to call you."

"Thank you, Mrs. Handler."

Ari Engel headed into Boro Park, growing more annoyed by the minute.

First the guy sets up signs and banners as if this was some kind of Chol Hamoed carnival, instead of a highly professional, New York State government-sponsored facility, and then he keeps the residents up half the night as if this were summer camp.

This was clearly not working.

He parked the way he always did, at a haphazard angle that proclaimed that he hadn't the time to straighten it out, three wheels in the small parking lot adjoining the building and the last one on the sidewalk.

The boss was in.

Chevy had finished making the coffee just as he stormed into the office. She had been working for him for long enough to know that he wasn't in the best of moods, so she placed the steaming mug on his desk next to his pile of messages and hurried out.

He nodded to her as he passed. "Please get a message over to Wasserman over at 18th Avenue that I want a meeting with him. Today."

He closed the door and looked at the pile of green post-it notes that she had neatly assembled on his desk.

Call Dr. Shindelheim, said the top one.

Now there is a professional, thought Ari as he dialed the number, *a man who takes his job seriously.* Larry Shindelheim was the clinical director of Mishkan Shalom and consistently reviewed the medical condition of each patient. He made sure that their prescription medications were working for them and that the doses were being administered on time, and he was a frequent visitor at each of the Mishkan Shalom locations.

Ari reached him on his cellphone and the two men exchanged pleasantries, chatting briefly about family and the weather.

"Anyhow, Ari I just had to tell you something interesting. The new rabbi fellow that you got working over at 18th, he isn't exactly the conventional type, and at first I was skeptical about him. I mean, what's his training and experience in dealing with this type of person? But these last few days, he has the residents there on some kind of high, it's like color war. They're always happy and upbeat, and I am not seeing any of the usual mood swings that are so common there. It seems that he gave them something major to look forward to, and that's energizing them. It's fascinating to see these same people, who I have been speaking with each week, some of them for years, suddenly alive and vibrant."

Ari wasn't sure how to respond. He had been expecting criticism and been prepared to agree that Wasserman wasn't the right man for the job — instead he was hearing compliments.

"Uh, right, doctor; I hear exactly what you are saying."

"I thought that you deserved some *nachas.* You picked a winner, Ari. It might be worth it to write up a memo about what he is doing and distribute it to all the case workers and staff members."

"Yeah, that's definitely something to think about."

Ari hung up the phone. He was the type that thought in black and white; either someone was good or bad. He wasn't sure what to make of this Mendel character turning the place upside-down.

He needed another coffee.

"Hold all calls," he instructed Chevy, "I need some quiet time to think."

But it wasn't three minutes later that Chevy's voice came through the intercom. "Mr. Engel, sorry," she spoke with a sense of urgency, "but the Rebbe is on the phone."

"Which Rebbe, what Rebbe?"

"I don't know. The *gabbai* just said that the Rebbe would like to speak with you."

"Okay," sighed Ari. *Who knew what this was all about?*

"Hello."

There was a click as the phone was transferred to the Rebbe, and as soon as Ari heard the voice he knew which Rebbe. *The* Rebbe! Ari wasn't much of a chassid, but since the time that Naftuli had become part of Mishkan Shalom, Ari had become quite close with his father. They'd had many lengthy conversations, and Ari knew him as a man of great wisdom and insight.

"What can I do for the Rebbe?" he asked respectfully.

"I just had to share something with you, Reb Ari. At my age, you start thinking that there's very little that you can learn from other people. A wonderful young *talmid chacham*, Reb Mendel Wasser, came here and taught me something.

"I thank you for all that you do, and hiring this young man is just another one of your *zechusim*."

Ari hung up from the phone call a little less confused. He had found the clarity he sought.

Mendel Wasser was gearing up for his big day. Last night, he had hung up the beautiful banner that Gitty had made, and this morning, he was planning on ordering refreshments for the event. He also needed to set up chairs for the crowd, and he planned to borrow them from a local *gemach*.

There was an urgent message on his voicemail from a Zalman Finestone, who needed to meet with him as soon as possible.

Mendel called the number.

"Oh, Reb Mendel, thanks so much for returning the call. I don't know if you remember me, but I met you outside of the building where you work and you told me all about the wonderful little *beis medrash* that you are opening."

"Oh, sure," said Mendel, not really sure that he remembered him at all.

"Anyway, do you think that we can meet, Reb Mendel? It's very important to me."

"Okay. When and where?"

"I could come to you right now. Where are you?"

Mendel was actually in the corner of a large shul, learning by himself. He told Zalman where to find him and turned back to his Chumash, preparing a nice *vort* to share with his boys.

Mendel sat silently when Zalman finished talking. The whole story of Reb Anshel moved him, and he wanted badly to meet this elderly Rav.

He wasn't anticipating the next question. "Do you think that my father-in-law could sort of be a rav for your new shul? Obviously, you wouldn't have to pay him or anything. It would be more like giving him *kavod* and asking him to speak."

Mendel was caught off guard.

"I mean, our residents aren't on a very high level of learning. What could he say to them?"

"He would be able to relate to them too, I am sure. I have never seen anyone with whom that my *shver* couldn't converse."

Mendel began to think. He loved learning with the men, but it would be nice to have a real rav, someone to sit in the front of the shul and wish them a good day and speak at *shalosh seudos* and … he was getting ahead of himself again.

He dreamt of *shalosh seudos* and Shabbos *tefillos,* but they had neither a real *minyan* nor a Sefer Torah.

He turned back to Zalman. "We don't really have the basics of a shul, no *minyan,* no Sefer Torah. I just wanted a place for the men to learn. What kind of job are we offering?"

Zalman's eyes glinted. "What about if I got you a beautiful Sefer Torah? Would you make it a package deal? My *shver* will be the rav — for whatever its worth — and the Sefer Torah will be a part of your project."

Mendel considered his words. He had to speak with Gitty. He had to ask Mr. Engel. "You know what? I have a meeting with my boss today. Let's hear what he thinks of the idea and then we'll speak again."

Neither of the men was a skilled or hardened negotiator. Neither had thought to bargain or haggle, neither knew that one wasn't supposed to give in too easily. The whole conversation had taken less than ten minutes and each got up feeling excited and optimistic.

The Sefer Torah had belonged to the rav, though it resided in the *aron kodesh* of the shul. When they had closed up the shul, Shaul Hammerman had lent to it to a friend who ran a *minyan* on the bus each morning, with the stipulation that he could take it back whenever he wanted.

He had just hung up the phone with his brother-in-law, Zalman.

He wanted.

Chapter 26

M alka had woken up with the sense that it was later than she wanted it to be. This had been happening with increasing frequency to her recently, now that Yom Tov was over and she didn't have much to do. The weeks before Pesach had been a whirlwind of joyous activity as she cooked and cleaned, anticipating Chavi's arrival, but now, she just couldn't get herself excited about anything.

She knew that her habit of sleeping late and then, after a cup of coffee, watching home videos of little Miri's antics wasn't a good one. It was an escape, a chance to hear the tinkling of genuine laughter in a home that was — of late — devoid of it.

She had once dreamed of a home filled with happiness and noise. Now, she was pleased when there was basic, civil conversation at the supper table.

It had been a strange few days in the Markstein home. Ezzy seemed happier then he'd been in a while, or at least Malka thought so. He seemed more at peace, more comfortable with himself, and had even told her that he thought that his weekly visits to Dr. Nikosi were a waste of time and should be stopped.

She was happy to hear him say it, even though she knew that Aryeh would insist that he keep on going. Aryeh liked it when things were dealt with by professionals and even though the doctor hadn't really done anything for Ezzy, Aryeh would say that they couldn't possible gauge what Dr. Nikosi had or had not done. When he signed the check for the doctor each week, he felt like he was helping his son, like he wasn't just standing idly by while ....

Well, while *what*? Malka couldn't for the life of her figure out why Ezzy wasn't just a regular teenager like a thousand other teenagers out there. She sighed. Was she, Malka of the sunny, optimistic disposition, getting depressed? She longed to call Chavi, just to hear her daughter's voice, but it wasn't fair. Chavi would hear the loneliness in her voice and it would just make her feel guilty. She knew how the thought of Chavi, sitting alone in the Ezras Torah Park hoping for another mother with a baby to come out, filled her with pity. Her Chavi, the most popular, energetic girl in her class — what was happening? Mother and daughter, at opposite ends of the world. Both so personable, cheerful, and ... lonely, so lonely.

Supper wasn't any better. Aryeh chose the worst possible moment — just as she served the main course — to broach the subject of camp with Ezzy.

"So Ezzy, have you given any thought to your summer plans?"

Ezzy looked up suspiciously. "Why?"

"I think that it would do you good to get away from the city a little."

"Why, what's wrong with the city?" Ezzy asked.

Aryeh grew uncomfortable and loosened his tie. "Well, everyone agrees that the city is not the best place for a yeshivah *bachur* during the summer months."

Ezzy's eyes narrowed.

"And?" he prodded.

Malka felt like she was going to cry. When had her son become so cynical? Were they all sinking together?

"Aryeh, perhaps you and Ezzy can continue this conversation a little later, after we are done eating."

Aryeh was actually grateful for the chance to delay the unpleasant task for a little longer.

"Sure, sure, Malka. That's a wonderful idea," he said, starting to eat.

Ezzy threw a pebble and watched it skip down the street. He was sitting with Moishy on the front stoop of his house and telling him about the conversation with his father.

"I'm trying to figure out why it means so much to him. He was adamant about it. And then, all nonchalantly, he mentions some rabbi-friend of his that has a camp and 'happens' to need waiters. Come on! Do you expect me to believe that? My father isn't the type of person who shmoozes with people for no reason, and there is no way that he found that out if he didn't actually call and ask for a job for me."

Ezzy involuntarily winced at the memory; he had turned to his father then and asked, "Why does this Rabbi want to hire the boy who stole?' Thankfully, Malka hadn't been within earshot to hear the hurtful words.

There was also a whole other part to the conversation, one that Ezzy would not share with Moishy.

Aryeh had been forceful, convincing Ezzy that being home for the summer would be detrimental to him.

Finally, Ezzy could control himself no longer. "You just want to keep me from Moishy, isn't that what this is really about?"

"Well, yes, a little bit," Aryeh had admitted, glad that it was out in the open.

"Tatty, I don't want to go to camp, and I like Moishy. He is my friend."

That was the part of the conversation that Ezzy had left out, but Moishy was no fool.

"Ezzy, I think I know what this is about. Can it be that he just wants to keep you away from me?"

Ezzy felt a stab of pain that he had indirectly caused Moishy to express the thought.

"No," he assured Moishy, "it has nothing to do with you, nothing at all."

Ezzy had a sudden brainstorm. In one move, he could convince Moishy that it wasn't about him and also make sure that his father would drop the idea just as abruptly as he had brought it up.

"Moishy, would you consider coming to camp with me if I went?"

Moishy leapt as if bitten by a snake. A look of sheer horror crossed his face, and Ezzy shrank back, scared. "No," said Moishy more vehemently than Ezzy had ever heard him say anything before, "I wouldn't. I would never go to camp."

Reb Anshel Hammerman may have been old and feeble, but he was no pushover. He was looking guardedly over his glasses at his daughter and son-in-law, trying to make sense of what they were saying. "Tatty, it's really just a small shul, not even a real *shtiebel,* and they can't afford to bring in a rav and pay him, so they want you to serve as rav."

Reb Anshel was getting agitated. "What, all of the sudden there is a shortage of rabbanim in the city of New York that they should have to *schlep* in an old man with half a mind."

"Tatty!" protested Frieda, laughing in spite of herself.

"No, I am serious, leave me alone. You brought me here to say a little Tehillim and sit in the sun, and now you come to me with crazy ideas like this? What do they really want?"

Zalman tried speaking. His *shver,* like his wife, was clever and astute, while he was more naive and uncomplicated. He knew that in this situation, his *shver* was more likely to listen to his voice than Frieda's, more likely to believe that he wasn't being taken for a ride.

"Tatty, it's not a shul. It's a facility for developmentally delayed adults that —"

"So that's what this is about? You want to put me in a facility? You think that I need to be there, watered like an old plant three times a day and then ignored? I didn't have to leave the Lower East Side for that!"

"Please, please," said Zalman soothingly, rising to stand next to his father-in-law. He placed a comforting arm on the old man's frail shoulders, "That's not what I was saying at all."

"Tatty, it's a place for adults who suffer from various delays, emotional and mental. They have a member of the staff there who thought of this idea, that it would be nice for the residents to have a shul, that it would give them a reason to hold their heads a little higher. It isn't a real shul, but it is something. He plans on having a *minyan* for Maariv every night of the week, and maybe to gather there for *shalosh seu-dos* — and he wants an older, experienced rav who could lead this whole thing. Tatty, he wants you."

"What do I have to do?"

Zalman sensed victory. Frieda came in to finish the job.

"Tatty, just do what you do best. Love them, smile at them, care about them, the same things that you've always done."

Reb Anshel shifted his body so that he could see her more clearly. He looked her up and down, as if looking for a clue as to what the catch was.

"I just have to go there? Are you sure that there's nothing else?"

"Yes Tatty, I am sure. And Tatty, it's right across the street from our house, so it will be easy to get there."

Mendel had risen early, and was trying to sneak out of the room without waking Gitty. She worked so hard and needed her sleep. But he was excited about tonight, and when he reached for the deodorant in the darkened room, he accidentally knocked it over, and it, in turn, sent a mirror crashing to the floor.

Gitty sat bolt upright. "Mendel, what time is it?"

"Um, five-forty. I can't sleep, so I am going to say Tehillim for everything to work out tonight."

"Mendel, you need to rest, otherwise you will be too tired. What time did you come in last night?"

"Two-fifteen."

Gitty groaned. "You set everything up yourself?"

"No, not at all. Ezzy and Moishy refused to leave, and they were still there when I left. They are both coming over later today as well, to help with the last-minute details."

Gitty had too many questions to fall back asleep.

"Did you take care of a sound system? And of a *mechit-zah*? And what about a chair for the Rebbe; you know that you can't put him on a plain folding chair."

Mendel smiled. "Yes, Gitty, we took care of everything. Now go back to sleep. You can still get in a good hour before the kids wake up."

He left the room, savoring the feeling of being the one with the answers.

Chapter 27

It was Sunday afternoon, and Ari Engel was apprehensive. He never really liked it when Mishkan Shalom was in the public eye, when people had reason to sit and talk about how much money they got from the state and how it was spent. He himself wasn't sure how he had allowed things to spiral out of control the way that they had, and he wished only that the evening would pass quickly and quietly. He felt like wearing a sticker on his lapel that said, "I am Ari Engel and I have nothing to do with this whole event."

Mendel hadn't really consulted with him, and just seemed to think that he could make any decision that he pleased. He had assembled his own roster of speakers and basically brought it to Ari for his approval, just as he had with the idea of hiring a rav for the place. Well, not exactly hiring, but it was *like* hiring, another reason for people to talk about how they were drowning in money.

Every time that Ari had considered taking action, however, the words of the Rebbe and Dr. Shindleheim would come to mind, and he would feel his heart softening toward Mendel Wasser. It was clear that his sole motivation was the good of the residents and nothing else — it was just that he seemed to march to his own beat.

By the time Ari arrived at work (he always went in on Sunday, even if for a short time — there was work to do!) he was calming down somewhat, and even began to think clearly about how he could maximize the opportunity.

Mendel sat down on a bench, exhausted from setting up. He looked around with tired satisfaction. Ezzy and Moishy were up on tables at opposite ends of the room, affixing the makeshift *mechitzah* to the ceiling, and the others were setting up folding chairs.

The room, not very large when empty, looked tiny now that it was crammed with chairs, but Mendel had insisted that there be a microphone just the same. Gitty said that it made everything look more official and ceremonial. Ezzy had gone to borrow it from a *cheder* up the block, and it still needed to be hooked up.

Then there were the chairs that needed to be placed up front, a nice one for the Rebbe, one for Rav Hammerman, and, Gitty had suggested, another for Ari Engel. Mendel called out to the boys for suggestions, asking if they had any ideas where he could get nice chairs. There were some old armchairs around the apartments, but they weren't suitable.

Ezzy jumped down from the table he was standing on and jogged over to Mendel. Mendel was amazed at the boy. He

couldn't have slept more than four hours the night before, yet
he had been here five minutes after getting out of school and
hadn't stopped working. His eyes were shining and he looked
enthusiastic about this new challenge. Even Moishy, usually of
a grimmer disposition, was getting into the act, standing at
the old microphone and pretending he was Chazzan Helfgott,
making the residents laugh uproariously.

It was seven-twenty, and Mendel Wasser was nowhere
to be found. Ezzy, who had been unflappable all day, was
getting nervous. "Where could he have disappeared to?" he
asked Moishy as they searched the building once again. Guests
were beginning to arrive. An impressive contingent of elderly
women from the building had arrived precisely at seven-
fifteen, even though the program wasn't scheduled to begin
until eight o'clock. Mrs. Handler had shown them to their side
of the *mechitzah*, and the first six folding chairs were taken.

Minchah was called for seven-forty, and Ezzy figured that
Mendel was scouring the neighborhood, ensuring that he
would have a nice *minyan* on hand for the first *minyan* in
the new shul.

He was wrong. In fact, Mendel had locked himself in the
supply room off the apartment, reciting Tehillim with great
fervor and emotion. Somehow, he felt that he was building
something, and he was begging for Divine assistance that
something real and good would take shape here. He himself
was shocked to notice that it was seven twenty-three, and
he quickly prepared to go out. He straightened his tie and
adjusted his Shabbos hat. Then, he went to face his destiny.

At seven thirty-seven, the small room was full. Sure, there were the residents sitting in the front row, resplendent in their Shabbos finery. Leizer Krause was there, as was Dr. Shindelheim, and, of course, Ari Engel. Other staff members were there, as were assorted family members. The rest of the room was filled with neighbors and curious passersby.

At seven thirty-nine, Mendel rose to his feet and all the residents, prompted by Moishe and Ezzy, did the same. They stood as one and a hush came over the small room. Zalman Finestone led his *shver* into the room and the crowd parted to let the distinguished Jew pass.

Mendel and Ari Engel, who was clearly out of his element, rushed forward to greet the new rav and lead him to a place of honor along the front wall. By looking at his shinning countenance and tranquil demeanor, one would never guess that Reb Anshel had secluded himself in his room and refused to come out for several hours. It had taken desperate measures by Frieda to get him to cooperate and come to the ceremony.

After the rav was seated, Mendel gave a loud bang on the *shtender.* Ezzy had been given the honor of serving as *chazzan* for the very first *tefillah* and he shouted "*Ashrei*!"

Sara Gelber was thrilled. No, more than thrilled — ecstatic or even euphoric. Just a few short flights down, the welcoming ceremony was being held for Mishkan Shalom, while Jerry was in Cleveland. For weeks, she had been dreading this moment and the inevitable showdown that was almost certain to occur. She had clearly seen the Divine Hand when her husband's boss had called last night, just after Shabbos, and asked him to drive a truck to Cleveland. Sara had done her best to conceal her interest in the phone call, even leaving the room, as if she didn't really care what he would decide. Her heart had sunk as she had heard him growl about the last-minute notice, and when he said he would do it, she breathed again.

Or was it Detroit? Whatever, as long as he wasn't here.

Could it be, just maybe, that he was also happy to be spared this showdown?

Gitty thought that Ari Engel's opening speech was a little strange. It was as if he didn't understand why they were there and how important this little shul was to his people. He seemed more focused on the arrival of a low-level politician, whom he greeted warmly in his speech. He spoke about the relationship between Mishkan Shalom and the state, but he barely spoke about Mendel at all. Gitty was growing anxious. Could it be that all Mendel's talk about how enthusiastic Mr. Engel was about this had been another of his dreams?

The next speaker was the new rav, but he too seemed a little bewildered when Mendel introduced him. He looked around and actually scratched his head, as if wondering why he was there. Then, he smiled genially at the crowd and gave a *berachah* that the venture succeed. He sat down looking relieved.

The next item on the agenda was a song, written and performed by Benjy Biller, who stood up proudly, holding his old guitar. He walked up to the front of the room with all the confidence and poise of a seasoned stage performer. He looked around, and, in a loud, clear voice said, "Thanks to you all for coming here tonight. I want to give a special thank-you to our friend, Mendel. He knows what we really need."

Finally, thought Gitty, *someone is talking about Mendel!*

Benjy's voice cracked and he turned to his trusty guitar to express his feelings.

After three minutes of off-key playing, a commotion was heard from outside, and accompanied by two *gabbaim,* the Rebbe walked into the room. It was the perfect excuse for Ezzy to help Benjy back to his seat, and after embracing Naftuli and greeting the rest of them, the Rebbe was seated.

Moishy and Ezzy looked on with interest. They had both seen the Rebbe before, on Purim night, and even Moishy was respectfully silent. This man was nobility!

Mendel was speaking to the Rebbe quietly, and the boys were surprised when the Rebbe looked around the room, seemingly searching for them. His gaze rested on them. The trusty *gabbai* at his side beckoned them. Moishy was muttering to Ezzy as he rose,

"What does he want from us? Why he is looking here?"

Ezzy laid a hand on Moishy's arm. "Just come," he murmured.

They walked up to the Rebbe, and Mendel pulled them close. "These two boys are both extremely dedicated to the residents here, giving up all their free time in order to make their lives a little happier. Could the Rebbe give them both *berachos* for ...," Mendel looked at them searchingly, struggling to find the right word and finally settling on, "*menuchas hanefesh.*" Though from anyone else, that little speech would have sounded patronizing, from Mendel it was simply touching.

The Rebbe understood Mendel's request and he took each of their hands, first Moishy's, and then Ezzy's, and spoke. "*Berachah v'hatzlachah* to you both. You deserve to be happy and I hope that *HaKadosh Baruch Hu* grants you whatever it is that you need." Then, the Rebbe turned to face Mendel. "And to you, who realized that these wonderful men have *nesh-*

amos just like me and you, who was worried not only about what they will eat and drink but about how they will grow and develop … may *HaKadosh Baruch Hu* grant you true satisfaction, fulfillment, and joy in your work.'

Then, as a microphone was brought close to the Rebbe, he looked around at the crowd and smiled. "The *Aibishter* welcomes any sort of growth, any true show of desire to come closer to Him. May He fill this *mikdash* with His many *berachos.*"

Chapter 18

E zzy hated paperwork. Filling out long and detailed forms was the kind of thing his father relished, but he did not. He wished that he could ask his father for help, to read the fine print and navigate the endless questions, but he couldn't.

Mrs. Handler had explained to him that the State of New York wasn't some informal operation that would just wave his application through without issue; just the opposite. The people up in Albany were sticklers for detail.

Ezzy couldn't ask his mother either, but for an entirely different reason. She would be supportive of his decision, but she was equally inept when it came to this type of thing. Sometimes, when they would go to the doctor's office, he would watch her. She would doodle on the margins of the paper, and play around with the pen, but the task of filling in the correct information in each blank space was not for her. She would always joke that there should be classes in form-filling; she inevitably filled in her last name before her first name, or her address on the line reserved for her mother's maiden name.

So there he sat, three long pink papers in front of him, wondering how he would get through this on his own. He managed pretty well with his name, address, social security number, and institutions attended, but when he got to page two, he hit his first bump. "What qualifications do you bring to the job?" the paper challenged him. He called Moishy.

Moishy was having a much easier time of it. He had both his parents and his older sister working feverishly on the sheaf of papers. Even though they were laughing and sharing easy banter as they wrote, he could see how much they wanted to make it work for him. This was something new, that Moishy was actually taking the initiative and asking for their help in doing so.

Peretz Winternitz was writing with such force that his pen-point had gone right through the paper. Moishy was making summer plans! *Hashem is great*, he thought as he scribbled furiously. Summertime had always been the single roughest patch in the rock garden that was Moishy's life, the time when he would retreat even further into his shell. He wouldn't discuss going to camp like his siblings, refusing to even join his parents on visiting day. He would simply skulk around in the shadows of the house, home alone with his parents, a persistent reminder of their inability to reach him. And now Moishy himself had come home with these forms, the application for a summer job at Mishkan Shalom. The office staff had assured him that if he got state approval, then the job was his. The comprehensive forms in front of Peretz and his wife were as welcome as a perfect report card.

The only rough question was "Please provide a teacher as a reference for the applicant." Peretz scratched his head with the pen and pushed the paper across the table to his wife. She studied it for a moment and then shrugged. "We'll save it for last," she decided.

Ezzy felt like giving up. Moishy had his parents doing it for him and *he* couldn't even ask his father. Aryeh would insist that he go to camp, that there was no way he was spending the summer loitering around the city streets. Ezzy knew that he couldn't approach his father until he actually had the job in his hand. He turned back to the papers before him. "Please provide a teacher as a reference for the applicant," it mocked him. He stood up and stomped out of the room. Why couldn't anything go easy for him?

Eventually, the papers were mailed. The teacher reference came from Rabbi Mendel Wasser, with a long list of institutions next to his name, presently a program director at Mishkan Shalom. Now it was up to the Almighty.

The group of mothers watched the school bus drive off, and with it their precious children. It was the first really beautiful spring day, with the sky a picture-perfect blue and the gentlest of breezes. "Finally," said one, 'back to the real world. Yom Tov was great and I loved having all my sons home, but it's also nice that it's over."

The others laughed at her honesty. "No, don't say that. I wait for *bein hazmanim* a whole year. It's such a treat," one protested.

The first agreed, "I know, I know. It's just that they have these seemingly endless appetites and whatever I prepare isn't enough. And getting them up in the morning? Forget about it. I need a forklift!"

Chana Rivka Weinstein lingered off to the side of the group, having little to offer. Her children were still young, though she could relate to the comment about difficulty waking them up. Chaim had made it to the shul throughout Yom Tov before ten-thirty. She had no clue how to deal with it or what to tell the children. She had spent her morning's davening for both of them, clutching her siddur and pleading for Divine assistance. Aside from the fact that she so badly needed Hashem's help, it also allowed the children to see that davening was still on the program.

Lately, there was the faintest glimmer of hope, though it was still too premature to see how it would develop. Chaim, who never went to shul on time and never came home with a nice word to say about rabbanim — or anyone else for that matter — had fallen in to some new neighborhood *minyan.* He had gone there for Minchah and Maariv three times in the last week, which for him was a record, and each time he came home and shared something inspiring that he had seen.

She was experienced enough at this game to know not to push, or even react with excitement to this development. She would shrug and listen politely and try to pretend that her heart wasn't pounding as he spoke.

She was shaken out of her reverie by the realization that the other women were looking at her expectantly. "Oh, sorry, I was just spacing out for a moment. What did you say?"

"I just asked if you had summer plans yet," said one of the women.

Chana Rivka smiled. "No, not yet."

Summer! Hashem should just help her get through this day!

The secretary at the Albany office of the OMRDD filed through the pile of fresh mail in front of her. There was a new program that offered teenagers the chance to intern for the summer at the various OMRDD facilities, and it seemed to have generated lots of applications. She was surprised.

"Look, Carol," she commented to the clerk at the next desk. "There's hope for the world. All these kids want to spend their summers working with developmentally delayed persons. The pay is pretty lousy. They must be good kids to do this."

And with a tune on her lips, she quickly scanned each application and stamped it before putting it into the APPROVED pile.

Ezzy ran in from school, anxious to check the mail before his parents got home. His mother was usually home before him, but she didn't really look at it. She would do a quick check for wedding invitations and personal correspondence and then leave the rest for her husband.

He greeted his mother and found the pile on his father's desk. Sure enough, toward the bottom of the pile, he saw a green envelope with the symbol of the NYS OMRDD on it. He ripped it open the wrong way and took out the single paper.

> *Dear Ezriel:*
>
> *We are pleased to inform you that your application to join the Felix-Barber summer program has been accepted. We are pleased that New York State teenagers are taking the initiative and searching out opportunities to enhance the lives of their fellow citizens.*
>
> *You will be working at the Mishkan Shalom facility for the months of July and August under instruction from Mrs. Diane Handler, clinical director.*
>
> *We wish you the best of luck.*

Ezzy let out a little whoop and folded the paper carefully. He placed it in his pocket and went to call Moishy.

It was later that night when Ezzy sat down to talk to his father. "Tatty, you know how you've been saying that I need to have summer plans, some sort of schedule?"

Aryeh nodded vigorously. "Absolutely; unstructured time is the worst thing. You need a framework."

"Well, I had this idea. You know that I really enjoy helping out at this home, Mishkan Shalom, up in Kensington."

"Yes, I do," said Aryeh tersely.

"Well, there is a job available there for the summer, to help out and do a lot of the things that I enjoy doing." And before his father could interrupt, Ezzy played his final card. "And it's a chance to earn money as well."

Aryeh looked suspicious. "Is the Winternitz boy planning to do this as well?"

I should have known, thought Ezzy angrily. "Yes," he said, "Moishy also wants to do this."

Aryeh thought for a moment and then sat back, looking slightly amused. "Ezzy, Mishkan Shalom is a government agency, funded by the state of New York." He spoke slowly and patronizingly, as if he were addressing a child. "You don't just 'get a job' the way you would straightening out the *sefarim* at the shul. Jobs there are serious business, and most likely have to go through their office and be approved by the state. Your big plans notwithstanding," Aryeh's tone grew slightly derisive, "this is not child's play. Trust me; you will be better off clearing tables and playing basketball in camp. And there you will actually get the job."

Ezzy reached into his pocket and withdrew the folded paper.

He looked at his father. "With all due respect, Tatty, why don't you take a moment to read this?"

Aryeh put on his reading glasses and took the paper. He was silent as he read.

It took several minutes for him to read it and reread it. Then, he put the paper down and stuck out his hand.

Ezzy accepted it and they shook hands solemnly.

"Good work, Ezzy. I have to check out the place and think about it, but I have to commend you on your perseverance."

Despite his annoyance, Ezzy felt a stab of love for his father. He was just so ... himself.

Chapter 29

It was becoming a bit of a ritual on the Kensington street corner, their small way of celebrating the beautiful spring weather after a long, cold winter. The women would watch the school bus drive away and they would linger, chatting about this or that before hurrying off to jobs, chores, and responsibilities. Chana Rivka Weinstein was younger than most of them, and altogether more on the shy side, so she rarely contributed. Still, it was nice to be there, listening to their light banter and laughter. She didn't fool herself for a second; she knew that each one of them would return home to their trials and tribulations, some of them more daunting than her own. She knew that they all needed these few minutes, a respite from whatever faced them, so why couldn't she forget about her problems just as they were, why couldn't she seem to put them in the back of her mind just as they did?

Every conversation seemed to remind her about her situation, their situation — Chaim's and her own. This morning, each light comment was a dagger in her heart.

One of the more outspoken women, Aviva, was describing the trip back from Yom Tov at her in-laws in Toronto. "We were supposed to leave Toronto at nine a.m. sharp. One thing led to another, and we didn't end up leaving until five in the afternoon, and even after we left, we realized that 'someone' had forgotten my son's passport and we had to turn back. It cost us another forty-five minutes. Needless to say, things were tense in the car …."

The other women laughed, amused at the description of her trip and even more so, at her easy frankness about her family.

One of them was emboldened to tell how, "Once, when we were living in Israel, my husband forgot a suitcase in the taxi to the airport — the one with all our clothing — and we only realized after boarding. I was so miserable that I gave him the cold shoulder for three hours."

Another countered with a recollection of the time that she and her husband were at odds over something and not speaking. Their cold war had come to and end when their oldest child — a girl of three — asked innocently if she was allowed to talk.

This was too much for Chana Rivka. She excused herself and walked quickly towards home. *How could they laugh about these types of things with such ease, such comfort? Didn't they realize that this was real life for her, that the "cold war" was the perpetual state of affairs in her house?*

Sure, there had been a time when they had fought long and hard. She would plead and implore, patiently explaining to her husband that his way was not the way, that he had a wife and children and the responsibility to lead a Jewish home. He would rail back about pressure and how she was making his life unbearable and she wasn't his Mashgiach and she had to back off.

She longed for those days, because then, at least they had communicated. They both had expectations and demands, both had hopes that the other would change. Now, it was usually silent; his silence; accusatory and resentful, while hers was mournful and resigned.

What wouldn't she give for a good fight, a prolonged silent treatment that would culminate in embarrassed laughter and mumbled apologies?

Chaim Weinstein's desk looked like a hundred others on the floor. He was just another junior accountant at a huge firm, another anonymous figure on the eighth floor, unknown and unnoticed except by his immediate manager, who managed to make every moment of every day pure torture. Michael's own frustrations at not being promoted were poured out onto the heads of the hapless employees under his charge.

Chaim looked up from his computer just in time to see Michael headed his way. He gritted his teeth and waited for the inevitable.

"Hello there," said the manager with mock pleasantness. "How are we today?"

"I am doing fine, thank you."

"Well, that's just great then. Listen up." He placed one hand on Chaim's shoulder and another on the shoulder of Gary, at the next desk.

"Seems like you boys are going to have to stick around a little extra tonight. I hope that you have nothing planned."

This was nothing new. Michael habitually found reasons to keep them overtime, enjoying the looks of pure dismay on their faces. Chaim wouldn't give him the satisfaction. Gary emitted a long, low moan.

"Okay, so it's all arranged, just a few extra minutes to finish up those numbers before tomorrow. It's real important to the people upstairs."

Chaim knew that it was a bluff, that the mysterious "people upstairs" didn't even know he existed. More than once, he and Gary had already submitted letters of complaint to upper management, but had never received a reply. This was Michael's personal mission and it had already cost Chaim time with his children, it had cost him his wife's confidence, and it had cost him the ritual of going to learn and daven each evening.

But what could he do? He wasn't much of an accountant, had barely passed his exams. He had taken the first job that was offered and didn't really believe that he could do anything else. In the early years, Chana Rivka would assure him that he could and he would eventually go out on his own, that he deserved better. In time, however, as he lost more and more of his energy and grew increasingly disheartened and submissive, she stopped believing that things would ever change. Now, he just went to work and put up with it. He would do whatever was necessary to support his family and then he would go home, looking only for some blessed silence.

He turned back to his computer. These days, he no longer bothered to call Chana Rivka when he would be coming home late.

A few minutes later, his phone rang. He looked at the screen. Michael would be annoyed if he saw him on his cellphone during work, so he answered in a whisper. "Yes?"

"Shalom aleichem, Reb Chaim," an enthusiastic voice greeted him.

"Who is this, please?"

"It's me, Mendel Wasser. I just wanted to remind you that you are starting tonight with Benjy and he is super excited. That's all he talks about."

"I'm … what … tonight?" he finally managed.

"Yes, we made up for tonight at 8 in the new *beis medrash.* I hope it's okay."

Chaim suddenly remembered. Benjy, with his trusting eyes and hopeful smile. Benjy, who was so eager to make a *siyum* for his father's *yahrzeit* — the first *siyum* he would ever make. Chaim had also lost his father. He had also once made *siyumim* on the *yahrzeit.* Though Benjy was much older than he, Chaim understood exactly how he felt. He had so wanted to help ….

And then, Chaim Weinstein did something that he had never before done. He stood up and walked to the corner office, talking loudly enough that Gary's mouth dropped open. "Michael," he said in a confident tone, "I'm really sorry. I have a prior commitment for tonight and I won't be able to stick around late."

⬛▮▮▮ ▮ ▮ ▮▮▮ ▮▮▮ ▮ ▮▮▮

Night seder was beginning and Mendel was bustling around like a mother hen. "Ezzy, please go check if the hot water is finished boiling. Moishy, do you mind preparing some tea and bringing the cups around? Heshy, sit here, your *chavrusa* will be here shortly. Naftuli, come, I will learn with you at the corner table."

He stopped to greet some people from the neighborhood who had come in to learn until Maariv. "Hi, make yourselves comfortable; Maariv will be in forty-five minutes."

A father came in with his young son and Mendel showed them to a vacant table. He looked around with satisfaction; there was already a *minyan* for Maariv and they still had plenty of time!

And with true pleasure, he looked toward the front of the small room. The Rav's *shiur,* his pride and joy. Reb Anshel, or as they all called him, the Rav, had started to learn the *parashas hashavua* in depth with a small group comprised of the two most advanced residents, Pinky and Danny, Zalman Finestone, a brilliant fellow from the former Soviet Union who would write down every word that Reb Anshel said, and best of all, Moishy and Ezzy.

He knew that he really should invite Mr. Engel to come see the night seder program, but he wasn't sure that it was the right time. It was still too soon, too new of a venture, and he wasn't sure that it would last. It seemed to be working. Just last night an older gentleman from down the block had approached him with a generous check and thanked him for providing the neighborhood with such a wonderful place and such an illustrious rav.

Who knew where it would lead?

Benjy Biller could barely sit straight. He had lost his father at the age of fourteen, and there was a part of him that had never stopped mourning. He missed the gentle, laughing man and the way that he had made him feel: as if he were normal.

"Benji'le," he had called him. No one had ever called him that since.

This week, he had been chatting with Mendel and he had mentioned his father. Mendel had gotten a strange look in his eye and asked him when his father's *yahrzeit* was. It was on the 11th of Tammuz. He had told Mendel and Mendel had jumped to his feet.

"Benjy, this year you are making a *siyum* on his *yahrzeit.*"

Benjy hadn't been sure how to react to the announcement, but he liked the way it sounded.

Mendel had approached the first fellow that walked in to the shul, a young man named Chaim, and welcomed him warmly.

Benjy hadn't heard everything that he had said, but he had seen them turn to him and heard the words "father's *yahrzeit.*" Benjy had been a little embarrassed, suddenly worried that it wouldn't really work out, but a moment later, they were walking toward him.

"This is Chaim Weinstein; he is going to learn with you every evening until the *siyum.* Chaim, this is my friend Benjy Biller. He is ready and waiting."

They had shaken hands and arranged to start the following evening at eight o'clock. And now it was eight o'clock and there was no Chaim in sight.

The door suddenly opened and there was Chaim. Mendel flashed a greeting smile toward the new arrival. "I hope it wasn't too much trouble to be here."

"No," said Chaim, "no trouble at all."

Chapter 30

The lobby of the old building had been redone several times. In the Sixties, when "trouble" had consisted of mischievous teenagers coming in and pressing all the buzzers at once, laughing uproariously at the chorus of hellos, security had not been necessary. With the passage of time, "trouble" had taken on new meaning, as drugged-out teenagers needing a quick fix had learned how to break into the mailboxes and steal Social Security checks. The management had invested in new mailboxes and video cameras scanned the lobby.

Other than the new surveillance equipment, the lobby hadn't really been redone in years. The cracked linoleum floor, the poor lighting, and the sorry-looking fake plants in the corners were the same. The persistent droning of the fluorescent lighting and the jarring thud of the elevators coming to a halt created the background noise. And it was there, in this setting, that Ezzy and Moishy would sit, late into the night, after night seder was over and the residents were asleep in the quiet apartment.

These were exciting times for the two boys. They were feeling more alive than they had in years, more productive and necessary than ever before. For Moishy, this was huge; he was actually forming alliances with people based on trust, loyalty and respect, all things that had been hammered out of him so many years earlier. Sometimes, late at night, he still heard the echoes and could even feel the pounding on his back (*you're just a piece of garbage, do you hear me?*). Sometimes, the fury that had been his constant companion for so many years would come bursting out, like a volcano exploding. Sometimes, but not always.

He had discovered a new peace and contentment between the walls of this building. He had discovered the joy of a mutually beneficial relationship, had learned what it felt like to have someone's eyes light up when they saw you — the way Benjy's or Naftuli's did every single time that he entered their apartment. He had enjoyed Mendel's complete confidence and dependence, felt valued as a person.

Life was good.

For Ezzy, too, though it was less complicated, it was something new. Here, he was a successful yeshivah *bachur* who was giving up all his free time and energy toward the cause of bettering the sorry lives of the residents. They could never know how being in yeshivah, where he was viewed as a failure, had broken him. They could never know how the hours he spent here, where he was viewed with admiration, even adulation, were more therapeutic for him than any high-priced therapist.

It was working.

And these were the conversations that Moishy and Ezzy would have, late at night, on the faux-marble bench at the far end of the lobby, the one with the worn head of a lion at each end. They would sit there, two souls sharing a journey of self-discovery, feeling a hope and optimism that neither had ever known.

They never knew about the malevolent eyes watching them. Jerry Gelber had never gotten over the hijacking of his building, the way the staff and the neighbors had just swept in and treated these people like some sort of honorary citizens. Now, there was this new side entrance straight into their little shul, and there were cars parked there each evening. (*It's so nice; the building has become so alive!' Sara had made the mistake of commenting to him that morning.*) Jerry had had to park his truck up the block quite a few times already, but that was the least of his problems.

The bigger issue was the undesirables that they brought into the building, these good-for-nothing bums that they employed. They would sit there late into the night, talking loudly in the lobby and smoking. He, for one, was trying to raise young children in the building, and wanted them out.

If Jerry Gelber wanted them out, then out they would go.

He stormed into the building late that night, having just driven to Philadelphia and back through a rainstorm. He was cursing even before he entered the lobby, but the sight of the two boys sitting complacently — actually, sprawled out, as if they were at the swimming pool — infuriated him even more.

They were unaware of his presence, chattering obliviously even as he hovered above them, staring at them with undisguised disgust. They both became aware of Jerry's presence at the same moment. He was standing directly above them, a little closer to Moishy. "Get out of here, you despicable people," he hissed.

It was the look of pure horror on Moishy's face that caused Ezzy to spring into action. "Excuse me, what do you think you are doing, creeping up and shouting like that?"

"What do you think *you* are doing, you lowlifes? Don't you see the sign here? NO LOITERING!" Jerry jabbed his finger in the direction of the wall, staring hard at Ezzy. Moishy was cowering in the corner like a trapped animal. Ezzy couldn't understand what had come over his friend.

He looked right back at Jerry. "Fine, but there is certainly no reason for you to come in here screaming like a demented man."

Jerry looked as if he were going to lunge at him. 'DON'T CALL ME DEMENTED!" he shrieked. "It's the people in these apartments, the people that you hang out with all day; they are the ones who are demented."

Ezzy held his furious gaze. "No, sir. The people in the apartment, the ones that I hang out with, are not demented at all. *They* never raise their voices or lose their tempers. They are sweet and good-natured and don't expect anything from anybody; they are just content to live and let live. *They* are not the ones who are demented."

And with that, Ezzy grabbed Moishy's limp arm and walked right by Jerry Gelber. "Come Moishy, let's get out of here."

Reb Anshel was tired, but he was happy, happier than he had been in a long time. The new job kept him busy. He spent his mornings preparing — something he hadn't been forced to do in years, maybe decades. There were people at his Chumash *shiur* who asked all kinds of questions, thoughtful questions, the likes of which he had never before heard.

In the afternoons he would rest in anticipation of the evening, when he really worked. He would come before Minchah and learn privately with Mendel and the two boys. Then, after Minchah he would deliver the *shiur* for forty-five minutes until Maariv, but even after Maariv, they would be waiting with questions.

Now it was early afternoon and he was preparing for his nap. He first went through his ritual, checking the top of the closet for his envelope with the money, counting out the money, and then replacing it. Only then, feeling reassured, did he lie down to rest.

Ari Engel's desk was a picture of organized chaos. There were piles of papers and reports that needed to be looked at, commented on, and answered, but he didn't have the time. He would quickly scan each of them, usually while on the phone, and send them off to his trusty secretary with the appropriate instructions. The monthly reports mandated by the state were there as well, charting the progress of the various facilities and consumers.

Today, there was a fresh report, with a pink post-it note from Chevy attached, urging him to read it. It was a lengthy report from Dr. Shindleheim, describing the effect that the shul was having on the consumers at the Kensington group home, and recommending it as a model that should be followed elsewhere.

The report stated, *"The idea of having a common goal or objective that unites all the residents is different from that of each having his own job in the sense that they are learning how to work as a group, each of them accepting different responsibilities and roles."*

Who would have imagined? Mendel Wasser starting a revolution! Ari Engel, though still uncomfortable with the idea, was a results-oriented person. He couldn't argue that there were results. He dashed off an email to the bookkeeper inquiring how much Wasser was paid and if there was a way to give him a raise.

Malka accepted her change and thanked the young man behind the cash register. She studied the single dollar bill and heap of change in her hand, and decided that it would be too much trouble to unhitch the purse from her shoulder and dig around until she located her change purse, all the while holding heavy bags in her other hand. She looked around for the closest *tzedakah* box and noticed a cluster of them on a small shelf.

She felt like a little girl every time she had to decide who got a quarter and who would get only a nickel. She always felt guilty, as if it were presumptuous of her to decide who deserved what.

She scanned the colorful labels broadcasting messages for schools and shuls, organizations and foundations, and suddenly her heart gave a little leap. There, in the back, was a *pushkah* with the familiar blue-and-white Mishkan Shalom label.

She reached for it and deposited all the money into it. Then, she unhitched her purse and took out a twenty-dollar bill, which she crammed into the too-small bill slot.

There, she thought, now that was a *tzedakah* in which she wanted to have a share.

Though she was following from the sidelines, she had reason to cheer for the way the last few weeks had gone at home, and she knew who got the credit. She would never let Ezzy know just how closely she was watching and listening, but she was pretty up-to-date on his life, and had never been prouder.

Just before she left the store, she readjusted the position of the *pushkah,* moving it to a more visible spot near the front.

She was a mother, after all.

Chapter 31

itty had been debating all night whether or not to tell
Mendel about the phone call. She knew he would be
excited about it, but still, it would also confuse him.
She had discussed her dilemma with her older sister,
Rochel, who advised her to tell him. "Look, Gitty," Rochel had
said with the wisdom of years and experience, "this job he has
now, as satisfying as it may be for him, is not a real, permanent
job. When people ask you what he does, what do you say? He
considers himself a rebbi, and at least *that* is a real job, and
people know what that means. Trust me, Gitty, I have children
in *shidduchim* now and these things are very important," —
when Rochel said the word *very*, her voice dropped to a quieter, more urgent pitch, as if she was about to reveal exactly
in which cave Bin Laden was hiding — "you know, what you

do, where you daven, what type you are. Mendel has to decide who he is already and take a job with some permanence." Rochel finally stopped to breathe and Gitty took advantage of the lull.

"Yes, absolutely, but we are nowhere near the time of making *shidduchim* and Mendel is really enjoying what he is doing. Do you know, I was at a Chinese Auction last week and I met Simi Engel —"

Rochel interjected. "You know Simi Engel?"

Gitty could tell that she was impressed and briefly considered glossing it over and going on to something else. "Well, I don't exactly know her, but our husbands work together. (*Now didn't that sound nice?*). Her husband is the boss of Mishkan Shalom —"

"Of course, he is very well known. And she is also a big *ba'alas chessed*; she is honored every week by another organization."

"Right, anyhow so I met her and introduced myself. When I told her that I was Mendel's wife, I could tell that she was impressed. She told me that her husband says that Mendel is really putting Mishkan Shalom on the map — those were her exact words. You know Rochel, during those years that he was a Rebbi, he never really distinguished himself that way. Sure, he worked hard and all that, but when I would meet the mothers of his students, they never really seemed to know who I was. I was like a nobody, totally irrelevant. Sure, they would nod politely ..."

Gitty's voice trailed off as she recalled approaching the mother of one of Mendel's most beloved *talmidim* at a *chasunah*. "*Hi, I am Gitty Wasser,*" she had said, "*Mendel's wife.*"

The woman had looked confused for just a moment and then a look of familiarity had crossed her face. "Oh sure, Mendel from the silver store." The woman had turned to her friends, saying, "Ladies, her husband is Mendel from the silver store, the most helpful and patient man in Boro Park. And the way he was able to restore my mother's leichter? Just incredible, simply incredible!"

"I don't know, Rochel, I just don't know. I hear what you are saying, but Mendel is finally a somebody."

Rochel was the oldest of the sisters and not used to being doubted. "It's your decision, Gitty," she said, clearly miffed, "and I cannot tell you what to do, just that if you don't give him the option, you will never know if you did the right thing. It's his life, after all."

Gitty heard Mendel's footsteps just then, so she excused herself. Rochel hung up wondering when Gitty had become the type of wife who had to hang up the phone the moment her husband showed up. What was she, in the week of *sheva berachos* or something?

Mendel Wasser wasn't the most astute person, but even he was able to tell that his wife was distracted. He didn't have a chance to find out why, because they were both busy with the children during supper, and then as soon as the last one went to sleep, he had to hurry off to night seder.

He usually stayed after Maariv to put the *sefarim* back and organize the chairs, but tonight, he was too concerned about Gitty. He asked Ezzy and Moishy if they would mind closing up and rushed out just after Maariv.

Gitty wasn't like other women. He knew that. She wasn't usually moody or agitated; she was remarkably focused and single-minded. She woke up in the morning with goals, and she set out to accomplish them, one after another. She rarely had the time or disposition to indulge in dealing with her emotions, to consider if she was happy or sad. If she needed to talk, she usually spoke with one of her sisters. Mendel would sometimes overhear her and be surprised at the feelings she would express. He was happy that she had such a close relationship with them.

Tonight he was worried, however. Twice during supper she had looked as if she wanted to say something and then thought the better of it. He was concerned.

He entered his house and was glad to see that Gitty was still up. She seemed to understand that he was home early because of her, and she poured two glasses of orange juice. "Mendel," she said, "we have to talk."

"What's wrong, Gitty?"

"Nothing is wrong, nothing at all. Just that …."

And then, it all came pouring out. How the Menahel had called, the familiar number and name in her caller ID, and the familiar voice on the phone, and had asked to speak to Mendel. She had made it clear that he could speak to her, Gitty, if he wanted something. She could not know that the Menahel was no fool, that he had purposely called in the hope that she would answer and that Mendel wouldn't be home; he knew that convincing Mrs. Wasser was the way to convince Rabbi Wasser.

He had told her about the decision by his school's board of directors to open a new class, a remedial fifth grade, for the next year. It wouldn't exactly be made up of his star students, but it was a very nice group and the boys were eager to learn. Of course, the Menahel continued, Reb Mendel had proven himself as a dedicated and serious rebbi, ready to do whatever it took to get the children to learn, and the Menahel thought that he might be a natural fit for this new class.

Gitty was no fool. She remembered just how much Reb Mendel's seriousness and dedication had been worth when the Menahel had let him go a few months earlier. But she was also a practical woman, and understood that this wasn't the right time to become sensitive about that.

The Menahel let slip that really, there were a lot of people who would want the job, especially since the new school year was still months away and time was on his side; the only thing was that he felt very confident in Mendel. And also, that the board of directors wanted to get the class up and running before the end of this year, as kind of a trial run, and there was only a month left to classes. That meant that whoever would be selected for the job would have to start by ... let's see, what's today? Tuesday? Okay, then next Monday, at the very latest.

Gitty had understood. She was being pressured. If Mendel hoped to earn his way back into the Menahel's good graces and into the world of chinuch, he would have to take this lifeline. She had thanked the Menahel and promised to discuss it with Mendel.

"Okay then, please let me know as soon as possible. There are many others who are waiting for this very job," he reminded her one last time before hanging up.

And this is what Gitty told Mendel, for the first time in her life in a quandary and having no idea what was right. Usually when she presented him with a question, she had already decided the answer and would present it as such, but tonight, she herself had no clue about what was right. If she couldn't decide, how would Mendel?

When she finished sharing the conversation with him, she slumped back in her chair, exhausted. He looked at her thoughtfully. "Did he say anything else?"

"No, that was it. I told you everything."

"Okay, Gitty. You can call him back him in the morning and tell him that I have already made my decision. Actually, the *Ribono shel Olam* made it for me just a few months ago, when he led me into the place where I really want to be right now. Gitty, I love my job and am really happy, so thanks, but no thanks."

Gitty looked at Mendel, speechless. She had never heard him speak with such force before. "Yes, Mendel, I will call him in the morning."

Mendel smiled. "And Gitty, one more thing. Call him early. I wouldn't want any of those other people who are waiting for the job to have to be in suspense any longer than absolutely necessary."

Gitty smiled back. Mendel was not a cynical person; when he was even the least bit sarcastic, she found it strangely satisfying.

The phone rang just after nine o'clock. The Menahel saw who was calling and smiled to himself. "Good morning," he said as he picked up the receiver.

"Yes, hello. It's Gitty Wasser here."

Her voice was curt and confident and he knew at once that everything would be okay. He heaved an inaudible sigh of relief.

"Yes, Mrs. Wasser. I hope you are calling me with good news."

"Well, actually, it is good news for us, but I am not sure if it's good news for you. My husband feels very fulfilled doing what he is doing and, as much as we appreciate your generous and thoughtful offer, he wouldn't trade what he is doing for any other job in the world."

The Menahel was quiet, and finally stammered a weak, "Okay, I hear you."

Before Gitty hung up the phone, she allowed herself one more triumphant, "Thanks, but no thanks."

The Menahel felt an unexpected twinge of regret. He had never been at ease with his rough treatment of Mendel. It's true, he believed that Mendel Wasser would never be much of a rebbi, but he was an exceptionally fine and caring human being.

Oh, well, he shrugged, *no one can fault me for trying.* He shrugged once more before getting back to work.

Chapter 32

"It's an *ayin hara*, I'm telling you; I knew from the first second that something wasn't right with this whole plan. It just didn't seem right — it's an *ayin hara*."

Frieda Finestone was sitting at the table and tearing a paper napkin into shreds. Zalman was listening quietly, neither agreeing nor disagreeing; he knew there was no point.

"From the first second that I saw that banner draped across the street like that, I was nervous. This is a circus, not a real shul, and now my poor father has to suffer because of it."

Because of it, meaning me and my idea, thought Zalman. But still, he was silent.

In the next room, Reb Anshel, the subject of the conversation, lay on a small sofa, propped up on pillows. It had been two days since he had fallen, and the pain wasn't diminishing. He had been unable to leave the house, and though Reb Anshel wasn't a complainer by nature, the situation was clearly getting the better of him and he was sounding a bit cantankerous as he spoke to his granddaughter.

"I wanted *pumpernickel* bread! This is not pumpernickel. This is whole wheat or seven grain or whatever name they give it these days, but it's not the real thing. On the Lower East Side, they have pumpernickel."

His hapless granddaughter assured him that she would go to yet another bakery and get him pumpernickel bread. As she did, she passed through the kitchen where her mother was still wailing about *ayin hara*.

■■■■ ■ ■■■ ■ ■ ■■■

Mendel Wasser almost never noticed when people were upset with him. He simply wasn't that perceptive. From the moment that he heard about Reb Anshel's fall, he had been trying to reach him. He had called the Finestone home several times that first night, but they weren't answering the phone.

The next day the daughter had finally picked up the phone, but when she did, she was obviously in a big rush. She quickly informed him of the details: her father had been coming into the house from the night seder and had slipped and fallen on the steps. Hatzalah had rushed him to the hospital and though, *Baruch Hashem*, there were no serious injuries, he had sustained a pretty bad bruise on his hip. The doctor had told him that it would be a few days before he would be back on his feet, and suggested that he get as much rest as possible.

Frieda made it clear that there was no way — with wheelchairs or helpers or anything — that she would allow her father out, and she even said that she wasn't sure that she would allow him out when he felt better.

Mendel wasn't aware that there was any unkindness in the remark, and just reiterated his wishes for a speedy *refuah sheleimah*. When she hung up, she couldn't shake the feeling that she hadn't been clear and this irritated her even more. (*"It was on the tip of my tongue to tell him that it's all his fault, that he was the one who gave my father such an ayin hara"* she told Zalman later.)

Mendel had waited a day and then called again. He was in luck. This time, Frieda wasn't home and her daughter answered the phone. He introduced himself and asked how her grandfather was doing. She seemed friendly, so he asked if he might speak with her grandfather. She said *sure*.

Once Mendel was speaking to Reb Anshel, he asked if he might visit. Reb Anshel sounded overjoyed at the suggestion and they made plans for Mendel to come just before Minchah.

And so it had gone. Each evening, a group from Mishkan Shalom would fill up Reb Anshel's small room and listen to a *shiur*. Mendel would always come, as would Ezzy and Moishy, and then assorted other residents and people from the neighborhood.

As much as the traffic and noise made Frieda tense, she couldn't deny that her father looked forward to it all day. The two boys, Ezzy and Moishy, came at other times as well, sometimes in the afternoon and they had even walked over on Shabbos.

Frieda was softening toward them.

Delmy had come from the agency, just like Irena before her and Helena before *her.* Frieda never understood how it was that her friends just seemed to have *mazel* with finding and holding on to cleaning help while she went through hired help like other people went through tissues. No one ever stayed long. One took ill and another had an emergency back home in Poland. The next one developed a sudden fear of the United States government and its immigration policies and abandoned ship three days before Pesach, and there had even been one who developed an allergy to bleach and could no longer work.

Frieda welcomed Delmy with a businesslike air, too cynical to see this as anything more than another fleeting relationship, and within a few minutes, Delmy was parked in Frieda's living room, making her nervous. She was holding forth on the right way to arrange the pictures on the mantel, spicing up her lecture with various real-life examples from her very own family members. Frieda was growing tenser by the moment and finally cut the new cleaning woman off. "That's wonderful, really wonderful. Okay, when you are finished here, please change the linens in the children's rooms." Frieda hurried off to bring her father breakfast.

It was Delmy's third day on the job when she noticed the envelope on top of the closet. It was sticking out from under the hatbox and immediately, she knew that it was money. She just knew.

She continued dusting the shelf without moving the envelope, but she filed the information away in her mind. If the old man had money in an envelope squirreled away in his room, most likely the lady of the house didn't know about it. Delmy cast a furtive look at his sleeping figure before tiptoeing out of the room.

The second altercation was inevitable. Jerry had been steaming mad all week and was looking for an excuse; late one night, he found it. It was a beautiful night and Ezzy and Moishy were chatting out on the sidewalk, Moishy leaning casually against the side of a truck, an older, white model with the words EASTERN KOSHER DISTRIBUTION across the sides. It was *his* truck. He had come down from his apartment because he had forgotten to bring up his GPS. With all the objectionables in the neighborhood these days, he didn't feel good about leaving it there overnight. He had stomped down; irritated at having to go back out, and the sight of the two boys leaning against his truck put him over the edge.

Again, he started screaming even before they saw him, and again, Moishy retreated back with a look of pure fear on his face. "Who gave you permission to lean on my truck? Get your bodies off it now!" he shouted. Moishy stood there, frozen and again, Ezzy quickly rose to his defense.

He smiled coolly at Jerry and gestured at the series of stickers across the rear bumper. *Happy with my driving?* asked one, *then tell me.* It gave a toll-free number for the company. The next sticker was even chirpier: *Our guarantee — to be considerate, courteous, and competent.* Ezzy pointed with his thumb. "Look, maybe you are considerate and competent, but you are certainly not courteous!"

Jerry hated this kid with his big mouth. "You have a big mouth and I am going to shut it once and for all," he spat at Ezzy. At that point, Ezzy made a mistake. Had he remained silent, then Jerry's threat would have remained another idle warning, a blustery promise of revenge. Instead, Ezzy challenged him. He smiled even more sweetly and extended his hand.

"No problem. The name is Markstein, Ezzy Markstein."

Jerry's eyes narrowed. He knew a Markstein, that stingy fellow who ran the debt-counseling organization. Jerry had never liked that fellow, so puffed up with his own importance, lecturing Jerry like a schoolteacher. Jerry remembered how he made him bring in his grocery bills and given him a speech about his spending habits.

He felt certain that this kid was related to that guy. That's it. He would go to war. They didn't know Jerry Gelber yet.

A new ritual had evolved. Reb Anshel was simply too weak and exhausted to say the Chumash *shiur,* so he would tell stories. He had started one night, and the next day, they had wanted to hear more.

Frieda had overheard her father speaking and had been astonished. He rarely spoke about his Holocaust experiences with them — even at the Pesach Seder, they had to plead with him — and now he was suddenly speaking freely.

Reb Anshel was pleased that the boys were interested. He had always been ready to speak about it; he just needed to see a real interest. His years of experience in the rabbinate had taught him something; he had spent hours listening to lonely congregants. He had seen fathers try so hard to impart their dearest and most precious memories to disinterested children and grandchildren, people who opened up the innermost recesses of their souls to deaf ears. He considered that a violation of those memories. He had promised himself that he would never share his recollections unless he was convinced that he had an eager audience, unless he knew with certainty that they would be cherished and respected.

And so he didn't talk much about those years, even when asked by well-meaning grandchildren who were clearly being prodded by their parents. (*Go ask Zaidy to tell you about his yeshivah before the war.*)

But now he was old, very old, and also feeling tired. These boys were clearly anxious to hear every detail, Moishy in particular, so Reb Anshel spoke.

Last night, Moishy had asked so many questions, some of them quite strange. He hadn't wanted to know about the spiritual heroism of the great men in the concentration camps, nor had he asked about the cruel and inhuman conditions.

He had only been concerned with one thing: the beatings.

He wanted to know how often Reb Anshel had been beaten and how he had recovered from those traumatic experiences.

Strange!

Chapter 33

I t was almost ten-thirty and Chaim still wasn't home. For Chana Rivka, it was thrilling. The clock moving steadily forward was cause for inner rejoicing; she could barely contain her excitement. She had finished preparing the kids' lunches, done the laundry, called her mother, and even started polishing her silver. She would not, under any circumstances, fall asleep before he came home.

She knew that she had to play this smart. With a pang, she remembered a similar situation, two years earlier, when she had really messed up. Chaim hadn't been as down then as he had been recently, but he had also been going through a rough spiritual spell. There had been a bright spot when he had discovered a lecturer whom he loved and started to listen to his recorded speeches in the car. Chana Rivka had discovered his newfound interest and had been overjoyed that he was listening to Torah tapes. For Chanukah, she bought him the entire set of seventy-five tapes by that very speaker. Chaim had looked at her strangely as he thanked her, and he had never again listened to that lecturer.

She wouldn't make that mistake a second time.

It was close to eleven when she heard his key turn in the lock. She quickly busied herself with filling out the day camp forms for the kids — three weeks ahead of schedule, but he would get edgy if he suspected that she was waiting up for no reason — and pretended to look startled as he walked in.

"Oh, Chaim!" she exclaimed, looking up suddenly as he entered the kitchen.

"Hi, there. Why are you still up?" he asked suspiciously.

"I just got so busy, I had no idea how late it was. Is it really eleven already?" Then, self-conscious that she was talking too much, she turned back to the pile of papers in front of her.

"What are you busy with? *Day camp?* What's up with that? Camp isn't until six weeks from now!"

"You know, early start and all that. You want to make sure all the forms are in, right?"

"'Whatever.'"

Who would have ever believed that she, Chana Rivka Weinstein — the most *temimusdik* of them all — would operate and learn how to play these mind games? Yet somehow, she sensed that her newly developed shrewdness was reflective of her growth, instead of the opposite.

Chaim was looking around for something to eat.

Chana Rivka rose quickly, happy for the distraction.

"Hungry?" she asked, almost shyly.

"Yes, come to think of it. What do we have?"

"Well, there's leftover chicken and corn from supper and a little macaroni from lunch. There are apples in the fruit bin and" — she peered into the cookie jar — "some coconut cookies that I baked with the kids."

She hoped he wouldn't ask for them. There was really only one left, but she had been so proud to list off the contents of her bursting kitchen that it had come out differently than she had planned.

At the end, Chaim settled on a rice cake, and she sat down to join him.

It had been a long time.

Chaim usually fell asleep soon after the kids went to bed, or went to work on his computer. Late-night conversations in the kitchen were a distant memory.

Chana Rivka wondered if she should just chat or if she should continue to wait hopefully for Chaim to speak about his evening. She didn't have to wonder for long.

"You know about this guy, Benjy, who I learn with at night?"

How am I supposed to know, have you ever breathed a word about it to me? is what she felt like answering him. Instead, she shook her head slowly, "No, I don't think so."

"Well, he's this fellow who lives in Mishkan Shalom, you know, the facility just up the block, and he is a little delayed. Anyhow, however it happened, I got hooked up with him and we learn now and then."

Chana Rivka assumed a look of nonchalance and absently signed her name on a form, as if her heart weren't pounding loud enough for him to hear.

He wasn't even looking at her, but past her.

"His father passed away many years ago, and he wants to make a *siyum* for the *yahrzeit*."

Despite her careful efforts, Chana Rivka knew she was going to cry. What her husband was really saying was, "*I* have no father and *I* want to make a *siyum* for his *yahrzeit*." This Benjy was giving him the perfect opportunity.

"Okay," said Chana Rivka, hoping that she didn't sound pushy.

"Well, we learn mishnayos most nights and I kind of like it. Nothing too heavy, but there is responsibility on me to explain everything clearly and simply, which means that I have to know it as well. It is an interesting relationship, because he isn't really on the same learning level, but still, he is becoming a friend. When he talks about his father and how he misses him, I feel like he understands me."

Whoa! thought Chana Rivka, *that's a biggie!* She couldn't believe this entire conversation. Chaim didn't usually open up to her and he rarely spoke about the loss of his own father and how it had affected him.

He wasn't done yet. "Anyhow there's this real *chashuv* older person, kind of a rav really, who comes each night. He says a little *shiur* and answers questions. His name is Reb Anshel Hammerman. I never really spoke to him — I'm not exactly the close-to-the-rabbi type — but I would sometimes overhear his Chumash *shiur.*

"Last week, Reb Anshel fell and hurt himself pretty badly and he cannot leave the house. The one who runs the program there, his name is Mendel, arranged for people to go visit Reb Anshel — he lives at his daughter's house just across the street. I told him that I couldn't go, that it was hard enough for me to leave work on time to grab a bite before night seder."

Chana Rivka wasn't playing games any more. She was listening intently to every word. "So tonight," he continued, "Benjy is begging me to come and visit Reb Anshel with him and I have a really hard time saying *no* to Benjy. He says that he needs to introduce me to Reb Anshel. So after Maariv, Benjy is literally pulling my arm and I tell him that I will come, but just for a moment.

"We cross over to Reb Anshel's daughter's house and we go into this little room. There are like a hundred people there and he is telling a story. He is talking about his experiences in the war, and it was like nothing I have ever heard before."

Chaim was getting animated. *Hashem! Please don't let him grow self-conscious or moody now, please help him to keep talking!*

"He had this smile on his face as he spoke, not at all what you would expect. It was as if he was talking about someone else. I never saw someone who could describe such suffering in such a peaceful, accepting, matter-of-fact way. I couldn't help myself. I just couldn't leave and stayed after everyone left. I had to talk to him.

"So that's where I was until now, just speaking to this Reb Anshel. I was sure you would be sleeping."

That's it? He isn't going to tell me what they spoke about? Is the story over at the best part?

"Chana Rivka?"

"Oh, sorry, yeah. That is so interesting. He seems like an exceptional person. Maybe you should invite this Benjy to come eat with us on Shabbos."

But it was clear that the party was over. Chaim was already hurrying down the hallway to bed.

Chana Rivka cleared off the table, and, despite her frustration at his stopping the account in mid-story, there was a song of gratitude in her heart. *Chaim has a friend. Chaim spoke to a talmid chacham. Chaim was learning every night.*

It had been a busy week. There had been a steady stream of visitors and the old man hadn't gone out at all. Delmy had

234

heard Mrs. Finestone say that her father would soon be able to resume his schedule, and the maid was waiting anxiously for that day to come. She had managed to check out the envelope-there were several thousand dollars in there, all in cash. It was a perfect opportunity.

Mrs. Ruth Biller drew up a list for the fourteenth time. There hadn't been many events in her small apartment. She had never been one of those women who are always hosting parties and benefits, and rarely attended functions of any kind. She was a bright and able woman — a librarian at a high school in Sheepshead Bay, in fact — but she wasn't much of a social butterfly. Her life was her family, especially after her husband had passed away. He had left her three children, two daughters and a son, Benjy. Both girls were married, one living in Israel and the other over in New Jersey, while Benjy was in a facility just a few blocks away.

She spoke to him each day, and would have him home for Shabbos as much as the facility allowed. He was the only one — to her mind — who really needed her, and there was nothing that she wouldn't do for him.

His idea of making a *siyum* for her husband's *yahrzeit* had touched her more than he could ever imagine. The very thought that her Nathan would be remembered in a public setting filled her with bittersweet joy and since Benjy had shared his plan with her, she had been on a strange kind of high.

But … she was so intimidated! She simply wasn't cut out for entertaining and the image of people in her little apartment, crowded around her old dining room table, filled her with dread. Benjy had asked only one thing: that the *siyum* take place in her home, and she couldn't very well say *no* to him, not after he had committed to working so hard to make the actual *siyum*.

So she turned to the list before her and tried to figure out what she would serve at this *siyum*. She had no idea how many people Benjy would be bringing, but Benjy had said that he wanted to invite his friends. She needed paper goods, drinks, and food. It was all so overwhelming ....

But also, so touching. *That's Benjy, so sweet and sincere,* she thought. *Hashem should just watch over him.*

Chapter 33

T he doctor's appointment had gone well. The swelling on Reb Anshel's hip had receded and Frieda was gratified to learn that her father would be back to himself within a few days. Frieda couldn't understand why her father's face had clouded over and he suddenly looked anxious.

He had protested that he had things that he simply *had* to take care of outside the house and the doctor had looked at him strangely. "You will be as good as new in just a few more days. Just a little longer."

"No, not a few more days — I need to go out tomorrow."

The doctor had made it clear that he didn't recommend it just yet and Frieda hustled her father back home and into his room, insisting that he get some rest. He was agitated for the remainder of the day — he needed to get to the bank already.

His pension check had arrived and he wouldn't be completely at peace until he could add to his envelope. There were days when that secret stash of money was his only source of tranquility, his only guarantee that he would never really be a burden. Until he placed the bills into his envelope he couldn't relax.

He had thought about asking Frieda to go to the bank for him, but she would ask way too many questions. The last thing that he needed was that she should know about his envelope, find out about his little secret. She would laugh reassuringly and tell him that they loved him and would always take care of him, and he would feel like a small child.

At the end, in desperation, he sent his thirteen-year-old granddaughter to the bank with careful instructions. He made her repeat his directives several times: all the money into savings except one hundred dollars in cash, which she would be bringing home to him. That money, of course, would be added to his envelope.

Chaim had done a fine job of explaining the principle of "*dofen akumah*" in Mishnayos *Succah* to Benjy, but he himself wasn't really clear about it. How did it work? He resolved to visit Reb Anshel after Maariv and clarify it. He knew that Reb Anshel would have the right words to simplify the abstract concept and he was actually looking forward to hearing them. He couldn't remember the last time that he had been interested in learning, and couldn't help pondering if Benjy's simple and sincere desire to understand had brushed off on him.

He hurried across the street to Reb Anshel's home, lost in the intricacies of the mishnah.

Jerry's experiences with Aryeh Markstein and On Two Feet, the debt-counseling organization that he had established, had been entirely negative. Jerry had been forced by his daughter's school to meet with the do-gooders at the organization, as part of his tuition deal. He had refused to pay tuition on the grounds that his daughters didn't learn anything anyhow, the teachers were a bunch of inexperienced dopes, the building was a health hazard, and the principal was past retirement age. The school thanked him for his views and told him that if arrangements weren't made with the tuition office within one week, his daughters would no longer be welcome. Jerry had called the tuition office and left a long and hostile message on the voice mail ("They are just lucky that they didn't answer the phone — had it been a person it would have been really bad," he had boasted to Sara) and Sara, fearing that the school would make good on its threat, had called to apologize and set up an appointment. She did something she rarely did: she insisted that Jerry show up and behave with respect. When it came to her daughters, the woman could really put her foot down!

When it became clear that the Gelbers were not in a position to pay very much, the tuition officer worked out a deal with them. They had to meet with the people at On Two Feet, who would figure out how much income they had, how much they needed for living expenses, and what would be a fair amount for them to give to the school each month.

Jerry realized that he was being handed a gift, so he grudgingly allowed Sara to set up an appointment with the debt people. They were only open two evenings a week. Jerry usually worked in the evenings, so it was a real pain.

The office was a small, ugly room on the premises of a large medical billing office in Flatbush and there was vir-

tually no staff. ("The key to getting out of debt is lowering expenses," Aryeh always said, "so how can this office have high overhead?" Everything — the space, furniture and personnel — was donated.)

At first Markstein had been pleasant enough. "A tuition case?" he had asked. "Oh, that's nothing terrible. We get much more serious problems here." Jerry had liked that, the feeling that this was all a mistake and he didn't really belong there.

"Baruch Hashem, we have arrangements with most of the schools in Brooklyn and they allow us to finalize what the tuition payments should be, so if you'll just show me your file, I am sure that we will come to a satisfactory agreement," Markstein had said.

Jerry had started to feel as if he were a second-grader being summoned to the principal's office and he began to act belligerent. "I don't need you to get involved, and I am perfectly capable of working out my own arrangements." Markstein was a tough guy and he simply ignored Jerry as he ranted and raved against do-gooders out to save the world. He had spent the whole time reviewing the file that Sara had placed in front of him.

Then, Aryeh Markstein had stared right at Jerry. "Okay, Mr. Gelber, you make too little money to be —" and he proceeded to list a whole series of luxuries that Jerry should stop indulging in.

Jerry had grown furious. Who was Markstein to tell what he could and could not do with his money? If he needed tickets to a game so that he could relax with his buddies, who was this creep to decide otherwise? He was about to stomp out when Sara reminded him that if they were unable to work out a plan with Markstein, then the school would carry out its threat.

So Jerry had sat there, sat there like a sweet little kid, burning inside but nodding when Markstein needed him to nod and signing when he told him to sign. And he had decided that he hated Markstein and that one day, Markstein would be the one listening to Jerry Gelber.

And now Jerry Gelber had a new enemy, also named Markstein and also smug and insolent. It couldn't be a coincidence. Together, the two were ruining Jerry's life. It was because of the father that Jerry couldn't write a check or swipe his credit card until he deducted half his salary and gave it to the world saviors over at On Two Feet, and it was because of the son that his only place of solace — his apartment — had become overrun by nudniks who filled the lobby, took his parking spot, and chattered all night long.

They had made his life unbearable.

Chaim Weinstein walked out of the Finestone home and into the cool night air. He headed toward home feeling torn. On one hand, he felt great — light and happy. Reb Anshel had not only answered his questions, he had made him feel that his question were worthy of being answered. They had chatted for a few minutes as well; just small talk about work, family, and Reb Anshel's health, but to Chaim, there was no insignificant conversation with Reb Anshel, whom he considered a great man. Chaim was torn because he wanted so badly to share his feelings with Chana Rivka, but something was holding him back. He had been around the block enough times to know that there were cycles, and that just because things were going well now didn't guarantee that things would go well forever.

He wished that he could describe Reb Anshel to Chana Rivka and longed to bring his young son to meet this *tzaddik,* but that was all he needed; Chana Rivka would probably buy a full-size picture of Reb Anshel to hang in their dining room, or better yet, invite him to move into their house — and then the pressure would start building and the whole thing would just make him angry.

He was scared, too scared to confide in his wife about the feelings budding within him: feelings that just a few months ago were complete strangers to him; hope, ambition, optimism.

What was so beautiful about the whole Mishkan Shalom thing, about Mendel and Benjy and all the guys, was the total lack of pretentiousness and pressure. They welcomed him for what he was, and had no expectations or plans for him. He wasn't ready to commit to anything, and that's what made the whole arrangement so pleasant — there was no sense of commitment, nothing formal or official about it. Just he and Benjy learning because they both wanted to, really, really wanted to. They added vibrant colors to his life, Reb Anshel, Benjy, and Mendel, and their view of him had injected him with a new spirit. He felt that he somehow had a new strength, courage to hold his head high when speaking to Michael at the office, power to decide what kind of images would fill his computer screen at work, freedom to define what kind of life he would lead.

If he were to tell Chana Rivka how much it meant to him, then it would be kind of a commitment and he simply wasn't ready for that.

No, he decided as he walked up the steps to his house, it was better to keep it inside, as difficult as it was, rather than risk losing it all.

Chapter 35

Daniel Becker was acting totally out of character. He was shy and reticent, not one of the class leaders, so the fact that he had approached seven different boys after school and asked them to come to his home after supper was reason enough to make them curious.

They were all there, all the movers and shakers of the eleventh grade, gathered around his dining-room table and munching on fresh popcorn. Mrs. Becker watched from the kitchen, noting with no small degree of distress that many more kernels were falling to the ground than were being eaten. *Oh well,* she thought, *I guess that I should be happy that Daniel seems to be socializing with his friends and is even bringing them over here.*

For years, Daniel had been embarrassed about their spartan lifestyle and simple home. He seemed to be moving on.

Daniel sat at the head of the table, his eyes darting around nervously at the crowd in his dining room. He wasn't thinking about the torn upholstery or the peeling paint; he was much too nervous for that. They were all here, all the boys who seemed to move through life effortlessly, never having to consider their words before expressing them, never having to look over their shoulders and wonder what people *really* thought of them. Dovi, Nosson, Nachman, and Shloimy were all gathered around him, waiting expectantly for him to speak.

Dovi Berman, who had been a class leader since the first day in nursery, wiped some salt off his lips and motioned at Daniel. "Hey Daniel, what's up with the party? You wanna start a *chaburah* or something?" The other boys laughed easily.

Daniel shook his head. "No, nothing like that, just something that's been on my mind for some time that I wanted to share with you guys, and I didn't want to risk trying it in school where people would wonder what we were up to and all that."

The crunching of popcorn stopped and they leaned forward, intrigued.

"It's about Ezzy."

At the mention of their classmate's name, they all grew completely silent, an uncomfortable silence. It was clear that they all felt a little guilty about his plight. It was just that he had become so distant, so difficult to reach. Sure, after that crazy story with the theft they had all been a little leery of him — after all, what normal person steals from a *tzedakah* collector? They had been right to keep their distance. Their parents had told them so. Who knew what other issues he had?

And then, after the summer, when Ezzy had attempted to rejoin the group, acting as normal as ever, well, it just wasn't the same.

So now, they listened to Daniel with their defenses up, ready to protest their innocence.

"Well, we all see how he is drifting further and further away from us, as if he isn't really in yeshivah at all. He hangs out with street kids, like Winternitz, and spends time volunteering at a nursing home or somewhere like that. There is no question that he isn't the Ezzy that we grew up with, fast-talking, ball-playing, happy Ezzy Markstein. He walks around school like a ghost."

The boys were quiet. There hadn't been any accusations yet. Nosson even reached for more popcorn.

Daniel continued. "Here's the thing. I think it's my fault."

The boys exchanged glances. *His* fault? Daniel wasn't even a player in classroom dynamics. How could he have influenced Ezzy's status?

Daniel understood their unspoken question. He told them a little about his personal history with Ezzy and how Ezzy had hurt him badly when they were younger with an insensitive remark. "And then, this past Purim, after Ezzy had suffered through a miserable and lonely winter, he must have decided that he needed to shatter the wall that we erected around him for once and for all. He was looking for a group with which to collecting, thinking it would be a nice way to get back in. He knew better than to ask any of you to join your groups, so he looked around for a less 'happening' group."

Dovi Berman was the only one sensitive enough to note the catch in Daniel's voice and he reddened.

"He approached me, Daniel Becker, whom he had so thoroughly humiliated the year before and went out on a limb. He asked me to let him join my group. The thought that he humbled himself like that haunts me until today, and I should have just been big enough to see his plea for what it was: a sincere apology. He was down and I was up. But I just couldn't. I still had so much resentment toward him about what had happened that I rubbed it in his face."

The other boys, being confronted with the facts without being named as guilty parties, were able to listen objectively and Ezzy's pain filled each of their hearts.

Dovi Berman, a natural politician, found his voice. "Daniel, slow down. I remember what he did to you" — he had the tact not to review the details of the story — "and your reaction was perfectly normal. The blame is really on us, whom he never wronged, not on you."

Daniel held up his hand, looking miserable. "Thanks, Dovi, it's nice of you to say so, but it isn't true. The blame is on me, and I will tell you why. That Purim was the turning point in his life. It's as if that's when he stopped trying.

"On Purim night, after collecting, we all went to Rebbi's house and he didn't show up. Then, right after Purim, he just stopped being himself, hanging around with Moishy Winternitz — who is not even in yeshivah — and turning into a stone. He is always somewhere else, even when he shows up in school, and ..." — here Daniel, not one prone to drama, dissolved into sobs — "it's all my fault."

Leah Becker, peeking through the slit in the door from the kitchen, wished she could rush in and wipe his tears, but he had made her promise a hundred times that she wouldn't allow herself to be seen or heard.

Dovi smoothly took over the meeting, speaking in a comforting voice. "Okay Daniel, we hear you, but it really isn't as you say. We are as guilty, if not more guilty, than you. But anyhow, who really cares who is to blame? What can we do now?"

Daniel blew his nose, feeling less cool than at any other moment in his life, and spoke again. "So that's why I called you here. I spoke to Rebbi about this last week and he heard me out. He mentioned that Ezzy is actually learning much better now than he was in the winter, but he agreed that he has become kind of distant and that it's up to us to bring him back." Daniel flushed as he said the word *us*, as if he had no business including himself with such esteemed personalities.

"Rebbi suggested that I share this story with the more popular kids in the class, you guys, who have the ability to draw him back in, and maybe, just maybe, there's still hope."

His job done, Daniel slumped forward, leaving the rest of the conversation in the able hands of Dovi Berman.

The footsteps were too silent for Chaim Weinstein to hear, so he wasn't aware of Michael's presence until he was immediately behind him. "So how are we today?" asked Michael in a syrupy voice.

Gary at the next desk looked sick.

Chaim felt the familiar sense of confidence and buoyancy that he carried within him ebbing somewhat. Michael was a snake, and he made no pretense of being anything but. He had never forgiven Chaim for standing up to him on the first night of his seder with Benjy, when Chaim had rejected his suggestion that they stay late. Michael was out for blood.

"Just spoke to the people upstairs," Michael said casually, "and it seems like we are a little overloaded. It looks like we are here late tonight, gentleman, and I am sure that you will clear your schedules."

Gary ran his fingers through his hair, refusing to articulate his frustration. He looked hopefully at Chaim from the corner of his eye.

Chaim felt weak.

That first night, he had been propelled by a strange sense of bravado and daring; tonight, he felt like regular Chaim Weinstein, a loser with a loser job. Sure, there were times when the thought of his *chavrusashaft* with Benjy, his relationship with Reb Anshel, and the newfound respect he felt from Chana Rivka emboldened him, but right now wasn't one of those times.

He could hear Michael breathing behind him as he sat there silently.

"So, Chaim, what do you say? Are we going to party tonight? There is so much we need to get done."

Chaim couldn't look at Gary. He shrugged and closed his eyes. "Whatever you want, Michael."

Michael was surprised and relieved at Chaim's quick surrender. "Great, I am glad to see that we are all back to normal," he said in a snide tone before walking off.

"I am sorry, Gary; I know you were counting on me. I just don't have the strength today," Chaim said quietly.

"No, it's okay, man, I know how you feel. It's like you feel big for a bit and then, boom, you come crashing down. It happens to me all the time."

Chaim stayed late that night. Just like the old days. The only difference was that he called Chana Rivka to tell her. The disappointment in her voice was so acute that he felt a stab of pity for her, despite the fact that he would be the one in the cold, dark office with only numbers for company. Then she said something uncharacteristic. Her voice became upbeat and she said, "Don't worry about it, Chaim, it's just one night and I will have a delicious supper waiting for you when you get home. Keep a smile on your face."

That was so unlike her — she of the mournful silences and disappointed looks — that he nearly dropped the phone. "Thanks, Chana Rivka," he said warmly, "I really appreciate that."

It wasn't until he came to learn the next night and saw Benjy's face that he really felt his anger towards Michael. Benjy's eyes lit up when he entered and he gave the most brilliant smile. "Chaim, you're back! I missed you so much last night. The *yahrzeit* is almost here and we have so much more to learn."

Chaim seethed inwardly. *Never again, Michael, never again*, he promised silently.

Chapter 36

F rieda Finestone's siblings appreciated what she did for their father, no question about it. They saw how devoted she was to his well-being and happiness and it put them at ease to know that he was being taken care of. But there was something in her attitude that could make someone a bit resentful, a certain smug and condescending tone she used when she would give them updates as to his condition.

Shaul Hammerman hung up the phone after one such conversation. He had called to know if he could come visit his ailing father, something he tried to do once a week. Frieda had told him it wasn't a good time.

"Frieda," he had said patiently, "I work for a living, actually quite hard —" Frieda had winced involuntarily, wondering if that was a jab about the checks that he sent each month to help with the expenses for their father— "and I cannot just come whenever it's convenient for you. Today really works for me."

Frieda bristled at the usage of the word *you*, as if this had anything to do with what was good for her. 'I understand Shaul, but Tatty is just getting ready to go to sleep. If you come, he will get all energized and will be up half the night; then it will be my headache. I really think it would be better if you were to come tomorrow."

Her tone made it clear that there was no room for negotiation, and Shaul, not used to losing, had slammed the phone down in anger and turned to his wife. "As if she was his press secretary and we were pesky reporters," Shaul had said in frustration.

If the other siblings had issues with Frieda's protectiveness, they kept quiet about it; they were all too overwhelmed by their own responsibilities to be anything other than completely indebted to her. She really was great, so on top of things, so committed to making their father's day as fulfilling as possible; she had gone and found him a job as a rav in a shul near her home, and he was so happy with the position and the responsibilities it entailed. He was constantly preparing for this *shiur* or that *chavrusa*. Now, when he was ill, there was a steady stream of visitors at her house. *Only Frieda could pull off something like that*, they would say admiringly, shaking their heads in wonder, grateful that she was bearing the burden that they all shared.

So it was only Shaul who was uneasy. It had always been that way, that mild strain of competition between Shaul, who was the most accomplished and successful among the children, and thus used to being in charge of his father's affairs, and Frieda, who, as the youngest, had a special bond with him.

These last few weeks hadn't been easy on their relationship. They both knew that she needed his money — there was no denying it — and he had enough class not to make her ask, but she basically refused to listen to his opinions. Tatty was living with her, and that was it.

It wasn't much of a room, really. It was like an entrance from the street, and the landlord had put up some flimsy walls so he could add on rent. There was a long, tattered brown couch, faded from years of use, stained with a thousand spilled coffees and speckled with cigarette burns. There was also a collection of old leather executive chairs that were hand-me-downs from the offices upstairs, a donation from the people who spent their lives in warm, comfortable offices with handsome furnishings, never having to unload a skid, pack boxes in freezing warehouses, or drive massive trucks through snowstorms, as did Jerry and his friends. This was their room, the drivers, packers, and warehouse workers, where they sat between jobs and during breaks, chatting, smoking, and arguing. This makeshift room was the closest thing that Jerry had to a social life. He even had his own chair — a sign of seniority — a green captain's chair with one broken arm.

He was sitting in his chair surrounded by his people. There was Velvel, who had come from Russia three years ago and could drive for three days straight without blinking. He had just driven a truck to Chicago and hadn't been back for twelve hours, yet they were already sending him out again. He usually sat contentedly on a milk crate, humming to himself and peering through his thick glasses at whomever happened to be speaking. He had few opinions of his own, so Jerry considered him a friend. There was Mechel, an older chassidishe fellow who had never married and spent most of his time elaborating his hypochondriac fears. Today he was lecturing about a mysterious skin disease, spouting its Latin name with familiarity, (*Like some professor,* Jerry thought) that could look as harmless as a small cut, yet could eventually lead to complete paralysis. "There you are, driving along, and you notice a tiny little cut on your finger, so you cover it with a band aid, but really, it's eating you alive!" Mechel proceeded to show the group a variety of bruises and abrasions on his own skin that could very possibly be a symptom of that illness.

No one really paid much attention. Jerry got up to prepare himself a cup of coffee. He stood up with a sigh, as if to proclaim that he was way above the level of conversation and he was just humoring everyone by staying there, and walked over to the ancient machine in the corner of the room.

He pressed the buttons and the machine spit a sickly yellow stream into his cup. Jerry sat back down and sipped the hot drink, and then, as he did several times a day, he looked around in disgust. "This coffee tastes like mud!"

Erez, a young Israeli wise guy who was lounging on the couch, taking up three spaces, didn't miss his cue. "How do you know, Jerry? Did you ever taste mud?"

Jerry loved this part. "No, punk, but you will if you don't watch yourself!"

Erez had just returned from driving a freezer truck to Cleveland and he was telling a story about an altercation with a police officer on the Pennsylvania Turnpike. "So the guy tells me to show him my license and I pull out my Israeli army ID card, so he looks at it and looks back at me, and then he says —"

Jerry snorted. "You took the turnpike? That's crazy. It just shows how young and stupid you are. If you were doing this for more than three minutes you would know you should *never* leave the 80!"

Erez laughed easily. 'That's your opinion, Jerry. Just your opinion."

Jerry bristled. This was a new breed of person. If someone had attacked him the way he had just attacked Erez when he was new, he would have been shattered. Instead, this kid just shrugged it off and went back to his silly story — *it probably never happened anyway* — with the cop.

Jerry crushed his coffee cup and interjected with a cop story of his own. That got the men going and one of them, a bookish fellow named Sidney who claimed that he was in law school at night and just helped out here to cover his bills, began to speak about the difficulty of being a policeman. Jerry grew irritated and wandered over to the secretary to find out when he could get back on the road. "Oh, they are just packing up an order that has to go to Lakewood now; it should be ready within minutes."

Lakewood, thought Jerry, *just what I need! A million new stores added to the route each week and these crazy developments that all look the same!*

He sat back down to wait and was glad to see that his friend Abie had come in. He was a nice fellow, had been here as long as Jerry, and they understood each other. Abie greeted him and offered him a cigarette.

Jerry accepted. "Abie, I gotta tell you something. Do you know those pesky kids I was telling you about, the ones that have overrun my building with all those undesirables?"

Abie nodded politely. How could he not know about Jerry's pet grievance?

"Well, get this. The kid, a real big mouth, is the son of Markstein, that crook over at On Two Feet who thinks it's his business to run the world."

Abie hadn't been expecting to hear that Jerry had found a cure for the common cold, but this was even less than interesting.

It was Sidney who perked up and turned to Jerry. What he said shocked Jerry, who made him repeat it again and then again. When the secretary called out to him that the order was ready and he headed out, he was still in a daze.

Frieda was telling Zalman about how badly she felt about Shaul. "It's just that when they come visit Tatty, I always feel like they are judging me, looking around to see that I am really taking good care of him. It makes me nervous."

Zalman stopped stirring his tea. "Frieda," he said, "Tatty is his father. You can't keep him locked up."

"Yes, I know that. But if I let Shaul come too often, he will start telling me that Tatty needs a better bed, nicer window shades, cleaner linens, whatever, and all at his expense of course — I *hate* it when he says that — and it makes me so uneasy."

Zalman understood his wife, but he also felt for Shaul, who was just trying to be a good son and meant no harm. He had an idea. "Frieda, when is Tatty leaving the house next for an appointment?"

"Well, he wants to go to New Jersey on Thursday, someone from the Lower East Side passed away and the children are sitting *shivah* in Passaic. I was planning on taking him."

"Frieda, why don't you let Shaul take him? It's a perfect opportunity for you to let him have time with his father without you getting nervous."

"But Tatty wants to go in the morning, because he is more alert then, and Shaul won't want to go until after work."

"Did Tatty tell you that?" asked Zalman.

"Well, no," Frieda admitted, "but that's the way it is."

Shaul was gratified to receive the call from his brother-in-law, Zalman, asking him if he was available to take his father to New Jersey. "I would love to, thanks for asking — but I can't make it until later in the afternoon."

"That's fine," said Zalman warmly, 'just perfect."

Chapter 37

There's a certain way that elderly people leave messages, as if they are not really sure if the machine picked up or if there's a real person there. Reb Anshel was no different. It took Mendel Wasser a few seconds to figure out whom the message on his voicemail was from. "Hello? Hello? Hello? Mendel?" it started, and then there was a long silence, followed by shuffling and a muffled conversation. Then, "If you are there, Mendel, it's me, Hammerman, just to let you know that I won't be at the *shiur* tonight, perhaps you can say it instead. *Zei gezunt.*"

Reb Anshel missing night seder? thought Mendel. *How strange!* It had only been a few days since Reb Anshel had returned to the evening program, and the place had filled up again. His Chumash *shiur* was drawing a nice crowd and he had managed to form a meaningful relationship with almost every one of the home's residents. He was the Rav.

Mendel looked at his watch. If he would be delivering Reb Anshel's *shiur,* he would need to start preparing.

Jerry Gelber had learned his lesson the last time he had tried to meet with Ari Engel and been soundly rebuffed. This time, he made an appointment over the phone.

"Can I ask what this is about?" a brash young secretary asked him.

Jerry swallowed a hundred answers that came to mind, with *No, you can't* being his most obvious choice. "Yes, sure you could. I have some information for him which he might find extremely interesting."

The girl gulped.

"Um, I need to you to be more specific," she replied, struggling for composure.

"Let's just say that it concerns one of his personnel and it can put him and the whole organization in an embarrassing light."

As smoothly as she came across on the phone, Chevy was really just a Bais Yaakov girl who had taken a three-month secretarial course and had made it all the way to the boss's office. She had no clue if this was a hoax or serious enough to merit real panic; Mr. Engel had been unequivocally clear that there were to be no interruptions or phone calls.

"Can I ask you to call back in an hour?" she asked, flustered.

Jerry was feeling good. "No, I am afraid not. It might be too late."

Ohmigosh! Chevy thought as she asked the caller to hold on for a moment.

She knocked hesitantly on her boss's door and, when she saw that he was in a meeting, grew embarrassed. She wanted to tell him about the phone call, but not in front of people.

"Can I ask you something privately?" she finally said.

He walked to the door. "What's the problem?"

"There's someone on the phone who says that he has important information about someone who works for you that can be very embarrassing."

Ari Engel furrowed his brow and asked his visitors to excuse him for a moment. He strode over to Chevy's desk and lifted the receiver. He knew how to handle a crisis!

"This is Ari Engel," he said curtly.

"Mr. Engel, we should speak, sooner rather than later," said the anonymous caller.

"Who is this?" asked Ari, as if he hadn't heard the caller's words.

"Mr. Engel, trust me, this is important. I know how hard you have worked over the years to build up the outstanding reputation you enjoy, and it world be tragic if it were to be lost because of one person."

"Listen, my friend, I don't have much time for guessing games. If you want to come here and speak with me face to face, I have an opening at —" Ari looked at Chevy, but she was biting her nails nervously in the corner — "at twelve-thirty. It's quieter then."

Jerry wasn't happy with this development. He had been expecting more respect. Now he was being told what to do.

He went back to intimidation mode. "You don't *want* to wait until then."

"Like I said," Ari replied smoothly, "twelve-thirty is great. If not, it will have to be some other time."

Then he hung up. Click. Just like that. Conversation closed.

Jerry had been hoping that he would be the one to end the conversation and now that pleasure had been denied him as well.

Delmy was growing anxious. It had been obvious that the old man was planning on leaving at some point, and she had been sure that today would be the day. Alas, two o'clock approached and he hadn't yet left. She would soon have to go, and he was still home, sitting by the window.

"Tatty," she heard Frieda call, "Shaul isn't coming for another few hours. You can take your coat off."

The old man had shrugged, and kept watching.

Delmy finally left, frustrated and annoyed.

Driving along the New Jersey Turnpike with his father at his side, Shaul Hammerman was a little boy again. Normally reserved, even taciturn, this evening he was chatty; it was so thrilling for him to be able to just schmooze with his father, like the old days, before Frieda had taken charge and was always fussing in the background of every conversation.

His father was just such a pleasure to speak with! It was amazing that someone could be so wise and understanding even while being accepting and nonjudgmental. Reb Anshel listened to his son with a little smile on his face, never speaking unless he was being asked a question.

Shaul was telling him about different business deals he had made, some profitable and some not. Oh, how he had missed this! Shaul updated his father on his own children and the progress that each of them was making in his or her own life. Again, Reb Anshel nodded silently, listening intently, but rarely speaking.

As they neared Passaic, Shaul was suddenly struck with a thought. What if his father wanted to talk to *him?* He hadn't really given him a chance to get a word in, and perhaps just as he had been longing for some quiet time, his father also had some things to get off his chest.

"What's doing by you, Tatty?" he asked.

Reb Anshel laughed. "Oh, lots of things. Don't you know that I am the Chief Rabbi of Kensington?"

He told Shaul all about the schedule at Mishkan Shalom and about the *shiur* he gave. He described the interesting people he had met, speaking with obvious pride and satisfaction.

After Reb Anshel finished speaking, he paused. It was obvious that there was something else on his mind.

"Yes, Tatty," Shaul prodded.

"There is another thing, but I am not sure if I should discuss it."

Shaul turned to look at his father, an apprehensive expression on his face.

Suddenly, Reb Anshel looked sheepish. "Nothing, Shaul, forget it. Are we almost there?"

"Yes, Tatty, just five minutes away."

"Okay, so let me collect my thoughts about what to say to the family, okay?"

Shaul let the matter, whatever it was, drop, but his concern only grew.

Jerry had decided not to go meet Ari Engel after all. If the man couldn't show him a little more respect, than he didn't deserve the visit. Jerry would find a more willing audience for the information he possessed and *then*, they would all wish they had listened to him.

Ari Engel had noted the fact that this anonymous caller had neglected to show; he had been mildly irritated by the disturbance and the questions that it raised, but Ari Engel wasn't someone who agonized over problems he couldn't solve. Did he think that the caller was for real? Maybe, but he couldn't very well sit and wonder which of his staff had a dark secret and what it was, could he?

He had a large staff and he was a busy man.

It was only on the trip back to Brooklyn that Shaul had opportunity to bring up the topic again.

"Tatty, was there something else that you wanted to discuss?"

Reb Anshel looked confused for a moment, and then ashamed again.

"Oh, it's nothing, nothing at all."

"Tatty, tell me. Please."

Shaul's mind was racing with possibilities. What secret could his father be hiding?

"You look too serious, Shaul. Don't worry, I am not getting married again—" Reb Anshel laughed heartily at his own joke while Shaul smiled uneasily, "—and I am not leaving you millions of dollars in a Swiss bank account."

Then Reb Anshel looked uncomfortable again. "It's just that ... just that I had my own little secret, and I am going to tell you, and only you, about it.

"Over the years on the East Side, in the shul, I was involved with many, many *niftarim, rachmanah litzlan.* I saw first-hand how important it is that these things," Reb Anshel was speaking quickly because Shaul was clearly ill at ease with the conversation, "be planned in advance. There is so much unnecessary tension and heartache in the heat of the moment.

"Shaul, it's important to me that, when that time comes, there will be no needless aggravation.

"On top of the closet in my room, next to the box with my Shabbos hat, there is an envelope with cash. It isn't much, but it is mine and I have been saving up for some time. I want that money to be used for my *levayah*!"

There, he had said it.

Shaul's initial reaction was one of hurt. Did his father not realize that finances were not an issue, that he had, *Baruch Hashem*, plenty of money? Then he immediately felt selfish and petty.

"But … why, Ta? Why is that on your mind?"

Reb Anshel was quiet. Could he ever share his worst nightmare with his son? Could he express his fear that, at that time, Shaul would be the one footing the bill, thus putting Frieda, who liked to be in charge, at a disadvantage? Who knew what would happen then? *His* children would not fight!

"I don't know, Shaul, I don't know. But this is important to me, and I wanted one of you to be aware of it. The money is there, a few thousand dollars, enough for what you will need."

"Look," Shaul would later tell his wife, "a father likes to provide for his children."

But in truth, it was more like a father *knows* his children.

Chapter 38

S haul had gotten the call early in the morning, very early. He had been fast asleep and was only dimly aware of his phone ringing. His wife had shouted out, waking him, "Shaul, the phone … maybe it's one of the kids." But even as Shaul had reached clumsily across his night-table for the phone, he knew that it wasn't about the kids. It was about his father.

And thus, he was overjoyed when he heard his father's voice at the other end. At least he was alive! Shaul was too sleepy to hear the aggravation in the old man's hoarse voice. "Shaul, come here, come here as fast as you can."

Shaul groped for his glasses and looked at the clock next to him: 5:34 AM. "Tatty, is everything okay? What happened? Are you feeling well?"

"*Oy*, Shaul, I feel fine, *Baruch Hashem*, but something terrible has happened, and I can only tell *you* about it." Reb Anshel was whispering.

"Um, Tatty, whatever it is, why can't you tell Frieda?"

"Because it's about the money, about my envelope — and only you know the secret!"

Shaul was frustrated. Again with that ridiculous money. Ever since his father had confided in him, he would mention the money at every opportunity and Shaul didn't like it one bit.

"Tatty, what will Frieda think if I suddenly come barging in to her house in the middle of the night —"

"It's not the middle of the night," Reb Anshel interrupted, "I am up for close to an hour already. And anyhow, this is an emergency. Come, come now."

Shaul looked at his wife in exasperation, but she had decided that whatever the emergency was, it wasn't that serious, and had quickly fallen back asleep.

Shaul sat up, still shaking his head and muttering, and prepared to take on the day.

When Shaul pulled up in front of his sister's home at a quarter to seven, he was dismayed to see his father standing at the front door in his pajamas and a robe, looking disheveled. He looked … he looked like he wasn't well and it distressed Shaul to see that.

He hurried up the front stairs and was shocked to see that his father had a wild, unnatural look in his eyes, so unlike his normal calm disposition. "Tatty," said Shaul cautiously as he leaned over to embrace his father. Reb Anshel fell on his shoulder and burst into tears.

There were people on the sidewalk, men headed to shul or work, and they were staring.

"They took my money. They took my money. I am a prisoner," Reb Anshel was shouting. A small crowd was gathering.

Shaul led his father into the house and sat him down. Then, he looked cautiously around for Frieda and was relieved that the house was silent. He poured his father a glass of water and sat down next to him. "What's this all about, Tatty?" he asked gently.

Reb Anshel spoke in a strange voice, a voice choked with fear and anguish. "Don't you understand? *They took the money!*"

Shaul had seen his father in his bad moments, seen him hallucinate and slip out of reality, but that had been when he was living alone in his apartment and had been in a perpetual state of confusion. Also, then it was never so scary! His father was clearly befuddled, and Shaul was growing increasingly nervous. He was actually thrilled to see Frieda appear in the room, a look of pure astonishment on her face.

"What's going on here?' she demanded.

Reb Anshel suddenly shrank back in horror. *"You took my money,"* he shouted hoarsely. "Give it back to me."

Frieda was stunned into speechlessness.

Reb Anshel began to ramble, looking first indignant, and then contrite. It was as if he himself didn't believe the things he was saying. He was looking up, past both of them, at some faraway place and speaking. He was talking about the concentration camps and how they took away his things. Then he would look accusingly at his two children and tell them not to take his money.

He was clearly delirious and Frieda didn't waste any time calling Hatzalah.

In the interim, her children began to wake up and she busied herself with shooing them into the kitchen and away from the action. What a nightmare! Her father was slipping out of reality and saying the most ridiculous things!

She had picked up the phone to call her other siblings (*last time she hadn't called them right away, and they had been so insulted!*) when two Hatzalah members burst in. The sight of the medics threw Reb Anshel into a fresh panic, and he began to shout that he didn't need police; he would deal with his children by himself.

One of the Hatzalah members led Reb Anshel to the couch and did a quick checkup. He nodded at his partner. The burly fellow stood in front of Frieda, blocking her view of the room and they worked quickly, Reb Anshel rambling throughout.

Then it was quiet.

"Your father seems okay, except for his high blood pressure. He is suffering from some sort of shock, and you should probably call his doctor and describe what happened to him. For now, though, he will be okay. We were able to give him a relaxant, and he should rest for a few minutes."

Shaul was grateful for the professionalism and courteousness of the volunteers, even as Frieda bristled at the invasion of her privacy.

Now came the hard part. He would have to tell her whatever he knew.

Malka had never been much of a formal "davener." It wasn't that she didn't daven; sure she did, all the time. It was just that structured *tefillos,* at specific times, were hard for her. Even so, she had taken upon herself to daven Shacharis with a siddur each morning — it was all she could do for Ezzy.

There had definitely been some improvement. Even Aryeh had agreed that there was no longer any reason for Ezzy to go for therapy, though Aryeh wouldn't go as far as to say he was healed. Aryeh preferred to call it a trial period. Her husband.

He liked when problems ended in neat little solutions, like his math, but problems rarely ended that way; usually, things just resolved themselves. Like Ezzy.

She picked up her siddur at seven forty-five, confident that her good works, her *tefillos* and *chassadim (she gave money to every single meshulach last week, even when Aryeh wasn't home and she didn't like to open the door!)* were turning the tide for her beloved son.

She wasn't wrong. Things were getting better.

But first they would get worse.

By eight o'clock in the morning Frieda was in a state. She had gotten all the details from her brother, and her hurt at not having been privy to the existence of the envelope mixed with worry about her father, who was clearly not himself. *He had accused her of taking it!* She knew that he didn't really think that, that he had simply been reacting to the fear and confusion, but still, it hadn't been pleasant.

She knew exactly who took the money and she would get it back. Well, not exactly, but almost exactly. There had been so many people in his room over the last few weeks, of course this had happened, and it really was her fault. She had been silly enough to open her home to all these people, and who really knew what sort they were — well, now she knew, and she was going to the bottom of this.

She would also ensure that her father would no longer be a puppet in their play. It was simply too much for him. *Zalman and his bright ideas,* she thought.

By mid-morning, the news had spread. Frieda Finestone had stormed into Mishkan Shalom before the residents had left to their day jobs and made a speech. She had tried to sound calm, even encouraging — she had once been a teacher, she knew how to do this — but instead she had sounded hysterical. She had gotten into a shouting match with Mrs. Handler, who didn't like the way she had made all the residents nervous, and in no time, the neighbors knew about it. Old Mrs. Herskovits was on the phone with her friends, piecing together whatever information they had. *It seems like there was some really terrible theft, someone from the home on the first floor robbed the old man across the street of his life's savings. His daughter thinks that maybe one of the residents took it and now she has them all up in arms. Terrible!*

Even Sara Gelber, who really wasn't in the loop as far as building politics went, knew about it. There had been no police, but there was enough activity and conversation in the lobby that, while waiting with her daughters for the school bus, she had heard about the robbery across the street, something to do with the distinguished-looking Rabbi.

She wasn't sure if she should tell Jerry. Why give him more reasons to get angry? Then again, she thought, he would find out anyhow, so why shouldn't she tell him? She liked it when she spoke and he listened. The opportunities were all too few.

She decided that she would tell him.

Delmy was on vacation. She had quit three days earlier, telling the lady that she needed to be home with her daughter. It wasn't the greatest of excuses — I mean, what had she done until now? — but the lady hadn't even been listening to the reason. She had just nodded miserably and said, "Another one."

Delmy had thanked her and left, the envelope at the bottom of her purse.

She had boarded the bus, secure in the knowledge that she was home free. Now, there was nothing anyone could do to her.

And thus it was that by nine-thirty in the morning, Jerry Gelber was marching triumphantly toward Ari Engel's office, appointment or no appointment. This was his day.

He had schlepped an unwilling Sidney, the law student who worked with him, the one who had told him the whole story. Sidney had protested vigorously, but Jerry wouldn't take no for an answer and Sidney, who saw Jerry every single day, wasn't about to make an enemy out of Jerry Gelber.

Malka finished davening. She had davened for a long, long time. Who knew what the day would bring, after all?

Chapter 39

There were three men gathered in Ari Engel's office, but they weren't talking to each other at all. Ari himself was pacing back and forth, chewing nervously on a pen; something he rarely did, and certainly not in front of people.

Jerry Gelber was sitting on a large, comfortable chair. This was his moment of triumph. The revenge he had longed for so badly was within his grasp. Yet, instead of feeling good, he felt horrible. Even in his righteous indignation, he felt a certain sense of revulsion, but it wasn't for Ezzy or his father or any of the Mishkan Shalom residents; it was for himself.

For the first time in his life, he was sensing who his greatest enemy was.

On the next chair, Sidney slumped over miserably. He looked terrified, and every few seconds he would gulp loudly, his Adam's apple bobbing as he did. It had been a rough morning for him.

He had come into work, like he did every day, and big Jerry Gelber had hustled him into his truck. "Come, Sidney, we have an emergency."

He hadn't given him a choice. Sidney was scared of Jerry, of what Jerry could do to him, and he had barely even put up a fight.

"What about work?" he had whispered, gesturing around.

"I told them that we need a few minutes together, and they said it's fine. It's quiet this morning. Get into the truck."

Finally, after a few minutes, he'd found his voice. "Where are we going?"

"To see justice served. Some poor, defenseless old man was robbed by a teenage hooligan and we have to help him out."

Sidney wasn't exactly sure what Jerry meant, but he was all for helping old men. Just … Jerry didn't seem like the protector of the elderly and defenseless. *Oh well, people were full of surprises, right?*

Jerry had parked next to a long, low building and led Sidney by the arm through a maze of offices. Jerry had confidently approached a secretary guarding a large corner office and said to the girl, "Tell your boss that Jerry Gelber is here. He wants to see me. Trust me."

Chevy hadn't even hesitated. She knew what Mr. Engel would want.

"Go right in."

Ari Engel had been in the midst of trying to reach Mendel Wasser when his visitors barged in. Of course, he had heard all about the theft. Mrs. Handler had given him a detailed report, sparing nothing. Ari Engel had smelled a crisis brewing. All he needed was a neighbor to drop the idea that one of the residents had taken the money and Ari would have a full-blown catastrophe on his hands. If Ari Engel had achieved anything over the years, it was that he had convinced the inhabitants of New York City's frum neighborhoods that Mishkan Shalom residents were good neighbors. He had overcome their hostility, fear, and uncertainty and succeeded in convincing the people that this was an opportunity; he had an entire folder filled with letters from people who testified that their lives has been changed as a result of having a Mishkan Shalom facility next door. They wrote how their children and themselves had become more giving, compassionate people, how the sweetness, sincerity, and willingness of the residents to help had touched their lives.

It was Ari's pride and joy. All it took was one story like this to destroy everything he had worked so hard to construct.

Ari Engel knew that the whole story was rather silly. The amount was just a few thousand dollars, an amount that he could easily replace, but it wasn't about money. It was about the daughter's insistence that it was one of the residents that had taken her father's money — "intruders," she had called them — and he was afraid of the rumors that she would spread. He wouldn't offer her money, because then she would almost certainly go around claiming that she had been a victim of Mishkan Shalom.

There was another reason that he wouldn't pay her; he was certain that none of the residents had taken the money. He had spoken to Dr. Shindelheim several times, and the doctor, who was intimately familiar with each of the residents and their emotional issues, had assured him that it was a virtual impossibility. He would not admit guilt when he wasn't guilty, even if it was convenient. But the alternative was no less unattractive. The unsolved mystery would attract rumors like flies to a corpse.

He imagined the comments. *Such a chashuve Yid, he gave everything he had over to the poor people there, nebech. They learned with him and sat in his room, talking, at all hours of the day and night. He was like their father, and what thanks did he get? They stole his life savings. You have to be so careful these days, so many dangerous people ....*

Or, *You know, some people just don't know how to retire. He had a long and successful career on the Lower East Side; why couldn't he just relax? Such an old man, and not well either. It's never smart to try to do too many things ....*

So Ari Engel had been agonizing over how to proceed when his two uninvited guests had entered. He knew instinctively that their visit was connected to the morning's events and he welcomed them to sit.

So Jerry had told him everything. He spoke about all that he had endured throughout the years from the residents and their noise. Then he spoke about the mess and inconvenience of their renovations and the new shul. Ari winced at Jerry's coarse, foul-mouthed way of speaking, but he did not interrupt.

He noted that Jerry seemed to have a special arsenal of vitriol reserved for the staff at Mishkan Shalom. His fury grew as he described the brazen way that the two boys that hung around had spoken to him.

"And I said to my wife, these boys are up to no good. Always laughing at everyone else, loitering and laughing in the lobby late at night."

Ari was upset. This was a government funded agency with a squeaky-clean image, and these were the boys who had been approved by the State for summer internships. Loitering on the premises simply wasn't acceptable!

Jerry had continued with his story, relating how he had shared his frustration about one of the boys — Markstein — at work one day. Here, Jerry off on a tangent about the senior Markstein and his save-the-world tactics. Ari had been surprised to learn that the boy was Aryeh Markstein's son. He knew the father, a serious, driven sort; the son seemed quite the opposite.

"So listen to this," Jerry was saying, "I am at work, telling my buddies all about the grief these kids put me through, and listen to what Sidney here tells me."

Jerry indicated the short, stocky fellow who sat there mutely. "*Nu*, tell your story already."

Sidney felt like he was going to be sick.

The other two looked at him expectantly, so in a faltering voice, he began.

"Last year, at about this time, I was in law school, just like I am now, and I was looking for part-time work. I saw an ad about a yeshivah that was looking for a geography teacher and I grabbed it. I mean, I am no geography major, but it just meant reading the next few chapters in the textbook and it helped pay the rent. It just so happens that the Markstein boy, Ezriel his name is, was my student, and he was a nice enough boy, if a tad arrogant."

Sidney blushed involuntarily at the memory. Ezriel had been more than a little arrogant. He had quickly perceived that the new teacher knew little about geography, and had never tired of exposing the fact. "Sir," he would call out, "is the North Pole really a pole? What does D.C. stand for, in Washington D.C.? Why is there a West Virginia but not an East Virginia?"

Sidney would laugh weakly, never quite sure how to reply to the attempts to humiliate him. He hadn't really liked Ezriel at all.

"So, one day, I came to school and I heard in the teacher's room that the boy, Ezriel, had stolen money from a visiting *tzedakah* collector from Israel. The whole staff knew about it."

Ari sat bolt upright! He remembered that story. He remembered hearing about the boy that had cleaned out the *meshulach's* box in shul.

It couldn't … wasn't possible … the same boy?

Did Wasser really go and hire a boy with that kind of history to work at Mishkan Shalom.

Ari's anger was mixed with relief. At least they had solved the mystery. While this wasn't the conclusion he had hoped for, at least it wasn't one of the residents.

That's when he asked his secretary to dial Aryeh Markstein's office.

It had been a typical day for Aryeh Markstein: perpetual motion. He had hurried out of shul, dropping coins into the outstretched hand of a *tzedakah* collector without actually making eye contact with him. He made it to the subway station just in time for the train and within minutes was ensconced in his seat reviewing his *daf yomi.*

He had arrived in Manhattan with just enough time for a quick coffee before his first meeting of the day, and had been going from meeting to meeting since eight-thirty. It had been that kind of morning.

He was in intense conversation with the top administration of a large construction company when his secretary buzzed in. "Mr., Markstein, someone on line three says it's very urgent."

With an annoyed shrug, Aryeh pressed the speakerphone button. "Yes."

"Reb Aryeh, this is Ari Engel, over at Mishkan Shalom."

The two men were only distantly acquainted, but Aryeh knew who Ari was. He wondered what he could want. Was this about a community thing? Did they serve on any boards together?

"Oh, how are you? Listen, Ari, I am just in the middle of an important meeting now. Perhaps we can speak later."

Engel's voice had an edge to it. "No, we need to speak now. And it had best be in person."

Before Aryeh could protest, Engel continued. "It's about Ezzy."

"What about Ezzy?"

"I think you should come down here as soon as possible. It would be best for everyone."

Aryeh Markstein was no pushover, but he was no match for Ari Engel. He didn't even try to argue. There was something in the other man's tone that told him that this was for real.

He looked apologetically at his clients. "Family emergency," he explained as he rose and put on his jacket.

He left the room without looking back.

Chapter 40

Things were better than they had been a long while. On Shabbos afternoon, Dovi Berman had dropped in for a visit. "I mean, it's such a long day and I am in the neighborhood, I figured I would come say hello."

Ezzy had stood there, stunned. In the neighborhood? Dovi lived a block away from him! This was huge. Ezzy had welcomed him in and the two boys had spent a pleasant half hour chatting. There were moments when the conversation was strained, when Ezzy wondered if things would ever really return to normal, but it was still thoroughly enjoyable. Eventually, Dovi had excused himself to go learn and invited Ezzy to join him. Ezzy had walked alongside with a wide grin on his face. This was really nice!

278

Then, in school, some of the other boys — boys who generally nodded at him, or just said uncomfortable hellos — were out-and-out gracious to him. They joked with him and one even teased him about needing a haircut, the kind of barb that only a friend could make.

Was the tide shifting?

Ezzy didn't know, but he intended to enjoy it.

Sure, Moishy was a dear and trusted friend, and the residents of Mishkan Shalom were his buddies, but this was ... different, real, normal.

Maybe his penance was complete.

· ·

Aryeh Markstein and Ari Engel had much in common. Both were driven and successful at what they did. Both were focused and goal-oriented, interested only in getting things done and not in niceties and small talk, so, in theory, their conversation should have gone very well.

The problem arose as a result of yet another characteristic that the two men shared: they both needed to be in control. Ari would talk in his matter-of-fact, this-is-the-way-it-is, manner, and Aryeh would respond as if he were the one being asked for advice.

Ari had started their meeting by describing how hard he had worked over the years to build up the Mishkan Shalom reputation and how he had finally succeeded in making people understand that a Mishkan Shalom facility was not a threat to the neighborhood.

Aryeh had nodded sagely.

Ari briefly described the set-up at the Kensington home regarding Reb Anshel. Aryeh interrupted to tell him how his Ezzy had been instrumental in developing the whole program, and of course he knew all about it.

Then, without preamble, Ari looked right at him and told him about the stolen money and his worry that it would reflect badly on the organization.

"I mean, that's all we need after all our hard work, and the woman, Mrs. Finestone, is running around shouting that it was one of our people, and then rumors spread ..."Ari's voice trailed off.

Aryeh felt sick. *Again?*

Ari continued. "This morning, a fellow from the building came to see me" — Ari wisely neglected to mention his name — "and he isn't so happy with Ezzy, feels that he isn't behaving with total professionalism and courtesy. He brings in another guy, an old teacher of Ezzy's, and he says that Ezzy has some history with this type of issue."

And here, Aryeh made a big mistake.

He was so anxious for the upper hand, so anxious to be the savior marching in to help beleaguered Ari Engel, so anxious to be the one deciding on a course of action, that he nodded vigorously. He wasn't one of those softy fathers who couldn't face reality!

"Yes," he said, "I understand. You think that Ezzy should be considered a suspect."

Ari Engel — practical, determined Ari Engel — was shocked at the reaction of this father. Where were the screaming protests, the offended arguments?

But Aryeh was just sitting, nodding efficiently.

Inside Aryeh Markstein, a storm raged, but Ari Engel would never see it. His world was turning upside down in front of his eyes. *Ezzy!* What had happened? Could Ezzy have some sort of disorder, some sort of psychological condition that made him take other people's money? Why hadn't any of the many professionals that they had sent him to picked up on it?

If he had been thinking clearly, he might have questioned the other man's assumption. He might have stormed out in protest of the baseless accusation. But he wasn't thinking clearly; he was too focused on being the savior, on answering the question, and this was clearly the neatest solution to a thorny problem. Ari Engel was desperate for a guilty party; then he could get the money back and put the whole story behind him without any more unwanted attention. It just made sense.

Aryeh squared his shoulders and sat up straight. "I will have a talk with Ezzy, and if he is responsible, then we will do whatever we have to do to make things right."

Ari Engel looked at him gratefully. "You have no idea how much I appreciate your willingness to work with me on this. It's very big of you."

Good! thought Aryeh. To Ari, he said "Why shouldn't we deal with this in a mature fashion? Would it really help to let our emotions get mixed in here?"

Ezzy was surprised when someone told him that his father was looking for him. His father? In school? It made no sense. Had something terrible happened? He hurried into the hallway and saw his father coming towards him.

"Ta, what happened?"

Aryeh attempted a smile and put his hand on Ezzy's shoulder. "Nothing, Ezzy, nothing at all. I think I need you to come with me a bit. Can you get excused?"

Ezzy looked at his father uncertainly. *What was this about?* He went to get an excuse slip and headed off with his father.

This was weird, thought Ezzy. His father was walking beside him in silence and had turned off his cellphone. *Was someone sick?* Suddenly, like a little child, Ezzy was overcome by a powerful longing for his mother. He wished she was by them now.

Aryeh fidgeted a little more, and then stopped suddenly.

"Ezzy, I am coming here directly from a meeting with Ari Engel."

The first thing was struck Ezzy was the fact that his father's tone was accusatory, as if he, Ezzy, had done something wrong.

Then, he was immediately overcome by a sense that his privacy had been invaded. Ari Engel? Mishkan Shalom? Those were *his* places, his people! Why did his father have to mix in there?

Calm down, Ezzy, he told himself. *Maybe they serve on some board together; who says this is about you?*

Ezzy was quiet, wondering how to respond, and Aryeh couldn't handle it.

"Do you have anything to say?"

Now Ezzy was really surprised.

"What should I say? That's wonderful that you met him, really it is."

Aryeh looked at Ezzy searchingly.

"Apparently, the old man, Reb Anshel, had an envelope filled with money, where he kept his savings."

Ezzy felt desecrated. Just hearing his father drop Reb Anshel's name — *his Reb Anshel* — like it was a cumbersome, heavy object, was irritating. What was this about?

Ezzy didn't like the way his father was staring at him pointedly.

"So your boss suggested that perhaps it was an inside job, without mentioning names, of course, and that if it was, it could look very bad for the organization."

Ezzy's head was swimming. Was this really happening?

Aryeh misinterpreted Ezzy's silence, and he made his second mistake of the day.

"Ezzy, all I am saying is this. I have no idea who took the money — or even if it really happened — but these are the facts the way I heard them, and as a responsible person, an *ehrliche* Yid I have a responsibility to act on them."

Ezzy was in total shock. Emboldened by Ezzy's silence, Aryeh continued.

"Ezzy let me tell you how much I love you. Mommy and I will always be there for you no matter what, and whatever we do is motivated by our love for you."

His voice grew warm and tender. To Ezzy it felt like cold steel pressing against his heart.

"Ezzy, if this is somehow connected with us, we will do whatever it takes to make it right. I have already told Ari Engel that the money is not an issue, that we will take the appropriate measures to rectify the situation, okay?"

Ezzy had no words, and even if he had, he lacked the strength to express them.

He simply turned around and began to run, faster than he had ever run before.

Malka and Aryeh didn't fight; they just didn't have that type of marriage. Malka had once attended a *shiur* where the lecturer had said that a marriage without passionate fights is a sterile relationship, lacking in real feeling. Fighting is a sign of life, he had said.

Malka had walked out of that *shiur* feeling cheated. She had mentioned it to Aryeh, who had shrugged it off. "Sure we fight, we fight plenty," he had said. "Don't you remember, this past Shabbos we argued about who took that picture of the kids on our summer vacation. And this morning, I was upset that you had finished the milk and there was no more, and you could have just told me to buy some on the way home for Shacharis. And you said that I could have bought some anyhow, what would be so bad if we had two bottles … see, we fight a lot!'

Malka hadn't been convinced. She thought the lecturer had meant *real* fights, about issues and ideas, not practical disagreements.

That had been years ago.

Tonight, when he had tried to tell her about his meeting with Ari Engel and the subsequent conversation with Ezzy, they had fought: a full-blown, heated, passionate argument.

Malka had cried and accused, Aryeh had defended and accused right back.

He was too rigid, she was too dreamy.

It was terrible. His voice was raised. Malka found herself wishing that they had closer neighbors who could overhear his wounded shouts. The person inside Aryeh Markstein was emerging in all its pained glory.

But at what a cost ….

The text message on her cellphone screen pierced her anew each time she looked at it.

Hi Ma, came by 2 get stuff-sorry missed u- need some time away from home- call u 2moro-bb4n-:)

The 'bye-bye for now' she was able to figure out; it was the smiley face that left her guessing.

Was he saying that he was okay? Was he saying that he was okay with *her?* Was he telling her not to worry, that this would soon pass?

Or was he saying, *Ma, I am hurting like you can't imagine and the smile on my face is just about as convincing and genuine as this silly little icon?*

Chapter 41

A house in the depth of the night. Every home has its own sounds, the noises, hums, and whispers that fill the heavy silence. Maybe it's the satisfying ripple of water running through pipes or the gentle swish of a ceiling fan. Perhaps it's the eerie creaking of a loose floorboard or the distant drone of a nocturnal neighbor starting a car. It's the sounds of night.

From the moment that Malka Markstein had become a mother, the sounds that formed the background noise to her night's sleep were those of her children; first crying, then whimpering, then simply breathing. In later years she would wake at two in the morning to hear Chavi on the phone with her friends or Ezzy puttering around the kitchen, but that was fine too. As long as she heard them.

Tonight, she couldn't sleep. It wasn't like Ezzy was away in camp or on a trip — it was as if he had been swallowed up by the deep, dark night beyond this house, by forces stronger than the love and warmth of her home, and the silence that he left behind was deafening.

She needed to hear his breathing in distant corner of the house, needed to know that he was okay, needed to know that he knew how much she loved him.

She had studied his text message a hundred times, wondering how — and if — to reply.

She could tell him that she loved him and was thinking of him, but that wouldn't be enough. He would be waiting to hear her denounce her husband's accusations, her fervent assurance that she knew he was innocent; she did, in fact, believe that he was innocent, but she was torn by her loyalty to Aryeh. Deep down, she also sensed that, as much as Ezzy wanted her on his side, he would derive comfort from her alignment with her husband, the way that things ought to be. She believed that a child would prefer that his parents turn on him — together — rather than see a show of disunity.

She could text him that she wished he would come home, but in her heart of heart, she understood him. She would stand loyally by Aryeh, but she appreciated what her son was doing; proclaiming his deep sense of hurt and betrayal at his father's baseless accusation. A part of her wanted to shout to him, "Run, my son, run …."

So, though she wondered where and how he was, she opted to wish him well from afar, willing him to work through the issue his own way.

Malka wasn't the only one unable to sleep. Mendel Wasser was also up in the middle of the night, lost in thought. It had been quite a day for Mendel. Mrs. Handler had called him early in the morning to inform about the theft, and also about Mrs. Finestone's hysterical accusations.

Mendel had hurried over and tried to visit Reb Anshel. Frieda had unequivocally refused to allow him entry, telling him to go find out who stole her father's money. Mendel had been hurt.

He had gone across the street to the facility and found the residents in a state of agitation. They understood very well what had happened. They too were hurt. Many of them had stayed home from work, nursing their grievances, and Mendel had spent the morning reassuring them that it was all a misunderstanding and of course, Mrs. Finestone was simply a bit high-strung and didn't mean the words she was saying.

By late morning, when things had calmed down somewhat, he got a phone call. It was Ari Engel.

Mendel heard the censure and indictment in the other man's *Hello*.

Hello, Mendel; hello, dreamer; hello clueless person who messed up as a rebbi and now messed up my facility. Hello, Mendel, who has caused me nothing but grief ....

"Hi," said Mendel.

"Well, it's been quite an exciting morning," said Mr. Engel.

Mendel was quiet.

"I have some disturbing news," Mr. Engel continued. "It seems that Mrs. Finestone's accusations were not totally baseless and it is likely that one of ours is responsible."

Mendel felt faint.

"We are not accusing anyone, and of course, every Yid is innocent until proven otherwise, but until further notice, we are considering one of your staff, Ezriel Markstein, who spent a lot of private time with Rabbi Hammerman, as a suspect. Please ensure that he takes a few days off and doesn't come on to the premises of Mishkan Shalom until all this is resolved."

"Ezzy didn't do it," Mendel's words came out before he could even consider them, a torrent of passion and feeling.

"Rabbi Wasser, I have neither the time nor energy to explain to you how I arrive at my conclusions. But, out of curiosity, are you aware of the fact that the boy has some history with this type of corrupt behavior?"

Mendel suddenly felt silly. "Um, no, I am not," he stammered.

"Well, be aware, and, like I said, he isn't welcome for now.

"And Rabbi Wasser, one more thing; no one has to know about any of this, of course."

Mendel gulped. "Right."

Feeling like a chastised little child, he hung up.

Ezzy!

But of course, the news spread. Pinky had overheard Mrs. Handler on the phone saying that there were some issues with Ezzy, and Heshy, another one of the residents, had gotten a call from his mother who warned him that she had heard from good sources — *very* good sources — that one of the staff at Mishkan Shalom was a serial thief. "Heshy, you had better hide that expensive new sweater I just bought you," she said.

They huddled together and discussed it. Ezzy? *Their* Ezzy? It just couldn't be.

And they, too, unsure of whom they could trust, ran to Mendel, hoping for reassurance that it wasn't true. He had done his best.

And after the long, painful day, who should ring his bell? Ezzy.

But Mendel Wasser practiced what he preached. *Hevei dan ess kal ha'adam lekaf zechus* was real to him, not simply a catchy phrase. He smiled broadly at the forlorn-looking teenager on his doorstep and welcomed him to his home.

"Come on in, Ezzy."

The long, painful night came to an end with a bright sun rising lazily in the spring sky.

A new day.

Thwack went Ezzy's head as he sat up. He knew where he was, but had forgotten about the bunk bed.

When he had come to Mendel's house yesterday, he had merely been looking for a place to calm down, to wait out the storm. With each passing hour, however, he had grown angrier and more resentful, less willing to return home and face the disapproving, condemnatory silence. He had nowhere else to be; Moishy's house was too crowded and noisy, and Moishy himself felt like a guest there. He had briefly entertained the idea of sleeping at Mishkan Shalom, but that was just too strange.

So, with few options, he ended up sleeping at Mendel's. Mendel, of course, had welcomed Ezzy with his usual warmth and sincerity. At least he was the same.

And sometimes, there is nothing more comforting than someone who stays the same.

Benjy looked in the mirror yet again. He was wearing his Shabbos hat and suit, with his best tie and freshly-shined shoes. He was ready, but first he had one more call to make.

His boss.

He worked at a kosher caterer, sticking labels on small salad containers, a job that he did with conscientiousness and care. But everyone is entitled to some time off, and this morning, he needed a few hours.

'Hi,' he said to the manager, 'it's me, Benjy. I will be in late today, and maybe not at all. I have an important meeting.'

Ari Engel parked the Highlander at the usual angle, blocking a few feet of sidewalk in front of the Mishkan Shalom offices, and entered, walking quickly. The clicking of his heels seemed to be announcing to one and all who dared to wonder, "It's business as usual, we've moved on, don't bring up the events of yesterday, it's behind us."

He nodded his good-mornings without stopping and closed the door to his office behind him.

It was a brand-new day. Yesterday's nightmare was over. He had spoken with Mrs. Finestone and promised her the missing money, had spoken with Aryeh Markstein who would bring over the check. The boy's *chinuch* wasn't his problem.

Hopefully, he could concentrate on other business today.

He turned to his pile of paperwork when Chevy knocked at the door with an apologetic expression.

"There's someone here who needs to see you; he's a resident."

A resident? At the office?

"Show him in, please."

Ari Engel looked up to see a familiar face. A short, chubby fellow with curly graying hair stood before him. His face was scrubbed and shiny and he wore a gray suit and striped red tie.

"Hi there," said Ari warily. "What's up?"

"Shalom aleichem, Mr. Engel. You don't know me, but we all know you. You are the boss of Mishkan Shalom. My name is Benjy Biller and I live in the group home over in Kensington."

Despite his curiosity, Ari had more pressing concerns. "Does anyone know that you are here? How did you get here? Did you get permission?"

Benjy looked proud.

"No, I kept it a secret. I said I was going to work, but I called in for a day off. Then, I took a car service all the way in to Boro Park."

Benjy suddenly looked nervous. "But don't worry; I paid for it myself with my spending money."

Ari made a quick note on his pad and turned back to Benjy.

"Sit down, Benjy, make yourself comfortable."

This was still one of his boys and he felt a pang of paternal love for the hapless man in front of him.

"What's on your mind, my friend?" he asked.

Benjy looked right at Ari Engel.

"I have to tell you something important."

"Okay, what is it?"

"Yesterday, people were talking about the money that was stolen from Reb Anshel. I know who stole it."

Ari looked annoyed, then interested.

"Oh?"

"I do. It was me. I took the money one day when we were visiting Reb Anshel."

Ari stared at Benjy, uncomprehending.

"You stole the money?"

Benjy's eyes were bright.

"Yes, it was me. It wasn't Ezzy. Ezzy would never do something like that."

Ari wanted to speak, but he couldn't.

"And Mr. Engel, I know that I might have to go to jail, but I am ready. Just please find someone else to work at Mr. Klein's, because he really needs someone to do the salad containers."

Chapter 42

Moishy was no stranger to guilty feelings; he had spent a good part of his sixteen years feeling blameworthy and at fault, but the intensity of these feelings was something new, even for him. He felt as if he were somehow responsible for the plight of his best — and only — friend. Not through anything he had done, of course, but rather, because, deep in the recesses of his troubled soul, he felt a strange kind of relief at Ezzy's situation.

Over the past few months, as Ezzy and Moishy had grown closer and closer, Moishy had always felt this odd sense of dread, of impending doom. He wasn't worthy of a friend like Ezzy Markstein, and he knew it. At first, he had thought Ezzy was just using him to get through a tough time, but as the weeks had passed and they had become "partners," so to speak, in their work at Mishkan Shalom, he had wondered where it was going.

The beatings of long-ago never really stopped reverberating within him, and the pounding of fists on his back had driven out any sense of self-worth; he kept waiting for Ezzy to dump him.

During the last few weeks, he had sensed that the tide was turning. He had watched Ezzy's face brighten as he would mention his friends at school, and when Ezzy had innocently and guilelessly mentioned that Dovi Berman had come to visit him, Moishy knew that his time was over. He would go back to being a street kid and Ezzy would go back to being a regular yeshivah boy; sure, Ezzy would wave when he would see him, and maybe even visit Mishkan Shalom on Purim or something, but that would be it. He would be alone again.

Then, Ezzy had called him and, in about three sentences told him what had happened; Moishy had been hurt for his friend, filled with resentment toward Aryeh Markstein and his inability to see things in more than one dimension. But, deep down, he had also felt relief, reassurance that Ezzy, who had been perched on the top rung of the ladder back into society, would now fall so low that he would be his, Moishy's, friend again. It was a relief that made him even more miserable than he already was.

And so, when Ezzy called to meet him at their usual place, the corner table of the old pizza shop, Moishy, with his troubled conscience, was glad to be able to help his friend.

Each week, the old Spanish woman would come to the corner grocery store, Moishy read from the papers Ezzy had photocopied, a story from his high school literature text-book, *and each week the proprietor knew exactly what she was there for. She would come every Wednesday, at four o'clock, and place two dollar bills down on the counter.*

"What are you going to do with the money, Grandma?" he would ask her, just as he did every single week. And the hard lines in the grandmother's face would relax as she would begin to discuss what she would do with every single penny.

"First I will send some money back to Mexico for my sister, she needs a new knee and she has no money for surgery. Then I will take some money for my grandson — he is such a smart boy — so that he can go to college and become a doctor. I will give money to his mother, my sweet daughter, who works so hard all day at the restaurant, and I will use a little for my old age."

The proprietor knew what was coming. "An old woman deserves to relax a little bit. Maybe I will go to a big hotel on the beach and just sit there, sleeping in the sun."

The proprietor would look at her earnestly as he handed her the garishly colored piece of cardboard, nodding along at expressed fantasies. 'I hope you win, Grandma, you deserve it," He would say.

She would bless him before taking her purchase, a scratch-off lottery ticket, to the photocopy machine in the corner and putting on reading glasses for her weekly ceremony.

Then, when she was finished scratching the small piece of cardboard, which had gone from promising to pitiful in just a minute, she would carry it with dignity to the wastebasket and shrug at the proprietor.

"Looks like my sister is going to have to wait another week," she would say.

"Next week you will have better luck," he would assure her.

Then she would step out in to the cold streets and hurry back to the nursing home where she worked, in time for supper.

But one Wednesday things went a little awry, not according to the plan. She had come in after her work and placed her two dollar bills down on the counter. The proprietor had selected the lottery ticket with his usual solemnity and handed it to her.

She had gone to scratch it, but instead of the usual x'es and $5 symbols, there appeared the smiling face of a joker and then another. This was more than she had ever seen. She began to scratch furiously, sending up a hail of latex, and uncovered the third joker.

She had won.

The grand prize.

Fifty-thousand dollars.

Enough to fulfill many of her dreams.

The old woman had looked at the proprietor, to see if he was watching her. He was busy with a customer and wasn't focused on her. So she took the small cardboard, and unlike other weeks, she didn't drop it into the wastebasket, but placed it in her pocket and carried it out of the store. Then she walked over to a wooden garbage pail near a bus stop and began to tear the hard cardboard with urgency. It wasn't easy, but she tore with fierceness, piece after stubborn piece, the joker's eyes and elaborate chin, the numbers, all of it. She dropped each piece into the large garbage pail, willing them to be swallowed up by the mess of beer bottles and cigarette butts.

Then she hurried off on the cold streets toward the nursing home where she worked, in time for supper.

That was the end of the story. Ezzy hadn't understood it at first. Then, the teacher had asked the boys what they thought the theme of the story was and each of them had offered suggestions.

Ezzy had suddenly been struck by inspiration and raised his hand.

"Maybe the old woman didn't really have the energy to deal with change, maybe she was settled in her life and wanted to *talk* about change, to daydream about better times, but was too intimidated when the opportunity presented itself to actually realize those dreams. She didn't really think it was possible, and interpreted the winning ticket as some sort of cynical mockery of her and her situation."

The teacher had walked over to Ezzy's desk and slapped him on the shoulder. "Ezriel, it is astounding how perceptive you are," is all he said.

Ezzy had smiled shyly, but inside his head, he had only one thought: Tatty.

After class, Ezzy had photocopied the papers and folded them carefully in his pocket. He had to send the story to Chavi. She would understand.

Moishy had finished the story and was looking at him quizzically. "It's a real sad story, Ezzy."

Ezzy sighed. "Don't you understand? My father talks about me changing and growing, and all that, but really, he long ago decided how things are, what I am, who I am, and he doesn't really believe that anything can change. It's much easier for him to assume that they will always remain the way they were. It's like the lady in the story. She is such a victim of routine, too hardened and cynical to *really* believe that her dreams can come true, so she would rather not pursue them past the talking stage."

Moishy nodded slowly. "I hear you. You think that your father is incapable of getting past what happened last year and immediately assumes that you are the same person?"

The thought was horrible. Ezzy, who gave time, energy, and encouragement to the often-demoralized residents of Mishkan Shalom in his every free second, the same boy as the popular, happy-go-lucky, self-absorbed class leader of last year?

Then, deep in Moishy's unconscious, another thought struck. What about *him?* Was he like that grandmother, unwilling to believe in change, in dreams being fulfilled, in new beginnings?

Chaim Weinstein was confused. Things had been going better for him than they had been going in a long time. His nightly learning sessions with Benjy had given him a new reason to go on, a sense of meaning and purpose in his whole day — in his whole life! He had enjoyed his budding relationship with Reb Anshel and even felt like he actually had a place in the neighborhood. The small room was starting to feel like his spiritual home, and he found that he was able to daven there the way he had once davened.

The effects of his growth were being felt at home, too. He knew that Chana Rivka was proud of him, and her pride was like water on a plant; he grew still further.

And now, everything seemed to have come crashing down. Night seder had suddenly stopped. Well, it hadn't really stopped, but it had lost a lot of its flavor without Reb Anshel and the boys there. Mendel Wasser was still trying valiantly to create an atmosphere, but the residents seemed demoralized.

He still learned with Benjy each night — the *yahrzeit* of Benjy's father was just a few days away and they still had an entire *perek* to do — but even Benjy wasn't the same. He told Chaim about how Reb Anshel's daughter didn't really like them at all, none of them, and wouldn't let her father come out anymore. Benjy said nothing about Ezzy and Moishy; it was too painful for him to talk about it. He knew that Ezzy had done nothing wrong, even though some of the residents had heard from their family members that he had.

The only reference that Benjy made to the whole episode was when he commented to Chaim that he hoped that they would actually learn together until they finished the *mesechta*.

"I might be going to jail any day," he had said.

Chaim had turned to regard him with interest.

"Not because of anything I did, but don't tell them I said that. It's just that something bad happened and they are accusing someone else. But that person is a big *tzaddik,* and he for sure shouldn't go to jail, so I want to go."

Then Benjy burst into tears.

Chapter 43

Malka felt self-conscious, plain and simple. She felt silly sitting in her car, like a cab driver waiting for a fare, casting furtive glances in each and every direction. Each time a car slowed down next to her, she would stare straight ahead, hoping they wouldn't notice her, hoping they wouldn't wonder — even worse, figure out — what she was doing there.

She had checked her appearance in the mirror and straightened up the glove compartment, but now she was out of time-wasting activities. This would never have happened to Aryeh, she thought. He had the car equipped with various resources that ensured he would never be bored. He had a mishnayos and a daf-yomi Gemara in the pouch behind the driver's seat, and even kept plastic cutlery in the glove compartment so that he could use time spent waiting in the car for a quick bite. Between his *sefarim,* Blackberry, and food, he was never bored. Why couldn't she be more prepared? There she was, trapped in her car, on the verge of tears, with absolutely nothing to do!

She glanced at the clock. Five-fifteen. It was almost time. She looked up and down the sidewalks again and whispered words of Tehillim.

Ezzy walked down the quiet street, the weight of the world on his young shoulders. How pitiful it was to walk home after a long day of school toward someone else's house. He wished he could just turn around and run back home, but there was something keeping him. He sensed that this was something he had to do. If he wasn't going to respect himself, then he couldn't expect others to respect him.

He walked reluctantly down the unfamiliar block, headed towards the Wasser home. It seemed that every house he passed was welcoming its own, inviting loved ones in with a happy embrace. A father parked his car and hurried up the front walk of a house to his left as a gaggle of young children tore out from inside, laughing excitedly. An elderly man walked haltingly up the stairs as his wife waited expectantly by the window, watching his every step with loving concern.

It's just me who has nowhere to go, he thought. Occupied by that unhappy reflection, he suddenly stopped and stiffened. The gray Camry parked a few feet ahead of his was too familiar.

Mommy! He felt a pang of affection.

Without turning his head, he checked if she was alone; she was. His heart leapt, and he unabashedly ran toward the car. He threw open the passenger door and plopped down. Malka reached out and embraced him.

░▌▐▌▐░▐▌▐▌▐░▐▌▐░

Malka wasn't sure what to say to her son, but in truth, she was ecstatic just to sit with him in silence. She kept reaching out and touching him, and, uncharacteristically, he didn't shrug her off.

Suddenly, she burst into tears. "Oh, Ezzy," she said and started to weep.

He looked at her and it was clear that he was struggling with his own tears.

He didn't speak, however, and she finally voiced the questions that had been weighing on her mind for the previous two days — *was that all it was? It seemed like so much longer* — since he had left home.

"Ezzy, when will this be over? How long will you punish us? Are you ever planning to come home? Are you sleeping well? Eating well?"

And she burst into a fresh round of tears.

"Oh, Mommy. I can't stand it here anymore. I came because I had nowhere else to be, but I didn't stop to think what it would be like. I mean, they are wonderful people, the Wassers, they really are, but it's a little kid family. There are so many of them, always asking me why I am there, if I have a Tatty and Mommy, if I am going home ….

"Ma, I was starving the night I came, and do you know what Mrs. Wasser served for supper? Macaroni and cheese. You know I hate macaroni and cheese, and all the kids were grabbing and mixing it with all kinds of strange stuff, so I lost my appetite."

Ezzy paused as Malka burst out laughing. *This* was her Ezzy speaking.

"Ma, I sleep on a bunk bed and at six o'clock in the morning, the little boy on top, Shmuli, jumps down on me and asks me if I want to wash *negel vasser*. They try so hard to be nice to me, and will do anything to make me feel comfortable, but it's not home. I miss your food, the way my pillows smell, everything. I can't take this."

Was it really going to be this simple? Malka exulted. "Okay, so you'll just take your stuff and go say thank-you, and we will go back home. I will make you anything in the world that you want for supper and then you'll take a good hot shower and sleep in your bed."

Ezzy was quiet as he visibly sobered up.

"What?" Malka asked. "Do you want me to come in with you and say thank-you as well? Obviously, it's hard for me, but I will do it if it's what you want me to do."

"No, Ma, it's not that at all. It's that I can't — won't — come home yet. I don't think you realize what this is about. I don't want to hear from Tatty that he is there for me, or that he will make things right — I only want to hear one thing; that *he knows that I didn't do it.*"

"Okay, Ezzy, no problem. You didn't do it. Now let's end this little nightmare and come home with me."

Ezzy spoke with a maturity beyond his years, and despite her anguish, Malka felt her heart soar with pride. "Ma, it's not enough to say it, I need you both to believe it. Until then, I am not coming home."

For the first time, the message penetrated. "What are you going to do, Ezzy?" Malka finally asked.

"Well, school is over in just a few days, and then I will go far away. If you are willing to pay for my ticket, I would love to spend a few weeks with Chavi in Yerushalayim. I need to get away. After that, we'll see."

"Please, Ezzy, just come home. Your father will come around. We are convinced that you did not do it."

As Ezzy contemplated her words, she ruined everything. "Ezzy, I don't care if you *did* do it; we want you with us, at home."

Ezzy looked at her. "See, Ma? You just said it. Loving me doesn't mean not caring if I did it. It means believing that I didn't."

He leaned over and gave her a kiss before opening his door. "See you Ma. Thanks for the visit."

Malka looked at him. "Are you serious? You are going back there?"

"Yup. I will go back. *They* may serve macaroni and cheese and have a noisy home, but *they* don't think I did it."

It had been a rough week for Chaim Weinstein. The last few *mishnayos* of the *mesechta* weren't going well; Benjy was simply too depressed about Ezzy. Chaim missed having Reb Anshel around and the sparse, lackluster crowd at night seder was making it difficult to finish up. The *yahrzeit* was two days away, and they had to finish, but Benjy had lost much of his resolve. Chaim decided that he would have to give Benjy a pep talk.

"Benjy, you are doing this for your father's *neshamah*. Think how proud he will be up in *Shamayim,* if you push through."

"I know, I know, but I so badly wanted to have a real *siyum,* with Reb Anshel there, and Ezzy there."

Benjy was still miffed that Ari Engel didn't believe his admission of guilt and when Benjy had insisted that he had taken Reb Anshel's money, he had merely told him that he was very sweet for trying to take the heat off Ezzy.

"Benjy, you learned this *mesechta* for your father. Let's stay focused on the fact that the holy words of Torah join together and lift his *neshamah* so much higher. That's the important thing."

But even as he reassured Benjy, Chaim was determined that Reb Anshel would be at the *siyum*. He had to be. For Benjy's sake.

Gitty Wasser was a creature of the night. Her most productive hours were late at night, when the rest of the house was silent. It was then that she prepared her lessons for class and then that she had time to think.

She tiptoed up the creaky hallway of her home at one forty-five a.m., looking in on each of her kids as she passed. They were all sleeping soundly. She paused by the door of the boy's room, and her gaze rested on the sleeping adolescent in the bottom bunk. Even in sleep, Ezzy's' features were uneasy.

Hashem should just have mercy on that boy! she thought as she continued toward the kitchen. She wasn't completely sure what he was doing in her home, and knew just that he felt more comfortable with Mendel than with his own father. It seemed that his father believed that he had taken the money from Reb Anshel — everyone believed it. She had heard it from so many different sources.

She didn't believe it, however. Mendel had assured her that it was impossible, but she knew it even without Mendel's assurances. Gitty Wasser was a very perceptive woman, and she was certain that this boy was not a thief.

And there, in the middle of the night, as Gitty Wasser poured herself a drink and contemplated Ezzy's situation, she made a commitment. It was so simple. She would find out who really stole the money, and that way, Ezzy would be off the hook.

Why hadn't she thought of it earlier? It was obvious. She would call her sister as soon as it was light outside and they would leave no stone unturned. Together, they would find the real culprit and Ezzy would be revealed for what he really was: a sweet, innocent kid.

She could hardly wait for morning!

Chapter 44

Malka was strangely conscious of being watched, and it was bothering her. When she finished washing her coffee mug, she turned from the sink and was unnerved to see Aryeh just sitting there, staring straight ahead.

It irritated her. Were they some old, retired couple with nothing to do but sit and gape at each other all day? *Run along,* she wanted to say. *Don't you have work to do, a daf to complete, a meeting to attend?* This was so not Aryeh, so not her busy, self-demanding husband.

Having him home made her especially insecure, as if he would suddenly start questioning how she spent her mornings, if she was really as productive as she could be, if maybe she should take a part-time teaching job, just to have a schedule ....

Though Aryeh sometimes came back home after Shacharis for a quick bite, he would never stay more than a few minutes, and would rush, rush, rush through breakfast, the frantic rustle of newspaper pages the only background noise. This morning was different. He hadn't eaten anything at all, just sipped his coffee so slowly that it had grown cold, and sat there in morose silence, looking at her.

He had been this way since the night before, when she had shared her conversation with Ezzy with him. He had listened in disbelief, his expression alternating between raw pain and stunned incredulity. She had actually been pleasantly surprised at his reaction.

He hadn't checked his Blackberry, looked pointedly at his watch, brushed his hat, or done any of the other things that he usually did when a conversation got too personal for him. For the first time in over twenty years, she saw her husband *there,* emotionally there, living a situation along with her, feeling the pain as acutely as she did. They were joined, joined in pain.

They had both slept little throughout the night, and this morning, after Shacharis, when she had been sure he would hurry off into the welcome distractions of a new business day, he had instead come home. And home he had remained, following her like a little puppy, and to be honest, she found it unsettling. First of all, she wanted to cry, and she couldn't allow herself a good cry with him around. Then, she wanted to reach Ezzy, to tell him how his father was suffering, to beg him to accept their *teshuvah.*

Aryeh finally spoke. "Malka,' he said, still wearing his shell-shocked look, "let's go find Ezzy and bring him home. I will apologize. I am sorry. I love him and want him back here, under our roof."

He somehow sensed that, in this entire situation, it was Malka who had the answers and not he, and, uncharacteristically, it was he reaching out to her for help.

She sat down and looked right at him, speaking slowly, as one might address a child. "Aryeh, Aryeh … he doesn't want your apologies. He wants you to feel his pain, understand his anger, to experience what he has been experiencing for the past few days. Maybe then he'll listen to your apologies."

Aryeh was quiet, and then he stood up and walked to the window, still lost in thought. The street outside looked as it always did at nine-thirty in the morning. Across the street, a gardener worked on a lilac bush with intense concentration, and on the sidewalk in front of the house next door, two elderly women chatted in the bright sunlight.

Aryeh tuned back to her, but his eyes were elsewhere. "Malka, since the day my father died, when I was just eleven, I have never really had the luxury of 'feeling,' or 'understanding,' for me things were always how they seemed. It wasn't that I *felt* like an orphan, I really was an orphan. I didn't have time to experience pain; I was too busy running to make money so that my mother wouldn't be thrown out of another apartment. No one asked me if I was angry about never even having time to enjoy a simple punch-ball game, because anger wouldn't have helped; I had no time for friends and games. It wasn't about feelings."

He paused, and Malka suddenly grew worried that he would stop talking. She had never heard this type of talk from him. Each time he said the word *felt* or *feelings*, he would draw it out sarcastically, as if feeling were a new luxury that only she and Ezzy found necessary, but still, she wanted him to continue.

He did. "I trained myself to stay focused on my goal, to learn Torah and get good grades so that I would, one day, be able to provide for a family and help my mother out. I never looked past what I saw, because that would have been dangerous for me, it would never have helped. It wouldn't have brought my father back to life or kept pushy landlords off my mother's back. I learned to deal with what I saw in front of me, to see things in black and white.

"Then, when, with Hashem's help, I realized my dreams, when I can finally taste tranquility and security, my sixteen-year-old son wants me to do it the other way. Malka, I don't know if I am capable of that. I work with what I see on the table. Maybe, hopefully, I am wrong about Ezzy and he had no part in taking the money. I am willing to apologize to him, but I am not sure how I can feel what he feels. I wouldn't know which button to press."

Malka wiped the tears from her eyes. She knew that there was only one way to bring Aryeh around. He would have to *see,* with his own practical eyes, that he had been wrong. Now the only question was how in the world she could make him see.

There was only one way. The Aryeh Markstein way — in black and white.

Frieda Finestone was irritated. She has just attacked a pile of dirty laundry when the doorbell rang yet again. She was downstairs in her basement and now she would have to climb up the narrow staircase to see who it was.

She opened the door to a youngish woman of maybe thirty or so, with a sensible, no-nonsense look about her. "Hi, Mrs. Finestone. Can I ask for a minute of your time?"

Frieda stared at the visitor in wonder. *Life insurance? Nah, couldn't be. This woman was very yeshivish, and also, she didn't have any blue plastic folders filled with papers under her arm.*

Tzedakah? No, also not. The woman was too put-together for that.

Frieda tried to look gracious. "Um, and you are?"

The woman held her gaze. "Oh, I am so sorry, didn't I say? My name is Gitty Wasser. May I come in?"

Frieda realized that she had little choice.

"Okay then, I guess you could, but don't look around. The house is a total mess."

Gitty nodded at this timeless introduction of women throughout the ages, replying in kind.

"Oh, you should see my house. It's a lot worse."

Frieda showed her to the living room and offered her coffee. Gitty shook her head determinedly. "No, thank you. I would prefer to get straight to the point."

Frieda didn't like the way this Gitty woman was making her feel like a guest in her own living room.

"Mrs. Finestone, are you familiar with the *parashah* in the Torah of *eglah arufah*?"

Frieda wondered if this was some kind of joke.

She didn't even bother being polite. "Did I call rent-a-*shiur* or something?"

Gitty just smiled, brimming with self-assurance, and continued, as if Frieda hadn't said anything at all.

"So after the dead body is discovered, the *zekeinim* from the city from which he left must seek atonement for not having accompanied him. They have to proclaim that their hands didn't spill blood — *Yadeinu lo shafchu ess hadam hazeh.*"

Gitty had taught *Parashas Shoftim* that year and the words rolled off her tongue. Frieda was fidgeting uncomfortably.

"What do you want?"

"Mrs. Finestone, I have a young boy in my home. His name is Ezzy Markstein and his own father, as well as many, many other people, believes he stole your father's money."

So that is what this is about!

Frieda was struck by a sudden thought.

"What did you say your name was?"

"Wasser. Gitty Wasser."

Frieda smiled smugly. "Oh, so your husband works over there ... at that place."

"That's right."

Frieda crossed her arms. "Well, you sure stick together."

It was Gitty's turn to stare at her.

She went back to her original speech.

"Mrs. Finestone, I just want to ask you one question. Ezzy has left his home, because he has been deeply pained by the accusations. He is hurting badly, very badly. I want to know if, when these wounds become too much for him to handle, will you be able to stand up and say '*Yadeinu lo shafchu ess hadam hazeh*'?"

Frieda let out a little gasp and Gitty knew she had gotten through.

"What are you suggesting? I *certainly* didn't accuse him. What does this have to do with me?"

Gitty placed her hands on the other woman's shoulders. "What I want from you is to sit down with me and, calmly and methodically, try to figure out if perhaps there's someone else who might have taken that money."

Frieda held her head. She felt a migraine coming on.

Our hands have not spilled this blood ....

"Oh, alright then. Come to the kitchen and let me make you a cup of coffee."

Gitty followed Frieda into her kitchen and gingerly sat down. She removed a pen and paper from her purse and started to write with a flourish. She started with the date and then spoke enthusiastically, as naturally as if they were working on a high-school yearbook together.

"Okay, tell me anyone who came into the house over the last few weeks who was not from your family — and leave out the Mishkan Shalom people, please."

Frieda closed her eyes and leaned her head back against the wall.

"Okay, there was a plumber, and also a washing-machine repairman. My father had some visitors from the old neighborhood one day, and there was also the cleaning lady, Delmy, but she's already gone ...."

Chapter 45

The day off couldn't have come at a better time. For the students in the middle of final exams, the break was most welcome, but for their teacher — Gitty — it provided the perfect opportunity to follow her lead. And so, at eleven o'clock on a Tuesday morning, she was navigating traffic, construction and aggressive driving on the BQE, very much enjoying the feeling of playing sleuth. She looked at the small scrap of paper on the seat next to her as if for reassurance and felt a little stab of pleasure, like a child discovering the next clue in a treasure hunt.

She followed the exit through the industrial scenery and into chassidic Williamsburg: laughing mothers steering double strollers through crowded sidewalks, beautiful children chattering animatedly as they lingered in the early summer sunshine.

Gitty pulled over and then took the first available parking spot. How big could the whole neighborhood be already? Two blocks?

Ten minutes later, she was hot and exhausted and realizing just how big the neighborhood could be. Though she didn't really like asking for directions — it just wasn't something that came naturally to her — she finally stopped a teenage girl and asked her how to get to 317 Wyeth Street.

The girl stared at her silence, and Gitty's discomfort grew. Had she said something wrong? Wasn't it pronounced Wy-eth? Finally, the girl shrugged and pointed her in the right direction.

And so it was, when Gitty Wasser finally came to apartment 7D, she was already at a disadvantage. She had been walking for twenty minutes and it showed. When she had finally found the building, the elevators had been out of order and she'd had to walk up fourteen flights of stairs.

Now, as she knocked at the door with the modest "Mishpachas Horowitz" plaque on its door, she was overcome by a very rare spell of self-doubt. Was this really her business? Why hadn't she been content to just let things be?

A little boy who couldn't be more than two years old opened the door and led her toward the kitchen, where his mother sat at the table. Gitty was already apprehensive about coming, and the sight of Bleemy Horowitz only made it worse.

The tall, black-kerchiefed woman at the table radiated strength and capability. She was speaking into one phone and holding another, with two cellphones on the table in front of her. Her kitchen was immaculate, as was the entire apartment, and the smell of fresh cake wafted from the oven.

To add to Gitty's discomfort, her hostess barely acknowledged her presence, and just went on speaking in exaggeratedly loud tones. She was using the English that people use when addressing foreigners who hardly know the language, as if her listener's lack of proficiency had suddenly rendered her unable to speak English as well.

"Listen, Marina no come anymore by bus; Marina come by taxi and lady pay," she shouted.

It sounded like Marina was either crying or laughing, but Gitty couldn't make out her response.

Bleemy was still shouting, but with forced calm. "What? Marina husband drive taxi? So then Marina go husband, me no care, just Marina come to lady eight o'clock, no later."

Bleemy turned back to the other phone. "Mrs. Hirschberg, I don't want to threaten you, but if you persist in paying Anna more than your neighbors and friends, even if she gives you her extra hours, you will lose in the long run. I, as well as every single other agency with which I am affiliated, will blacklist you and you will never find help again."

Mrs. Hirschberg was obviously arguing, but Bleemy had no patience for it. "No, Mrs. Hirschberg, not a tip, not a Chanukah present, not anything — if you go above the going rate, you will regret it. We are doing our best to satisfy a huge number of clients — please don't break our rules. Goodbye, Mrs. Hirschberg."

Bleemy hung up and looked at Gitty with humorless eyes. "Hello, how can I help you?"

Gitty felt like a shy little girl introducing herself to the head counselor. "My name is Gitty Wasser and I need two minutes of your time."

"I don't have two minutes," said Bleemy, and it was clear that she wasn't being facetious, only stating the obvious.

Both cellphones were chirping, her baby was howling and the two-year old doorman was clearly hungry.

Gitty had no smooth arguments for a woman far smoother than she, and no strength against this picture of confidence.

She looked into the other woman's eyes and whimpered, "Please. It's important."

Bleemy Horowitz studied Gitty for a moment and obviously decided that she deserved a chance. She placed the phone in her hand down on the table with a bang, lifted her baby in a seemingly effortless motion and, with her free hand, took two glasses from a cabinet.

Glasses? Had this woman ever heard of plastic? Gitty thought as Bleemy poured her a generous serving of home-made iced coffee.

Bleemy gestured toward the sofa at the end of the living room, which was really part of the dining room. There were high *sefarim* shelves reaching to the ceiling, every inch crammed with holy books, but here there was order. Gitty couldn't help thinking of Mendel's mismatched sets, orange *sefarim* next to blue ones, tall ones leaning on short stubby ones.

"Yes." It wasn't a question, but a statement.

Gitty spoke hurriedly. "Okay, I will try to make this fast. I have a friend — actually my husband does, he — no, forget it. The main thing is that someone stole money from a woman and she is accusing a yeshivah *bachur* of it and he is innocent, so I am trying to find out whom else it could be and save this *bachur* from the false accusation. This woman mentioned that she had some cleaning help who quit shortly before the theft was discovered."

"Why didn't this woman immediately think of the cleaning help, then?"

Gitty was amazed at Bleemy's quick grasp of the facts.

"Good question. I think it's because her household help routinely quits on her, so she immediately assumes it's her fault, and also because the fact that the money was missing wasn't discovered until a few days after this cleaning woman quit."

"So why do you assume that it *was* the cleaning woman?"

"Because it wasn't Ezzy and the fact that they didn't discover the theft immediately means nothing to me, that's why." Gitty felt her confidence returning as Bleemy listened to her. "Mrs. Finestone simply doesn't see the whole picture, though–she is the type who makes up her mind right away and then sticks with it."

Bleemy interrupted. "Finestone; two in Boro Park, one in Crown Heights, one in Kensington, and one in Bensonhurst. Which one?"

Gitty was amazed. "Kensington," she said in breathless admiration.

Bleemy nodded. "Yes, she really doesn't have too much mazel with help. She is pretty demanding and it never really works out for her. I think my daughter handled that one, I have to ask her."

Her daughter? She has a married daughter too? She looks like she is twenty-five!

"Anyhow, how can I help you?" asked Bleemy.

"Well, I figured that, since it was your agency that sent Delmy, perhaps you have her full name and address on file. If you can give me that, I will handle the rest."

"Oh, Delmy, I remember that name. Let me ask Toby."

Bleemy reached into the pocket of her housecoat and pulled out a cellphone.

"Hi, *sheife'lah,*" she said, "do you have the name and address for Delmy in your files? Is she still with us?"

Bleemy listened for a minute and then wrote something down.

She hung up and turned back to Gitty. "She is no longer with our agency. I don't know what she does, but after quitting Mrs. Finestone, she informed us that she wanted to do other work, and my daughter doesn't know what she does now."

Bleemy was speaking pointedly, as if they were suddenly partners in solving this crime, and this new information was crucial. Gitty was thrilled at the thought of joining forces with this dynamo.

"Here is the address," she said, handing Gitty a perfect square of paper with a name and address written in impeccable handwriting.

Delmy Alvarez 354 Jefferson Street 718.386.3875.

Gitty accepted the paper from Bleemy as if it were some sort of precious gift, the gratitude welling up deep within her and rising through her body into a whispered "Thank you."

Bleemy responded with a dignified nod and turned back to her ringing phones and crying baby.

"Hatzlachah."

This wasn't easy for him, but for some reason, he was being made to suffer extra. Malka had waited for a few minutes before getting to see Ezzy, but he wasn't that fortunate. Aryeh had been parked in front of the Wasser home for almost an hour and Ezzy hadn't appeared, and now, when he had finally had enough and decided to ring the bell, there was no answer.

Aryeh stood there, at a loss as to how to proceed, when his phone rang. He looked down at the screen. It was Malka.

"Yes?" he answered.

Her voice was gentle. "I think you should come home now, honey," she said.

"But he isn't here and I want to see him."

Her heart broke for him. *When would this punishment end?*

"It doesn't seem like he's there anymore, Aryeh. I think he's moved on.'

She let the words sink in, and before he could reply, she continued. "Why don't you come home now and we'll discuss this further?"

It had been a long day for Gitty. It was late afternoon and she had already let Mendel know that he should be home to welcome the kids and give them supper. She was too focused on her goal.

She had bravely ventured down the streets of Bushwick, not the friendliest neighborhood, quieting her pounding heart with the reminder that *shluchei mitzvah einam nizakin*, and that she, who was on a holy mission, would certainly be spared any harm.

She had interrupted a policeman in mid-doughnut and asked him for help with directions — this wasn't Williamsburg, and she would *not* get lost here — and after looking at her curiously, he had wiped the crumbs from his mouth and instructed her to follow his car.

And thus, she approached the grimy building on Jefferson Avenue with hope in her heart and a prayer on her lips.

Chapter 46

The *gabbai* took one last look at the empty waiting room before turning off the lights. Another night, another stream of desperate Yidden seeking counsel and encouragement coming through the Rebbe's study. The *gabbai* stepped into the Rebbe's room and stood by the door.

"There is no one left," he said.

"Are you sure?" asked the Rebbe. This was a nightly ritual.

"I am sure," replied the *gabbai*. Only when the Rebbe nodded did the devoted *gabbai* depart. Now, at ten minutes to midnight, he would hurry home so that he might eat his own supper.

The Rebbe heaved a sigh and rose to his feet. He opened the door in the corner of his study that led to his home and smiled at the teenage boy who sat in the kitchen, sipping orange juice.

The Rebbe sat down at the table across from him and poured himself a drink as well.

"Okay, Ezzy, let's schmooze," he said.

Ezzy was not a chassid, nor was he descended from chassidim, but here he was, just the same. He had known throughout this ordeal that what he really needed was a Rebbe, someone to talk to. Mendel was wonderful, but he wasn't the advice-giving type. Ezzy had tried speaking with his rebbi at school, but the complexity of his issue made it difficult to express himself. This morning, when he had awoken and headed off to school, he had known with a certainty that he had spent his last night at the Wasser home. It was too much for him, the unfamiliarity, the noise, the confusion; what he really wanted to do was to go home, but with each passing day, he felt it harder to do so.

He had spent the morning contemplating a course of action. He had to leave Mendel's; he couldn't go home. He needed a quiet place where he could buy time to figure out a course of action. He needed someone who would listen to him — not sit silently, but *really* listen — and found himself wishing that he was a chassid with a Rebbe ....

Then, his thoughts had reverted to the *chanukas habayis* at Mishkan Shalom and his brief conversation with Naftuli's father, the Rebbe. It had been all too short, but Ezzy had felt a spark of connection, felt as if he were somehow understood.

So that's how it came to be that Ezzy slipped out of school, intent on finding the Rebbe. He remembered the *beis medrash* well — they had been there on Purim night — and he made the journey to Boro Park on foot, enjoying the sunshine on the back of his neck. He had arrived at the large building at about eleven-thirty and was suddenly overcome by self-consciousness. What *was* he doing? He shrugged his shoulders — this was a new Ezzy Markstein, on a new journey, and he was not yet sure where the path would lead — and pushed open the large door.

The smell was one of damp towels and coffee, but it was not at all unpleasant. It was, in some strange way, almost homey and Ezzy thought that he might cry. He ventured further into the building and was surprised to see the *beis medrash* alive with people, some learning, some davening, and some just chatting. His entrance attracted no attention, and he slipped into a corner, hoping to see the Rebbe. The Rebbe was clearly not in the room, however, and as he stood there uncertainly, a friendly young man came over and greeted him. "Hi, shalom aleichem. My name is Nochum. Are you looking for something?"

"Um, I would like to speak with the Rebbe," Ezzy said.

"Oh?"

The fellow's eyebrows arched as he studied Ezzy. Ezzy looked at the floor uncomfortably. He would *not*, under any circumstances, share his story with this guy. Nochum stood there expectantly for a few moments, hoping he would hear about Ezzy's connection to the Rebbe, but when he realized that no further details would be forthcoming, he shuffled off toward an older man in the corner of the room.

Ezzy felt their eyes at his back, and was soon called over. The older man, who seemed to be a *gabbai,* asked what he wanted.

"To speak with the Rebbe," Ezzy replied firmly.

"The Rebbe sees people after Mincha–Maariv on Mondays and Thursdays. Today is Wednesday and people are still davening Shacharis." The *gabbai* gestured at the activity around them.

Ezzy met his gaze. "This is an emergency."

The *gabbai* didn't move. "Who are you?" he asked.

"My name is Ezzy. I am a friend of Naftuli's."

There. He had pressed the magic button.

The *gabbai* hurried off into a different room, speaking heatedly into his cellphone.

Within minutes, he returned and beckoned Ezzy to follow him. Ezzy had gone after him and accompanied him into a maze of hallways and rooms. The *gabbai* stopped at one door and knocked softly; it was opened almost immediately by the Rebbe himself.

Ezzy was once again struck by the noble countenance. The Rebbe smiled warmly at him and ushered him in. The curious *gabbai* accompanied Ezzy into the room, but the Rebbe gestured to him and he stepped back out.

The Rebbe showed Ezzy to a chair.

"Remind me of your name, please."

Ezzy said his name and the Rebbe smiled again.

The Rebbe sat silently, but Ezzy felt emboldened to speak, to open up his heart and allow the raging river of emotion to come pouring out.

The Rebbe listened closely; a listening that was as comforting as an embrace and as refreshing as a glass of cold water.

The *gabbai* knocked softly at the door at one point, but the Rebbe ignored it.

The Rebbe never spoke, not once. Ezzy spared no detail, describing the bunk bed in the Wasser home and the little boy and the *negel vasser.* The Rebbe laughed heartily at the picture he painted, and then grew serious again.

Only when Ezzy fell silent did he speak.

"Your question, Ezzy, is not whether your father loves you or not. You know your parents love you and that you want to be home. Your question is just how far to go with this campaign you've launched."

Ezzy thought he heard a reprimand in the Rebbe's voice.

"So Ezzy, here's what we are going to do. I want you to sleep here tonight — don't worry, there's no bunk bed and you'll be comfortable — and call your parents and tell them that you're safe. Tonight we will work this thing through; later tonight, when I have time to talk. For now, go back to school and then get your stuff from Mendel's house."

The Rebbe reached into his pocket and handed Ezzy a $20 bill. "This is for a car service," he said.

Gitty was single-minded. She had found the apartment building on Jefferson Street and even located the correct apartment, but was having trouble convincing the old man who stood in the doorway. He was a wizened little man in an ill-fitting bathrobe, and kept asking her why she needed Delmy. He wouldn't listen to her answers though, and kept threatening that he would close the door. Gitty knew that she had him, however — if he really meant it, he would have closed it immediately — and wouldn't give up.

Finally, when she waved an assortment of cards from her pocket book at him — a driver's license, two bank cards, and a *tefillas haderech* and told him that she would call the police if he wouldn't help, he capitulated. He studied the cards with a dubious expression in his rheumy eyes, then cursed at her in his native tongue and spat on the floor.

"Dunkin Donuts," he finally said, "next block."

Gitty thanked him sweetly and turned.

Aryeh walked into the house, his shoulders sagging. "So where is Ezzy?" he asked.

Malka walked over to where he stood and he could see that her nerves were equally frayed.

"He seems to have left the Wasser's home and gone to stay with some Rebbe in Boro Park. He called and assured me that he's okay."

Aryeh exploded. "My son needs to sleep on a bench in someone's shul? Malka, the boy is deranged."

She felt for her husband, but he needed to hear it. "Aryeh, maybe not … maybe he's not deranged; just hurt, and this is the only way he knows how to make us listen."

Aryeh knew that she was being generous with the *we* and that she really meant *you*. He sat down heavily and looked at her. "Okay, okay. I believe," he said.

***

It was quiet when Gitty walked into Dunkin Donuts and she headed straight to the counter. "Delmy?" she inquired of the server.

"No, I'm not Delmy."

At hearing her name mentioned, a heavyset woman with large glasses turned toward Gitty. Her eyes widened in shock as she took in the Jewish woman and she stepped back.

"What do you want from me?" she whispered.

"Just a minute of your time, *Delmy*." Gitty drew out the name, as if to say, *I know your name and I know everything else as well.*

Delmy looked at her colleague, who nodded disinterestedly, and she came around the counter to where Gitty was.

"What?"

"Delmy, do you have children?"

Delmy's face was a mixture of distrust and bewilderment.

"Yes," she finally answered. "I do. A little boy, Aidan."

Gitty smiled sweetly. "That's wonderful. Now let me tell you a story about another boy. His name is Ezzy and he's someone's little boy. He also has a mother and she misses him."

Again, Gitty reverted to teacher mode, the words rolling smoothly off her tongue as Delmy sat and listened.

Tears formed in her eyes as Gitty described Malka's waiting in the car to see her son.

"Imagine that was your Aidan," Gitty said.

But tears or no tears, Delmy looked stubbornly at Gitty when the narrative was over.

"What does this have to do with me?" she asked.

"Oh, just that if I have to have the police launch an investigation into what happened to the money and they should find you guilty, well ... then you would miss Aidan just like Malka misses Ezzy, right?"

"Let's say that I tell you that I took the money?" Delmy asked.

"Then you will give it back and we will move on," Gitty replied.

"What if I don't have it anymore?" Delmy almost whimpered.

"You can take your time; pay back a little each month."

Delmy looked to the counter and then back at Gitty.

"I took it," she said quickly.

Gitty patterd her arm. 'Thank you, Delmy, that was very big of you. I hope that your Aidan will give you lots of joy. I just need one more thing of you for now."

Gitty dialed the Markstein home and handed the phone to Delmy.

"Ask for Mr. Markstein. If he's not home, leave a message. Tell him what you just told me."

Chapter 47

N ervous, nervous, nervous. Aryeh hadn't felt like this since he had been in *shidduchim,* the butterflies in his stomach, the anxious looks at the clock, the mild but unrelenting headache. And whom was he going to meet? His son. His only son. The one who was staying in the home of some chassidic Rebbe and couldn't take his phone call.

He had been brought to his knees yesterday by Gitty Wasser; she had put him on the phone with some cleaning lady who incomprehensively admitted having taken the money from the Finestone home.

Strangely, it had made sense to him. He hadn't been surprised at all. He had hoped all along that it wasn't Ezzy and had only been making sure. He had tried to call Ezzy and apologize, but hadn't reached him.

He'd had to resort to a tip from Mendel Wasser, (*look who was taking advice from whom!*) who had called this morning, speaking in his eager-to-please manner. "Mr. Markstein, I was just thinking; I am sure that Ezzy will be at Benjy's *siyum* tonight. He wouldn't miss it for anything. Why don't you come there?"

So here he was, sitting in his busy office, surrounded by ringing phones and paperwork, unable to do anything besides look at the clock and wait for seven-thirty.

Chaim Weinstein was surprised at how easy it had been. He had rang the doorbell of the Finestone home and explained that his *chavrusa,* Benjy, was making a *siyum* and that Reb Anshel's presence would make a world of difference. Mrs. Finestone hadn't even argued. She had asked him to wait for a few minutes while she got her father ready and then thanked him. What was that about? He had no way of knowing about Delmy's confession and the guilt that had followed Freida all day like a trail of black smoke.

Chaim had taken his Rebbi, Reb Anshel, by the arm and led him toward his car, feeling prouder than he'd felt in years.

Ruth Biller had been dressed in her Shabbos best since eleven o'clock in the morning and was sitting in her small kitchen, gripping the arm of her daughter, who had come in from Jersey especially for this event. Would there be enough room? Too much room? She rearranged the rugelach on a tray in front of her for the tenth time and peered into the oven again, checking the progress of her apple strudel. Would they eat?

Benjy was in his room, oblivious to her nervousness. He was practicing the last mishnah in *Mesechta Succah*, preparing for his big moment.

Nathan, she thought again of her deceased husband, Benjy's father, *this is all for you ....*

The room was filling up. All Benjy's friends from Mishkan Shalom were there, as well as most of the staff. Even Leizer Krause, Mendel's predecessor, had come from Monsey. Benjy's coworkers were there as well, as were some neighbors of his mother. His *chavrusa*, Chaim, sat next to him and at the head of the table sat Reb Anshel himself. Benjy had almost fainted when the old man with the flowing beard had entered, and everyone had risen to their feet in his honor.

Mendel wasn't there yet either, but Benjy wasn't worried about him. He always came through.

But Mendel *was* there. He was standing just outside the door with Ezzy and Moishy, trying to convince Ezzy, who had suddenly developed cold feet, to come in.

"I can't. Nothing is the same anymore. They believe what my father believes."

Mendel looked straight at Ezzy.

"The cleaning lady from Finestone's house called your father last night and admitted that she took the money."

Ezzy's eyes opened wide and he stood there limply. Mendel seized the moment to lead him by the shoulders into the crowded apartment.

The sad, basset-hound eyes of Benjy Biller lit up. "Ezzy!" he cried joyously.

Benjy had read the last mishnah perfectly and had even made it through the *ḥadran* and Kaddish. Chaim had stood next to him every step of the way, helping him along. The shouts of *mazel tov* filled the air and the participants began to sing, *"Siman tov u'mazel tov."*

As they sang, Mendel made two more phone calls. "Come, come already," he spoke urgently into the phone.

They began to dance, Benjy exulting in the moment. His father! He had done it for his father, and he was surrounded by his best friends, Ezzy, Moishy, Mendel, Chaim, Reb Anshel, and all the rest.

Ruth Biller relaxed. "They seem to be enjoying," she remarked to her daughter.

Chaim leaned over to the guest of honor, Reb Anshel, and asked him to speak.

Reb Anshel nodded.

As he began, Mendel noted with satisfaction that Ari Engel had slipped in, and right behind him, Aryeh Markstein.

"There was never a nice day in Thereisenstadt," Reb Anshel was saying, *"but I remember one particularly bitter one, and it was the day, so to speak, that I was born. I had*

already lost everything of meaning, my parents, my siblings, my strength … there was little left to keep me going. I lay there on the icy ground, enduring the vicious blows of a Nazi officer, wishing he would snuff the last breath out of me. I could think of nothing …."

The small room was totally still. Everyone was focused on Reb Anshel, who sat with his eyes closed.

"Then, five words crossed my mind: Neshamah shena-sata bee tehorah hee. My body is not my own. It houses a light that can never be broken or hurt, a fire that can never be extinguished.

"I suddenly felt charged with a sacred mandate to fight, to prove to the beast who stood above me that I had something he didn't.

*"And that was the day that I received a new life, a life of awareness that no one can really do anything to **me** …."'*

Reb Anshel was aware of his own voice, but he couldn't believe it was coming from within him. He hadn't spoken with this kind of passion in years, maybe decades, since the days when he would preach to a full shul, and even then, he had never shared so personal a recollection, though he would remember it anew each morning.

"The reason I mention this now is because my friend, our friend, Benjy, makes me think of that moment every time I see him. He, too, has received blows, hard ones. He lost his father at a young age. He faces all kinds of struggles that other people don't, yet he radiates the purest light in the world. When you see Benjy, you want to embrace him; you feel an instant love for him. Do you know why? It's because he represents 'tehorah hee', he is a pure light, unwilling to let external challenges sully him, break him.

"We all take our beatings, sometimes physical, sometimes spiritual, and sometimes emotional. Remember that

they can get in our way, but they can't touch our essence. Benjy has taught us that. This is his simchah, but it is really a simchah for all of us.

"*Mazel Tov Benjy, Mazel Tov all of you ….*"

The words filled the small apartment, surrounding the people who lined the creaky table and joining them together in a common thought.

Me, too …

Me, too, thought Pinky, Danny, Naftuli, Heshy, and the others from Mishkan Shalom, grown men who had never faced an easy day, who had to contend with doubt and derision, with tongues that couldn't express their eloquent thoughts and feet that couldn't carry out their desire to be swift.

But deep down, where no one can see, we are eloquent, deep down we are swift.

Me, too, thought Chaim Weinstein, who had been pulled down by spiritual failure and disappointment. Recent weeks had allowed him to see the great light housed in his own little home, the respect and steady, unwavering support of his pure wife, and indeed, the light within himself. Benjy had recited the words, *modeh ani lefanecha Hashem Elokai* in the *hadran,* but he spoke for his *chavrusa* as well. Yes, he had learned a lot about himself between the walls of the humble *beis medrash* at Mishkan Shalom.

Me, too thought Moishy Winternitz. He was also battle-scarred, he also bore memories of blows designed to break, but they hadn't reached *him.* He had heard Reb Anshel's words loud and clear: *pure, pure, pure.*

There was no more room at the table, and Ari Engel sat at an uncomfortable angle on the slipcovered beige sofa. He was engaged in a rare moment of soul-searching. He knew that he owed the Markstein boy an apology, and sensed that the Wasser fellow, though he still found him unnerving, was gold. Yes, he may have been guilty of poor judgment, but hadn't the Rav just said that deep down we are all pure?

Mendel Wasser stood by the door. He felt unworthy of being present for such a moment; it was really Gitty who deserved the experience. The looks on the faces of Marksteins, father and son, were only due to her persistence and hard work and he wished that she would be here to enjoy it. His wife ... he was truly blessed. He finally had a job that he loved, where he felt productive and useful. *There are many different ways to be a rebbi*, he mused. He hoped that Ezzy and Moishy would be able to move on, to rejoin his staff; and he would certainly make sure that Reb Anshel would come out again. They needed him, and no one could deny that he needed them ....

Aryeh and Ezzy had no words for each other. They could only sit near each other in silence, Aryeh's arm on Ezzy's shoulder. Reb Anshel had already spoken for them. Ezzy understood that he had been too harsh with his father, who had followed the only path he knew. He knew it now, when he saw the pain in the older man's eyes: *Tatty.*

Aryeh was moved to the very core of his being. The old Rav had shaken him up. Had *he* ever looked at people that way before? Had he seen purity and light, or drawn conclusions based on the facts as he saw them? He wasn't sure if he could change, but he could commit to looking deeper, to perceiving that beyond the black and white there was another dimension, many more layers than met the eye.

Hashem had been kind enough to give him another chance with his son, and he resolved that this time, he would see Ezzy through his wife's eyes, see the *tehorah hee* that she saw every time she looked at him. Together, he and Ezzy, and of course, Malka, would walk away from the past, away from the mistakes, off into a future. A promising future.

Glossary

achdus — unity.

afikoman — the portion of matzah hidden during the Passover Seder and eaten toward its conclusion.

Aibishter— (Yiddish) lit., the One Above; Hashem.

aliyah — lit., going up. 1. the act of being called to recite a blessing at the public reading of the Torah. 2. immigration to Israel.

almanos —widows.

amud — a podium or lectern where the leader of the prayer service (chazzan) stands.

aron kodesh — the ark into which Torah scrolls are placed.

Ashrei—a prayer recited three times daily, taken from the Book of Psalms.

askan (pl.) *askanim* — a community activist.

ayin hara — an evil eye.

ba'alas chessed—a woman who performs acts of loving-kindness.

baal korei — the one who reads from the weekly portion of the Torah.

bachur (pl.) *bachurim* — an unmarried young man, used to denote a student in a yeshivah.

bar mitzvah — 1. a 13-year-old boy. 2. the ceremony marking the coming of age of a Jewish boy.

Baruch Hashem — thank G-d.

bashert — fated.

be'ezras Hashem—with Hashem's help.

bein hazmanim — intersession.

beis medrash — a study hall.

bekeshes —traditional long coat worn by members of certain Chassidic sects.

bentsch— (Yiddish) 1. to bestow a blessing upon. 2. to recite Grace after Meals.

berachah — a blessing.

chaburah — a group (usually a group that learns together).

chanukas hayabis—a housewarming celebration.

chas veshalom — G-d forbid.

chashuv — important.

chassadim—acts of loving-kindness.

chassan — a groom, groom to be.

chassid (pl.) chassidim — a pious man; usually the follower of a Rebbe.

chasunah — a wedding.

chavrusah (pl.) chavrusos — a study partner.

chavrusashaft — (Yiddish) a study partnership.

chazzan — the leader of a prayer service.

chazzaras hashatz — the cantor's repetition of the prayer service.

cheder — school, usu. an elementary school (spec. for Jewish studies).

chessed — kindness.

chinuch — (Jewish) education.

Chol HaMoed — intermediate days of the festivals of Pesach and Succos.

Chumash — one of the Five Books of the Torah; the Five Books collectively.

chuppah — a wedding canopy; a marriage ceremony.

daf yomi — daily study of one folio of the Gemara.

darshaned — lectured, esp. on a Torah topic.

derashos — sermons or discourses.

dofen akumah — lit., bent wall; a halachic principle relevant to Succah.

eglah arufah —lit., calf whose neck is broken; a ceremony performed when a corpse is found between two cities.

ehrliche, ehrlichkeit — (Yiddish) upright; honest.

einekel (pl.) *eineklach* — (Yiddish) grandchild.

Eretz Yisrael — the Land of Israel.

erev — the eve of the Sabbath or a holiday.

frum — religious.

gabbai — synagogue sexton; attendant of a Chassidic Rebbe; person responsible for the proper functioning of a synagogue or other communal body.

gemach — a free-loan society.

gevaldig — (Yiddish) (interjection) great; wonderful.

gut yohr — (Yiddish) a good year.

gut Yom Tov — (Yiddish) happy holiday.

hadran — the prayer recited at the *siyum* (celebration) following the conclusion of the study of a tractate of the Talmud.

HaKadosh Baruch Hu — The Holy One (i.e., Hashem), Blessed be He

halachah (pl.) halachos — Jewish law.

hatzlachah — success.

hesped (pl.) *hespedim* — a eulogy.

hevei dan ess kal ha'adom lekaf zechus — the obligation to judge others favorably.

im yirtzeh Hashem — if Hashem so wills it.

kabbalas panim — a wedding reception that takes place before the ceremony.

Kaddish — prayer said in memory of the dead.

kallah — a bride; an engaged girl.

kashrus — Jewish dietary laws.

kavod — honor.

kehillah — congregation.

kevurah — burial.

kippah — a yarmulke.

kollel — an academy of higher Jewish learning for married students.

Kosel — the Western Wall.

kvittel — a written petition for help or spiritual guidance.

laining — (Yiddish) reading of the Torah in shul.

lamed — a letter of the aleph-beis.

laYehudim — lit., to Jews; the opening words of a joyous song.

leChaim — 1. party celebrating an engagement 2. toast over a drink of wine or whiskey

leichter — (Yiddish) a candelabra.

levayah — a funeral.

Litvak—of Lithuanian descent; non-chassidic.

ma'aser — tithes.

Maariv — the evening prayer service.

ma'avir middos — rise above one's instinctive behavior.

machutenesta — the mother-in-law of one's child.

makom — a place.

mashgichach (pl.) *mashgichim* — (often cap.) dean of students in a yeshivah who oversees students' spiritual and ethical development.

masmid — an exceptionally diligent student.

mazel — luck.

mechazek — to strengthen, often spiritually.

mechillah — forgiveness.

mechitzah — a partition.

mechutanim — the in-laws of one's child.

meis mitzvah—the mitzvah of arranging the burial in a case where there is no one else to do so.

melamed — a teacher.

menahel (pl.) menahelim — a school principal.

menuchas hanefesh—spiritual calm.

mesechta — a tractate of Gemara.

meshulach (pl.) *meshulachim* — an itinerant fundraiser.

mesibah — a celebration.

mesiras nefesh — self-sacrifice.

mesorah — tradition.

mezzuzos—small parchment scrolls affixed to doorposts, containing the first two paragraphs of the Shema prayer.

middah (pl.) *middos* — character trait or attribute.

mikdash — a temple.

Minchah — the afternoon prayer service.

minyan — the quorum of ten adult men needed for communal prayer.

mishnah (pl.) mishnayos — paragraphs of Mishnah, part of the Talmud; the teachings of the Tannaim that form the basis of the Talmud.

mishloach manos — gifts of food sent to friends on Purim.

mispallelim — those who are praying.

mitzvah (pl.) mitzvos — 1. a Torah commandment. 2. a good deed.

Mizrach — East.

mochel — to forgive.

modeh ani lefanecha Hashem Elokai — I thank you, Hashem my G-d.

mossad (pl.) *mosdos* — an institution; often used to refer to a yeshivah.

Motza'ei Shabbos — Saturday night; the time of the departure of the Sabbath.

nachas — satisfaction; pleasure, usually from one's children.

Ne'ilah — the closing prayer on Yom Kippur.

nebech — (Yiddish) (interjection) what a pity!

negel vasser — (Yiddish) water used to wash the hands ritually in the morning.

neshamah — a soul.

"Neshamah shenasata bee tehorah hee" — "The soul that You placed in me is pure."

niftar — a deceased individual.

olav hashalom — lit.,. "peace unto him"; may he rest in peace.

parashah — a portion of the Torah.

parashas hashavua — the Torah portion read during a particular week.

parnassah — livelihood.

paroches — the curtain covering the Torah ark in a synagogue.

perek — a chapter.

peyos — earlocks.

Pirkei Avos — Ethics of the Fathers.

pushkah — a charity collection box.

rebbi — a male teacher.

rachmaneh litzlan — 1. Heaven have mercy. 2. G-d forbid.

refuah sheleimah — lit., a full recovery; a blessing for a speedy recovery.

reshaim — evildoers; wicked people.

Ribono shel Olam — Master of the World; Hashem.

Rosh Yeshivah — the dean of a yeshivah.

ruach — spirit.

seder (pl.) sedarim — 1. study period. 2. (cap.) Pesach night rituals during which the Haggadah is recited.

sefer (pl.) *sefarim* — a book, esp. on a learned topic.

segulah — a spiritual remedy.

seudah — a festive meal on the Shabbos or holidays.

seudah shlishis — the third Shabbos meal.

Shacharis—the morning prayer service.

shadchan (pl.) *shadchanim* — a matchmaker.

shalom aleichem — lit., peace be with you; a traditional greeting.

she'eilah (pl.) *she'eilos* — a halachic query.

sheife'lah — (Yiddish) lit., little lamb; a term of endearment.

sheva berachos — 1. the seven blessings recited at a wedding. 2. the week-long festivities following a wedding.

shidduch (pl.) *shidduchim* — 1. a proposed marriage match. 2. one's betrothed.

shiur (pl.) *shiurim* — a lecture on a Torah subject.

shivah — seven-day mourning period immediately following the death of a close relative.

shlep — (Yiddish) to drag.

shluchei mitzvah einam nizakim — those performing a mitzvah will not come to harm.

shmuessen — (Yiddish) Torah discourses

Shomayim — Heaven.

shtender — (Yiddish) a lectern.

shtiebel (pl.) *shtieblach* — (Yiddish) a small synagogue, often situated in a house.

shul — a synagogue.

shver — a father-in-law

siddur — a prayer book.

Sifrei Torah — Torah scrolls.

simchah (pl.) *simchos* — joy; a joyous occasion.

simchas hachaim — joie de vivre; happiness in life.

siyum (pl.) *siyumim* — celebration marking the completion of a course of study.

tallis (pl.) *tallesim* — four-cornered prayer shawl with fringes at each corner, worn by (married) men during morning prayers.

talmid (pl.) talmidim — a student.

talmidei chachamim — lit., the students of scholars; term for Torah scholars.

tefillah (pl.) *tefillos* — prayer.

tefillas haderech — the wayfarer's prayer.

tefillin — phylacteries.

Tehillim — 1. the Book of Psalms. 2. psalms.

temimus — 1. integrity. 2. naiveté.

temimusdik — (Yiddish) having integrity.

teshuvah — repentance.

tisch — (Yiddish) lit., table; a chassidic gathering around a Rebbe.

Tosafos — 1. a group of medieval Talmudic commentators. 2. critical and explanatory notes on the Talmud by French and German scholars of the 12th - 14th centuries.

tzaddik — a righteous individual.

tzedakah — charity.

tzitzis — fringed garment worn by Jewish men and boys.

upsherin — a three-year-old boy's ceremonial first haircut.

vasikin — 1. the Shacharis service performed at the earliest possible time. 2. those who pray Shacharis at the earliest possible time.

vort — 1. a Torah talk. 2. an engagement celebration.

yahrzeit —(Yiddish) the anniversary of a death.

yarmulke — (Yiddish) a skullcap.

yeshivah — a Torah academy.

yichus — lineage.

Yid (pl.) Yidden — Jew.

yingelach — (Yiddish) little boys.

yiras Shamayim — lit., fear of G-d; connotes reverence for G-d, an all-pervasive attitude of piety.

Yom Tov — a holiday

zechus — a merit.

zei gezunt — (Yiddish) may you be healthy.

zekeinim — elders.

z'man — semester.

zocheh — to merit.